WHILE YOU WALKED BY

A NOVEL

REGINA FELTY

D1260914

To my mother, Donna Marie, who submitted my first poem to a publisher when I was ten years old.

It was rejected.

But my mother believed in me, and when your mother believes in you, anything is possible.

1

The tower bells from Our Lady of Hope could be heard from several blocks away on the morning that she left him. The deep baritone thrums of the bells echoed across the rooftops of the buildings, settling into doorways and holding everything captive until their announcement was delivered: *bong, bong, bong.* It was the morning after his mother's fated prophecy: *No more, Aden. I won't watch you grow up this way.* He hadn't understood the intent behind her words until now.

When she'd told him to get dressed that morning, he asked her where they were going.

"Out," she answered, curtly.

When she handed him his green backpack and told him to carry it, he'd asked her again. This time, she didn't answer.

They hopped on a bus a few blocks from their apartment building. Aden had only been on a bus maybe twice in all of his twelve years, but the adventure was lost on him as he worried about where they were going and why his mom was being so secretive about it. They rode for several minutes deeper into the city—places Aden had never seen before—before disembarking in front of a large stone building with an eye-level white metal sign pushed into the grass next to the parking lot. Its bold black letters read "Philadelphia County Clerk, District One."

His mom led the way for several more blocks without speaking. Aden knew not to ask questions when she was in a sour mood, so he kept his mouth shut. That is, until they arrived at the back of an unidentified run-down building. Aden took in the wide stripes of white paint carelessly rolled across the back wall, bright hues of red and orange graffiti still visible through the layer of paint. A narrow rusty pipe climbed the wall from behind a large metal shed, disappearing over the edge of the roof.

"Where are we, Mom?" Aden dared to ask, looking around for a sign or some other indication of their location.

She avoided looking at him, her eyes darting back and forth as if they were about to be attacked by an unknown predator, while her hands fluttered over the collar of her faded black trench coat. Aden studied the soft little balls that had formed on the surface of the coat. He felt like reaching over and plucking them off as he waited impatiently for her answer.

"It's a shelter, Aden. They help people. I…I don't have time to explain everything." She glanced around before leaning closer, her breath stale, sour—Aden resisted backing away. "Here's what I want you to do. Go in and tell them your mother is a drug addict and that you haven't seen her in days. That you have no other family and no place to go. They probably won't bother to look for me and, if they do, they won't find me. Don't give them my real name either." She reached up to touch his cheek. "Trust me on this, Aden," Tears were welling in her eyes, her words tumbling out frantically as she spoke.

"I…I don't understand. Mom, what are you *talking* about?" Aden suddenly felt like he was standing in a puddle of ice water as fear crept into his lower limbs. He waited for her to smile and punch his arm, telling him, "Oh, I'm joking, Aden, stop looking so serious." But she did neither.

"I *can't* go in there with you, Aden. They'd force me to take you with me, you just don't understand how hard...that I don't know what else to do. This is better, son..." Her breath caught. "You *have* to do this...for me." She was openly sobbing now, scaring him more than he already was, if being more scared was even possible.

Stretching out a trembling hand, she touched the backpack on his shoulder.

"There's an extra pair of pants in here. Also, a few T-shirts, socks, underwear—everything you need for a day or two until they work something else out for you." Watery black mascara streaks traced the lines of her thin cheeks as she attempted to smile at him.

"I also packed two of your favorite books. Remember *Where the Red Fern Grows* and *The Crossbreed*? You've always loved those."

Aden just stared dumbly at her. *Favorite books? Why is that important right now?* He couldn't make sense of anything she was trying to tell him right now.

"They won't turn you away, Aden. They know who to call, what to do. Go inside now. Go on..." She nudged him gently forward, causing Aden to fumble awkwardly. He was petrified—his legs refusing to move, his body lagging far behind his racing thoughts. After a shaky sob and a rough embrace, his mother turned and walked away.

Aden watched her walk away, the soft *patter* of her footsteps growing fainter with each step. It was several seconds before he found his voice.

"Mom...please...I don't...understand. I don't want to..." he called out to her. She hurried down the long back alley the way they'd come, giving no indication that she heard him, but Aden saw her shoulders quiver and knew she was weeping.

Many times over the past months, Aden had thought back to that moment and wondered why he didn't follow her—why he had just stood there doing *nothing*. Maybe he didn't believe she'd really just walk away like that. He'd imagined that she would get halfway down the road and beckon for him to follow. That she couldn't go through with it. Wouldn't expect *him* to…

But she hadn't done any of that. She had just kept walking, her awkward pace quickening the farther she went. Just before she reached the corner that led toward the main road, she looked back at him—but she didn't stop, didn't run back with open arms to embrace him and tell him how sorry she was for scaring him. Instead, she turned her face away and left him standing alone. Aden watched her go—dumbfounded and numb, his mouth slack with shock.

Aden stood rigid, frozen in place as he watched her weave… falter…struggle until she was out of view. He never cried out— never made a move to try and follow her. His mind was unable to absorb the shock of the moment and every sense in his body felt suspended in time.

It was the voices coming from the steps at the back entrance of the building that broke through Aden's trance as he frantically tried to process what was happening. He pulled his eyes away from the now-empty alley and the last image of his mother and saw that two older men sat on the steps in front of a set of heavy wood doors that appeared to have been painted red once but had long since been weathered down to a faded drab pink color. Aden blinked at the sight of the two men—he was sure they hadn't been there when he and his mom had arrived.

One of the men glanced casually over at Aden and offered a broad, friendly smile. He was an older man with a stooped back and eyes that sunk deep in their sockets. Bony shoulders drooped forward as if he carried a tremendous burden on his back. A cigarette dangled carelessly between the gnarled fingers of one hand and his lazy smile revealed a large, gaping hole where several teeth were missing. Aden stood paralyzed. His eyes dropped to the man's feet, shod in filthy yellow socks jammed into flip-flops that had chunks of rubber missing from the soles.

A younger man was seated on the step below him. His eyes were cold and hard as he scowled at Aden—a distinct opposite of the friendly man next to him. Puckering cracked lips, he spat a black stream of tobacco juice aimed in Aden's direction. The stream of sticky tar slapped the concrete a few feet shy of Aden's white tennis shoes. Fear churned in Aden's stomach. It burned like alkaline as bile pooled in his throat and tore through his chest. Sucking in a heaving gulp of air, Aden turned and ran deeper into the unfamiliar heart of the city.

2

*T*he hissing screech of bus brakes at the curb close to where Aden slept penetrated his dulled senses and stirred him awake. Crust caked the edges of his eyes as he struggled to open them. He pressed a cold, stiff fist to his eyes and tried to rub away the dirt that had mixed with the dampness of the morning. The rubbing only served to smear the filth across his face and scratch at his chapped skin. Slow, even breaths sent oxygen to his limbs and helped get the blood flowing enough for Aden to sit up. He blinked away his sluggishness and peered out at the empty street where the bus had just taken on its load of passengers and moved on to unknown destinations in the city. Aden felt like an invisible mass in the familiar fixtures of the bustling city. His existence was unnoticed by all the passersby who were already fixated on the here-to-there demands of the morning. It was as if the sun rose and set on Aden's days without so much as making a blip on the radar of a single soul he passed.

Muscles stiff and unforgiving, he sat for several minutes, quietly absorbing the disenchanting scene in front of him. Shades of mottled gray—from the trademark soot of the nearby shipyards

—and multicolored blotches of gum droppings from years-on-end spread across fractured concrete and crawled up building walls. Scattered paper scraps and crumpled plastic cups haphazardly littered the edges of the sidewalk and spilled over into the street. A metal trash bin, cruelly bent in the middle and overflowing with waste, sat posted near the corner by the crosswalk. Swollen, gluttonous gray pigeons blended seamlessly with the drab street they clustered on, cooing to one another as they surveyed the treasures left for them to forage.

Mixed with the diesel gas odor left in the wake of the departed bus, the air smelled of greasy food and musky body odor, no doubt permanently saturated into the concrete walls of the city structures from all the humanity that brushed by them endlessly day by day. Occasional hints of a mixture of coffee and baked bread drifted in the air but seemed to dissipate before Aden's next breath. His imagination lingered on the welcome scents.

Lost in thought, Aden jerked back into the brush when an old woman walked by. She was completely shrouded in a lumpy black jacket with her head buried in its hood, black pants covered with what looked like old food stains and mud, and thick dark blue gloves. She looked like a drifting shadow with no real form or substance—a shapeless figure shuffling down the empty sidewalk.. The paper cup she gripped in her hand sent out puffs of steam. *Coffee.* He could smell it—almost taste it—sense its warmth. He hadn't felt the hunger pains until the aroma of the coffee, mingled with the smells from nearby diners and street vendors, collided with Aden's senses, alerting him to his body's needs.

Time to find something to eat.

Aden waited until the woman turned a corner and the street was clear before standing and stretching. He leaned over to roll up his sleeping bag, wrapping its large band around it and pulling the strap over his shoulder. He had been so cold and tired last night that he'd used it as a blanket to cover himself rather than crawl into it. Aden reached down for his backpack and slung it over his shoulder next to the sleeping bag.

He weaved his way down the street, carefully avoiding contact with people. Wandering to a gas station on the next block, Aden huddled at a wall adjacent to the store entrance. Pressing his body against the wall, he waited. His body shuddered in response to the cold seeping through his clothes but he had to stay out of sight.

Travelers came and went all night and he'd have his best shot at finding something edible in the twin cans posted by the doors of the store. He was careful not to move too fast as he noticed two bikers clad in leather jackets dismounting their bikes on the sidewalk by the entrance. He didn't want to draw attention to himself. Bikers came with one of only two dispositions in Aden's mind: They either had a heart of gold or they were junkyard-dog mean. He didn't want to take his chances that he would run into the latter this morning.

The sun had started to cast its full glory over the roofs of the buildings and the city took on more life as businesses opened their doors and people hustled down the sidewalks for coffee and a quick pastry before heading to work. The buzzing hum of street traffic could be heard in the background but Aden tuned it out. His eyes were trained on the glass doors of the store just a few feet away, watching for an opening to make his move. When no one came or went after a minute, Aden hustled over to the two bins. His movements were sluggish and his muscles cramped in protest but Aden didn't have much time.

Reaching the first bin, he peered down into the crumpled mass of waste and noticed several torn plastic candy and pastry wrappers and empty cigarette boxes—nothing he found useful. He moved to the other bin. *This one looks more promising,* he thought as he spied several plastic cups and food bags. Aden shoved his hand deep into the pile and moved things around. Under a knotted grocery bag that Aden didn't have any desire to open, he spotted a brown deli bag with a large grease stain on it. Poking his fingers against the bag, it felt soft and pliable inside. He could only hope it was food. Yanking it out of the bin with a quick dart of his hand, Aden gripped the bag against him and rushed back to a fence at the back of the parking lot to survey the contents. *Bingo!* A half-eaten ham sandwich was crumpled in the bag along with a wad of greasy napkins and several limp French fries at the bottom. Glancing around, Aden went in search of a safe place to eat.

3

*I*t was freezing outside and Aden was tempted to find a place to huddle for the night to get warm. But he wasn't tired yet and needed a distraction from boredom.

Most of the small shops on the street had closed down for the night and fewer people roamed the sidewalks. Aden felt safer coming out of the shadows with less people mingling around. He wandered down the deserted sidewalk and stopped in front of a tattoo shop to admire all the design choices displayed in the window: skulls and crosses, one of an angel with enormous wings and a long spear in its fist. Aden's favorite was a drawing of an old lighthouse. He'd always thought lighthouses were like unsung heroes because they just sat quietly unnoticed until someone was in danger and then, suddenly, their light became a lifeline to the lost.

Aden shivered and moved on. *I need a scarf to keep the cold off my face,* he thought, pinching the end of his nose between two fingers to warm it.

When Aden turned the corner, he noticed an empty lot at the back of an old building. The edge of the lot butted up against a cluster of overgrown brush and trees. He saw steam seeping from a vent at the bottom of the wall at the back of the building. *Steam means warmth*, he thought and walked over to huddle down next to the vent. There was a stack of boxes on one side of the vent and Aden crouched next to them for extra warmth. He unloaded his packs off of his back, setting them down on the ground next to him.

The man appeared out of nowhere and scared Aden so badly that he knocked over several boxes, scattering them across the gravel like tossed dice. The man, eyes wild and one hand gripping his throat, looked just as startled as Aden, maybe even more. He was an older man, Aden noticed, and wore a thick black coat that hung past his hips and a dark blue beanie cap pulled tightly over his ears.

"It's alright, son," the man said, reaching out a hand to help Aden up. Aden ignored the outstretched hand and raised himself. "I just came out to get some fresh air," the man continued. "I'm guessin' you're back here lookin' for something to eat, although I think you're the youngest beggar I've seen come around here before." The man shrugged, obviously assessing that Aden was no real threat, and gave Aden a friendly grin. Every muscle tensed in Aden's body as he prepared to run.

It was the man's voice that had stilled him. The gentle compassion in his tone kept Aden rooted where he stood. It had been so long since he had felt compassion from another human. For months, he had been raged at and scorned by everyone and everything that he came near. He burned with shame under the scorching stares of people passing him on the sidewalks and the undisguised distrust of store owners when he walked by their open shops. Even dogs growled and snarled at him and trucks blared their angry horns if he got too close. There was something about the way this old man looked at him that made him feel, well, human.

His eyes drifted to the man's. Deep gray eyes blinked slowly, patiently, back at him as if waiting for a frightened doe to trust that he was not a predator to fear. "Are you alone?" the man asked. He'd made no move other than to tilt his head to look past Aden, as if searching for someone to emerge from the dark shadows behind him.

Aden didn't answer. He had no reason to. He didn't owe the man any explanation. The man didn't seem bothered by Aden's silence. He seemed relaxed, unhurried, without a care in the world other than to just stand there quietly.

"Aw, it's fine," he said, breaking the silence. "You don't need to answer, son." He looked back at the door he'd exited, a thoughtful expression on his face. Turning back to Aden, he told him, "Wait here a minute. I'll go see what I got left in the kitchen." He backed up several steps before turning to the stairs. At the top, he turned back to Aden and put up a finger to indicate that Aden should wait for him. Pulling open the heavy door, the man disappeared inside.

An ache formed in the back of Aden's throat when the man left. He didn't know why it affected him. In just a matter of minutes, the old man had appeared and disappeared before Aden could even process what had happened. Aden wasn't sure why he was still standing there, except that his desire for food outweighed his fear at the moment.

A slight breeze swept thin blond wisps of his hair into his eyes. Aden reached to brush them aside. His icy fingers brushing up against his cheek sent an involuntary shiver through his body. It was a reminder that he couldn't wait much longer to settle in a warm place for the night. The man reappeared in the doorway just as Aden considered leaving. A small, white bundle was tucked in his right hand, a large styrofoam cup gripped in his left. He'd paused and assessed Aden for a moment, reading his body language for clues on how to proceed.

Neither of them moved for a moment.

The man spoke first. "Good! You're still here," he said, a bright smile breaking out across his face. "I'm just a handyman 'round here, so I can't just help myself to whatever I want. But I did manage to rustle up a few leftover sweet rolls." He held out the white bundle to Aden. As an afterthought, he thrust out his other hand with the styrofoam cup. Both hands were suspended as the man waited for Aden to make a move. "And," he added, chuckling to himself as his head nodded toward the cup he held, "I don't know if you drink coffee, but it's hot and will warm you up real quick. Ain't no creamer in it—I don't drink the stuff—but it's got lots of sugar in it."

Aden's eyes fell to the bundle in front of him. He noticed that it really wasn't white at all but more like a muddy gray color. Peering closer, Aden noted that it was a kitchen towel blanketed around the bundle. *I hope it's clean*, he thought, then chided himself. *I've eaten food out of disgusting trash cans...*

They were at an impasse. The man was waiting. Aden knew it was up to him to rein in his fear. Breathing to calm himself, he stepped toward the man and lifted a trembling hand out for the bundle. The man leaned forward to place it gently in Aden's hands. Tucking the bundle under his arm, Aden reached for the coffee.

"Thank you," he whispered. The man laughed and grabbed at his chest with one fist, feigning a heart attack.

"You *do* speak," he teased, then added softly, "You're welcome..."

Rubbing his hands together to warm them, the man stepped back and lowered himself onto the porch edge—the smile fixed on his face. Aden looked around for a place to sit. Spying an overturned fruit crate that had been discarded near the edge of the property, he walked over and lowered himself onto it. The thick plastic creaked beneath him but held his weight. He arranged himself so that he faced the man while he ate. It made him feel better to be able to keep an eye on things.

Settling the warm coffee firmly between his knees, Aden began to unwrap the tidy bundle, edge over edge, until little brown mounds flecked with darker brown crumbles peeked up at him from beneath the last fold. He could smell the caramel scent of the yeast in the dough and the faint aroma of cinnamon. His stomach rumbled in anticipation. Lifting the first mouthwatering bite to his lips, Aden watched the man as he brushed loose dirt off of his pants. He wasn't even sure why the man stayed out here. *Didn't he have work or something else to do?* Aden wondered. *Maybe he's waiting for his towel back,* he thought, pulling the remaining two rolls out of the cloth and gently pushing them deep into his jacket pocket. He held out the towel toward the man when he looked up. The man waved him off.

"Nah, just leave it on the crate when you leave. I'll get it later."

With that, the old man stood and nodded at Aden—*did he just wink at me?* Aden thought—and went to straighten the stack of boxes that Aden had toppled over. Aden took another bite of his roll and reached for the cup balanced between his knees. He continued to watch the old man as he tugged and pushed to make the stack tidier. The man whistled as he worked, the soft tone filling the air between them. It was a comforting sound. Aden wondered if he might be seeing the very first angel among all the demons that haunted the streets of this city.

*a*den was tired of hiding. He could always go back to the shelter but was afraid of the kind of people he saw hanging around outside those kinds of places. Like the scowling man who had spit tobacco at him. If that hunched figure was a prelude of what life was like inside of a shelter, well, Aden thought he'd stand a better chance out on his own. Besides, Aden wasn't sure but assumed they probably didn't keep kids at shelters without their parents. He didn't know what they would do with him if he did decide to go back. His mom had said they would *help* him, but what was that supposed to mean? *Would the police come and take me somewhere else?* The thought made him even more anxious. *No, hiding just felt safer.*

During the months on his own, Aden had fine-tuned his instinct for survival. At first, he'd been careless about staying out of sight, mingling with the traffic flow of bodies in the city, his favorite place to visit being the Avenue of the Arts off Broad Street. You had to pay a fee to go into the museums and art centers but Aden still loved to look at all the advertisement posters for upcoming operas and plays and admire the displays in the windows as he walked by. Sometimes he would linger by the pretzel and hot dog stands on the sidewalks in case the vendors gave out free samples, which they'd been known to do when they were feeling generous. More often than not, though, he was chased off by an angry vendor who probably thought he was trying to steal something. He hated how they looked at him and treated him like he was nothing more than a filthy street rat that needed to be exterminated.

Many times during those first weeks alone he wandered close to colonies of thrown-together shelters: an odd mixture of nylon camping tents, threadbare blankets propped up by large sticks and poles, and all sizes of sheet metal and cardboard that served as walls of protection for the humanity that had nowhere else to call "home." Stolen grocery carts stood beside ratty tents, loaded down with plastic bags, milk cartons, and an assortment of other odds and ends—a summary of a person's life on four wheels.

Instinct warned Aden not to venture too close but he often found himself drawn to these strange little communities of people that took up residence in Philly's empty lots, under bridges— anywhere within walking distance of a busy area where there would be access to handouts and other freebies. Or drugs…which Aden had noticed was sold on most of the main city street corners. For many of the addicts Aden watched come and go regularly, the drugs seemed more necessary than food.

Aden was almost envious as he observed the people who shared a common hardship as they huddled together around small fires— which Aden was sure was not allowed in the city but they chanced anyway—sharing conversation and what little food and booze they had with one another. Aden had no one to share a fire or conversation with. He always felt lonelier after watching them and, after a while, he avoided going there altogether.

One night, he entertained himself by sitting on a bench outside of the Kimmel Center for the Performing Arts, a bustling venue close to the heart of Philadelphia, to watch the bustle of activity. The city came alive at night and Aden almost felt a part of the festivities while he watched the flurry of life go on around him. It was mesmerizing to observe all the people lined up between two thick gold ropes, shuffling forward every few minutes like cattle waiting to be branded. Even with their bodies crushed against each other and the long wait, Aden could hear laughter and saw smiling faces. A baby was crying somewhere in the crowd and a few younger kids chased each other, weaving in and under the ropes until someone put a stop to their recreation and sent them back to their parents.

Aden didn't notice the man until a haze of smoke floated into his vision. His eyes followed the cloud, which he now recognized as cigarette smoke, to a burly man leaning against the brick wall behind him. It was dark where the man stood and Aden struggled to make out details of his facial features. What Aden *did* notice were dark eyes boring into him as the man pushed off the wall and started toward him, the bright glow of the cigarette dangling from his mouth like a tiny beacon pushing through the shadows.

"You lost, kid?" the dark-eyed man asked.

The deep, husky voice was followed by a huge muscled body that reminded Aden of Hercules, the mythical half-god hero that he had read about during one of his trips to the library. But this guy didn't seem to be any kind of *hero* as far as Aden could tell.

The man stepped under the streetlight, where Aden could see him better. A faded brown jacket covered his massive shoulders and was zipped closed all the way to his thick neckline. He wore faded blue jeans draped over mottled brown work boots that looked like they'd seen some rough miles. He looked to be middle-aged, with dark brown hair that rolled back from his forehead in glossy waves and wispy gray curls near his temples. Aden couldn't tell the color of his eyes—they were so black and shrouded that Aden swore they were just empty holes pierced into the skull of a demon.

Hercules took a long drag on his cigarette, its glow brightening with the effort, before reaching up and plucking it from between his lips.

"Hey, kid, you lost or something?" he repeated.

"Uh, no…no, I'm not," Aden lied. "My dad's in line…over there," he said, pointing aimlessly to the ticket line behind the man. "I, um…I just got tired of standing so I came over here to sit. My dad knows I'm over here," he added, hoping the man would take the hint and leave. *No luck.* He didn't even bother to look behind him. Aden got the impression that the imposing giant didn't believe him as he stared vacantly down at Aden. Fear spread through his chest as his mind frantically sought for an escape plan. His eyes bounced between the man's stone face to the cigarette sandwiched between two massive fingers, the tip dimming as flecks of glowing ash floated to the sidewalk near his feet. When he flicked his cigarette to the ground and glanced down to crush it with his boot, Aden knew what he had to do.

He ran.

any times, over the long, solitary months of struggling to live on the streets, Aden had wanted to give up and just march into a random office building and ask the first person he met for help. But the first call they would make, Aden knew, would most certainly be to the police.

He imagined being hauled into the back of a police car—a thick metal screen imprisoning him in the backseat. *Where would they take me? Do they still have orphanages in Philly?* Images of being surrounded by stern-faced adults at the police station, strangers bombarding him with questions and becoming angry when he had no answers to give them flooded his mind, overwhelming him.

No, he thought. *I can't let the cops take me.*

His mother had been afraid of the police almost as much as the "bad guys" she warned Aden about. She'd cautioned Aden many times not to answer the door when she wasn't home.

"There's a lot of evil people in the world, Aden," she said. "People that wouldn't think twice about hurting a kid. You hear a knock on that door, and you hide yourself in the bedroom until they stop knocking. It might even be the cops at the door. They'd take you away from me. You want that to happen, Aden?"

It was only a matter of time before he absorbed her fears and no longer needed the reminder. Survival and staying free was all Aden lived for now.

And…looking for ways to ward off his restlessness. He had been so excited one afternoon when he'd found a deck of playing cards while poking through a donation bag someone had left at the back door of the Salvation Army. As he dug through the bag, hoping to find a fresh pair of socks or more shirts to layer under his jacket for warmth, he was disappointed to find it was mostly a bag of women's blouses and a few mismatched Tupperware containers. Dumping the rest of the contents on the ground, Aden smiled as a pack of cards tumbled out of the bag.

When he was seven, his mother had bought him several decks and taught him how to play Solitaire so he would have something to do when she was working. He would spend hours spreading the cards out on the coffee table in the living room, sometimes running two separate games just for the fun of it.

After shoving everything back into the bag and tossing it by the wall of the store, Aden unzipped his backpack and pushed the deck down into it. He waited until the sun had gone down and he'd found a secluded place to settle for the night before he pulled the cards out of his backpack. Laying out his sleeping bag, he sat down on it and crossed his legs.

It's a special occasion, he told himself when he also pulled out half a candy bar that he'd found the day before but wanted to save for a special moment. To him, finding the cards was a good enough reason. Shaking the cards out of the box, Aden sorted them into their suits to make sure he had a full deck before shuffling them and setting up a game on the ground in front of him. The cards were a welcome distraction from the cold and the drudgery of another long night alone.

———

ADEN WASN'T sure how long he'd been walking. That afternoon, he'd hunkered down into a restless nap underneath an overpass. He was relieved to find that there was no one else around, although piles of garbage, scattered cigarette butts, and a crushed hypodermic needle were evidence that someone recently had been. Kicking aside an empty cereal box on the ground, Aden lay down with his back against the side of a wall and slept. He had an hour of rest and the relief of being able to let down his guard for a while before night fell. Blessed peace from the haunting fears that drove his daily existence.

A few hours before dusk would cast its long shadow across the city, Aden awoke and shouldered his luggage. He crept away from the area and into the obscurity of the brush along the highway. He needed to move on. He couldn't stay by the overpass. He knew this area was a favored nighttime hangout for local gang members and other shady night characters.

He had a few hours to burn before he settled for the night but he liked to have a head start. Maybe find some kind of entertainment for a while. There was that fiddler who sat near the corner diner and played tunes while people danced and threw coins in the can at his feet. *I'll go by that way and see if he's there.* Aden also remembered that the diner usually had some good pickings in their trash bins after the crowds thinned as well.

Night was when the streets were most dangerous. Hustlers, prostitutes, dealers, and all sorts of dark figures who crawled through the streets and crouched in every dark alley and doorway.

You didn't walk the street at night if you wanted to see another day or didn't want to live with the demons that would haunt you if you did.

Aden stopped midstep and stared at his surroundings in confusion. He felt like a puppet that some entity had manipulated and steered to this place without his being aware of it. His eyes followed a familiar maze of jagged cracks on the ground that led to a line of empty plastic milk jugs neatly arrayed against the building's back wall like fat little sumo wrestlers awaiting their turn in the ring. Flattened cardboard boxes were towered together in a leaning pile. Three stone steps led up to a small porch with no railing. Framed into the concrete wall was a thick metal door.

The bakery door.

Large red faded letters painted on the wall above the door: *Angelo's Bakery*. The man with the white bundle. The warm sweet rolls and coffee. Why was he here—again?

6

*B*en pulled the frayed string suspended from the ceiling and waited for the light to flicker on. It always crackled and sputtered like an old man crawling out of bed in the morning before it finally sparked to life. It wasn't like the normal flipping of a switch that immediately flooded a room with illumination. Like everything else in this decrepit, ancient building, the light actually *working* was always a stroke of luck in itself.

Ben shuffled the large bag of flour he was dragging over to the back wall of the storage room and shoved it under the bottom shelf with his foot.

"I'm gettin' too old to be dragging around flour bags and hauling heavy pots all over the kitchen," he said to no one.

He was in a mood today. Sure, he had his moments of halfhearted sarcasm and suffered his share of cynicism, but today Ben was just downright surly and he wasn't quite sure why.

His coworker, Mia, walked into the storage room just as he was giving the flour bag an extra kick just because he felt like it. He looked up and saw her standing in the doorway, one thick hand leaning against the doorjamb, a scolding look on her face. Ben was embarrassed that Mia had caught him acting like a brooding teenager.

"What is going on with you today, Ben?" she asked.

Ben knew he wouldn't escape until he gave her a satisfactory answer.

"You've been walking around here growling at everything that crosses your path—including me—since you came into work today."

Ben reached up and began randomly organizing the spices on the shelf in front of him, anything to avoid meeting Mia's eyes.

"Nothin'…" he answered sourly. Mia walked to a shelf on the opposite wall and slid off a large can, tucking it up against her body. She turned away in a huff and marched back to stand in the doorway, again blocking any escape for Ben.

"Well, Ben Morgan, you need to adjust your 'nothin' attitude before you come into my kitchen. You're getting on my nerves."

Ben set the canister of lemon peel that he'd been holding back down on the shelf and leaned back against the wall. He and Mia had always gotten along well and had a mutual respect for one another. Her words stung.

It really was *nothing*—at least nothing Ben could put his finger on.

He considered how to answer Mia while he surveyed the inventory around him: wall-to-wall shelves stocked high with large cans of shortening, baking powder, extracts, and other staples necessary to run a bakery.

I'm gettin' too old to be dragging around flour bags and hauling heavy pots all over the kitchen…

I'm gettin' too old…

That was it. Ben was feeling his age and it wasn't his body that was taking it the hardest. It was his mind. He was getting older and it had been picking at the back of his conscience like a woodpecker on a tree trunk for weeks now.

"Fine, Mia, since you're just gonna stand there giving me the evil eye," Ben said with a sigh. He stared down at the flour bag at his feet, the telltale dent in the soft bag where his boot had landed mocked him. He resisted the urge to kick it again.

"I'll tell you what is botherin' me and then I don't want to hear another word about it. Deal?" he said, glaring at Mia.

Mia's face had softened to an *almost-not-so-irritated* look. She nodded, which Ben took to mean "go on."

Ben folded his arms across his chest and leaned his head back against the wall, his eyes focusing on the dangling light string. The knot at the end of it was beginning to come undone. *Like my life*, he thought.

"Well, it's like this, Mia." Ben unfolded one arm and swept it in an arch above his head. "Here I am, coming to work every day, puttin' in my hours, only to go home to space out in front of the TV or stare at the four walls. Don't hardly even see my roommate, Jake, most nights because of his haywire schedule." Ben tucked his arms back against his chest and looked at Mia, searching her eyes for understanding. The only encouragement she gave him was another head nod.

"Thing is," he went on, "after all these years of workin' and making my small contribution to society, I...well, let's just say I ain't getting any younger and I don't have nothin' to show for my life at the end of the day." Ben realized he'd just used the word *nothin'* again—his favorite word of the day, apparently.

Mia adjusted the large can she held, moving it to the other side of her body. A sad smile formed on her lips as she looked at Ben.

"I understand, Ben. I really do. I'm a few years younger than you but I feel that way sometimes. Do you think that when I was a young woman, I thought I'd be spending my middle-aged years working in a bakery, rolling out cinnamon rolls day after day for a living? I had bigger plans too, Ben: plans of college and a fancy career in a corporate office where I was the one *buying* donuts for everyone at the office, not *making* them. But I made some bad choices. I made the mistake of getting pregnant and marrying too young and life took a different turn for me. I left all those dreams behind. But I'm *happy*, Ben, with my life as it is. I have a nice home and a beautiful family. I can't complain. Maybe you should be looking at things a little differently, Ben."

Her expression was reflective, but not exactly sad. Ben appreciated her frankness—he really did—and her willingness to share her heart with him touched him deeply. But there was one gaping distance between their paths in life.

"Well, Mia, at least your mistakes *created* a family. My mistakes stripped mine from me. That's not an easy thing to live with."

Mia walked over and gave Ben a one-arm hug, the cumbersome can in her arms pushing into Ben's ribcage. "Ben, you are carrying burdens that are too heavy for you. I will pray for you to find peace."

She patted his arm and started out of the storage room before turning once more to deliver her final parting words.

"And, Ben…before you come out of this room, you need to put a smile back on that face. We can't have that scowl you were walking around with earlier scaring off the customers." Mia winked and Ben scrunched his face into a scowl just to make a point.

He heard her chuckling the whole way down the narrow hall, while Ben was left to sort through the "burdens" that Mia had referred to. He thought about Jake finding him on a barstool—after a three-day drinking binge when the bottom fell out of his world—

and dragging him along to one of Jake's AA meetings. Jake offered Ben a place to stay when he had no place else to go. That was fifteen years ago. After a few failed starts, Ben had been alcohol-free for nearly fourteen of them.

Ben was turning sixty this year and he was still sharing a house with his fifty-eight-year-old best friend. He should be on his own—creating a new life for himself.

After all these years of being sober, Ben struggled with the idea of going for a drink after work tonight. He shoved the temptation back into its dark place. The craving never went away but neither did the haunting memory of what drinking had stripped him of—had stolen from him. That's what kept him from ever taking that first sip.

Ben reached up and pulled the string above him. There was a final cranky *fzzzzt* sound before the light went out.

7

*H*e wasn't sure what he expected.

The man wasn't going to serve him pastries and coffee every night and was sure to start asking more questions. He'd called Aden a *beggar* last night. But Aden didn't think of himself that way. To him, beggars were dirty, hunched over, desolate bodies who sat on sidewalks and called out to people passing by, bumming "a few bucks to get something to eat," which Aden knew they rarely used to buy food with. He'd watched them curl their hand around the money and thank the giver like they'd saved their life. Then, they'd slip off to the liquor store or hit up a dealer as soon as their benefactor rounded the corner out of sight.

No, he wouldn't beg. *I'd rather pick through nasty piles of other people's castoffs to find my own food. I would never beg for anything from anyone.* It wasn't pride that kept Aden from asking for help. It was the fear of being noticed for what he was—an underaged kid alone on the streets. He knew he would either attract the eye of a concerned citizen who would call the cops on him or become the target of an evil child predator. Both were equally dangerous in Aden's mind.

Seeing adults sprawled on cardboard mats that cluttered the ground or loitering on the sidewalks was just a part of the fixed landscape of downtown Philadelphia. But Aden, who was on the smaller side for his age as it was, would stand out like a beacon for attention: a recipe for disaster.

Yet, here he was, standing at the back of the bakery again. Aden reasoned that he was only here because most restaurants threw out unused food at the end of the day. He would just hang out until it was fully dark and he was sure no one was around, and then just pop over to see if he found anything interesting in the bins. He'd had no luck tonight with the diner's cans and he was starting to feel weak from not eating for several hours. He didn't know what time the last of the trash went out for the night but he might find out by hanging in the shadows and watching.

It wasn't like he had anything better to do. Nothing else exciting was happening in the neighborhood at this hour. Even the street fiddler had already packed up and gone for the night. Aden had spied a covered area earlier behind an empty building nearby where he would spend the night. He'd head over there in a little while.

A lot of larger businesses kept locks on their bins to discourage trash digging but some of the smaller ones didn't. Looking over at the large metal bin pushed up against a gnarled chain-link fence, Aden noticed there wasn't a lock on this one. *Perfect.*

Hunkering in the shadows at the edge of the property, Aden waited. He settled himself back against a tree trunk, tucked his sleeping bag near him on the ground, and hugged his backpack to his chest. It made a little cocoon that trapped warmth against his body. He had to adjust himself as the tree bark stabbed through his jacket into his back, but he eventually found a sweet spot and melted into it as the anxiety of the day seeped from his body.

Slam!

Aden jerked awake, a searing pain shooting up his leg from being cramped in one position for too long. Aden set his backpack to the side and rubbed his leg while he looked around for the source of the loud noise.

The man had just come out of the bakery door. The old man from last night.

How long have I been sleeping?

Shrinking back into the foliage, Aden watched the man fumbling with several large black bags in his arms. After tackling each step carefully, he made his way toward the trash bin by the fence. "Guess I'm the only one that can take the trash out around here," Aden heard him mumble. A bag rolled off the top of the load in his arms and dumped onto the sidewalk. He left it. Lifting the remaining load over the rim of the trash container, the man gave it a final shove into the dark oblivion. There was a muted *thud* as the bags landed.

The man edged around and leaned back against the rusty bin. His head dropped to his chest, shoulders falling inward. Aden watched his eyes close, heard his breaths quicken and stutter. He looked sick. He hoped the man wasn't going to fall over with a stroke or anything. His own breathing slowed as time hung suspended, his mind rapidly shuffling between two possible scenarios: *Cut out of here before he keels over or sit here and wait to see what happens.*

He went with the latter—*wait and see what happens.*

Aden could see that the man was definitely still breathing. But he looked so shrunken into himself that Aden felt himself poise to run if the man fell over dead. He would be a hundred miles away before someone discovered the body.

The man had reached up to rub his cheek, then slid a wrinkled hand over his hair as he lifted his head and opened his eyes. Aden noticed that his hand was trembling. The man stared straight ahead into nothingness for a moment before slowly pushing off the bin and making his way back toward the porch. Passing the rebel black bag on the ground, he paused and huffed out a sigh. Shaking his head, he bent to retrieve it.

His hand stilled in midair as his eyes scanned the shadows surrounding the back of the property. Aden knew he couldn't see him. There was no way. He was camouflaged in the dead foliage with his dark clothes and dense layers of branches to hide behind. He hadn't made one sound to give himself away.

"Who's there?" the man called out. He didn't appear concerned —just curious. Aden chewed on his bottom lip, his eyes riveted on the man as he remained paused in motion. The urge to flee was even stronger now but Aden held it at bay while he tested the waters.

"It's just me," Aden answered from the brush, not that his answer was any help since it was obvious that he couldn't see him. "I just came to sit for a few minutes. Is that okay?"

The man's expression softened at the sound of the voice. "You that boy from last night?"

"Um, yeah."

The man reached down and retrieved the bag from the ground and swung it over his shoulder. Aden watched him make his way back to the bin with the bag. As he heaved the bag over the edge, he hollered back at Aden. "You don't gotta hide back there with the spiders and whatever else is creepin' in those weeds."

He turned to face the direction Aden's voice had come from. "Come on out, son. Don't nobody ever come back here but me anyways. I'm either haulin' junk out here for recycling or throwing trash out. Well…and I come back here to sit and eat most nights.

It's warmer inside but Mia's always askin' me to do this and that. Better to come out here and freeze just to have a few minutes of peace." A soft sound bubbled from his throat, his grin pushing his cheeks up into his eyes until they were thin slivers in his weathered face.

Eyes that had reflected pain only moments ago. Aden didn't know anything about this man except that he seemed to be kind and that he was hurting about something. Hurt was an emotion Aden understood very well. He pushed himself off the ground and brushed a stray leaf from his forehead. He stepped out to meet the man.

8

*B*en heard a faint shuffle and watched as a small shadow rose from the clump of bushes at the back of the loading dock. The young boy emerged, hesitant and wary, like a guilty dog who had just torn the couch to shreds and was about to face punishment. The boy paused to look behind him, then back at Ben.

Ben thought for sure he would race back to hide in the bushes, but he only darted in for a second before coming back out—a faded green backpack and lumpy blue sleeping bag draped heavily across one small shoulder.

He watched as the boy stepped out onto the broken concrete and walked toward him, stopping about five feet from Ben.

He wore the same filthy clothes from the other night and had the same guarded expression fixed on his face. Ben got a better look at him as he stepped into the light. His face was lined with faint streaks of dirt and his cheeks were chapped to a pink hue. Long golden hair framed his small face and curled slightly where it rested on his shoulders.

Ben noted his deep brown eyes shifted methodically as he

surveyed the world around him, poised for any unwelcome surprises that might show up unexpectedly in his path. He was a petite boy, with delicate facial features and small hands that were wrapped around the straps on his shoulders. Ben really couldn't guess his age with his body swimming under the coat he wore that looked to be two sizes too big for him.

His body was tense and bunched, ready to strike back at anything that came after him. Ben pitied the boy. *Where was his family? How was he surviving out here on his own?* Judging by the boy's rigid stance, Ben knew better than to voice his questions out loud.

"Should've let me know you were out here here sooner. I just threw a bunch of old bagels and whatnot in the trash." He gestured to the bin where he'd tossed the bags a few minutes before. "Got half a pastrami sandwich left over from my lunch. Want it?"

Ben noticed the subtle head nod but waited to see if the boy would speak up. After a moment, the boy nodded again, answering in a small voice.

"Sure, if you don't want it—I'm not here to beg for food, though," he emphasized. "I just stopped to rest for a while." He glanced back at the bushes, as if to clarify.

Ben didn't need clarification.

"Ain't no problem, son. Rest wherever you want to. Just you be mindful of whoever else might be hanging out in dark places like that." At the blank expression on the boy's face, Ben continued. "Anyhow, I didn't have much of an appetite today, so I saved the other half of my sandwich. You make yourself comfortable for a sec and I'll grab it. Ain't no coffee made but I got a box of hot chocolate packets if you're interested."

The boy looked eager. *Too eager.*

"Sure. Yes…please."

Well, he's got good manners anyhow.

"Oh," the boy continued, his voice more confident now, "can you make it extra hot?"

The boy ran an arm sleeve across his runny nose. Ben made a mental note to look for the biggest cup he could find and use several hot chocolate packets.

"You got it, kid. Be right back." He turned for the porch.

When he returned, Ben found the boy sitting on the same overturned fruit crate he'd sat on the other night. His backpack was tucked tight against his upper body and his sleeping bag rested on the ground next to his left leg. His gaze followed Ben's movements as he made his way over to him. The sandwich was wrapped in brown butcher paper and Ben's large metal thermos brushed against his leg as he walked. Ben was careful not to move too fast. *Poor kid looks as wound up as a fella on a first date,* he thought.

"Here ya go, buddy," Ben said as he handed the boy the wrapped sandwich and thermos. "Better wait a minute on the hot chocolate. It's too hot to drink yet."

Ben turned away and went to sit on the edge of the porch, watching the boy with curiosity. The whole scene felt like a repeat of their first meeting. He watched him meticulously unroll the sandwich from its paper, wrap his hands around the torpedo-shaped hoagie roll, and dive in, crumbs falling between his fingers as he tore off bites before swallowing the half-chewed food still in his mouth. When he looked up and noticed Ben watching, he slowed his chewing, carefully licking mustard off his top lip.

Ben lifted his head and pretended to study the moon. *Guess I wouldn't want someone to be watchin' me eat neither.* He heard the sound of metal dragging across the gravel and glanced over to see the boy pushing the thermos off to the side with his shoe.

Probably waitin' for it to cool.

Ben attempted conversation. "My momma used to tell me and my sisters that she didn't believe no man really ever walked on the moon," Ben said thoughtfully. "That no one really could prove it and those scientists that said it happened all made it up just to make people proud to be an American. What do you think about that?" Ben grappled to find common ground with the boy. He wasn't all that good at small talk himself and this boy was giving him a run for his money.

"I don't know a lot about people going to the moon," the boy said between chewing, "but I remember reading something about it happening a long time ago."

Ben had to strain to hear him, his words muffled behind a mouthful of food. He tried to mask his shock, tried hard to keep his facial expression neutral. *Don't they teach these kids nothin' in school these days?* Ben mused.

"Yeah, well, my sisters and I never cared what was happenin' or not on the moon anyway. We would lay on our backs out on the hay pile by the horse barn and try to find shapes in the clouds. Shoot, my sisters didn't have a spark of imagination in them. I'd be pointin' up there to the sky saying, 'You see that cloud up there? Don't that look just like Uncle Carl's horse cart?' And they'd never see a blessed thing," he huffed, shaking his head, staring up at the heavens. "Not a stitch of creativity in 'em." Ben ended with a final grunt and leaned forward, resting his elbows on his knees.

He glanced over to the boy. His backpack was back on his lap, arms wrapped around it. In his fist was the wadded-up brown paper. The thermos remained on the ground nearby.

"You don't want the hot chocolate?"

"You said to wait a little bit," the boy answered. His dark eyes never blinked as he stared at Ben and fidgeted with the paper he held, rolling it around and around in his fist.

"Well, it ought to be cooled some now. Go on, drink it."

Shifting the wadded paper to his other hand, the boy reached down to grab the thermos, but found the backpack too cumbersome. He slid it from his lap to the ground and jammed the brown paper ball behind it. Reaching for the thermos, he drew it onto his lap. He pulled off the plastic cap that also served as a drinking cup, searching for a place to set it down. Glancing at the ground, he changed his mind and pressed the cup between the thermos and his coat. It took him a few turns to get the metal thermos lid unscrewed but he managed and set the small lid on his knee. Pulling the plastic drinking cup from his lap, he poured a cup of steaming liquid and held it to his lips.

"Did we really go to the moon?" He asked.

Ben fixed his eyes on the thermos instead of just staring at the boy. He didn't know where to go with this. "You never learned about that sorta thing in school?"

"No, sir. I've never been to school—I mean, not like at a *regular* school or anything. My mom taught me to read and I worked in writing and math workbooks she picked up from the bookstore. She said I could learn more at home with her than in regular school. There was a lot of rough kids at school and…" He trailed off, looking surprised that he had rattled on as much as he had. "Anyhow, we never talked about anyone going to the moon" he trailed off. The boy poured a refill before screwing the lid back on the thermos and setting it on the ground. He took a long sip from the cup and looked over at Ben.

"Where's your momma now?" Ben asked, meeting the boy's eyes.

The boy went still, the cup lowering to his lap, resting there. A shadow fell over his face and his eyes clouded with a depth of emotion that pulled Ben into their dark vortex. When he answered, he spoke as if Ben wasn't there, looking past him to the wall at Ben's back.

"I...I don't know. She just kept walking until I couldn't see her anymore. She told me to stay. Said they would take care of me. She just kept walking and I just stood there and watched. I just... couldn't...move." He sucked in a gulp of air, his face a mask of anguish, and continued, "I never went in. I ran."

Ben's mind raced with a thousand questions but he didn't dare ask for clarification—not now anyway.

The boy's eyes shone with unshed tears. Along with the sadness Ben saw in those tears, there was a shadow of other conflicting emotions that concerned Ben. The boy looked down into the cup he held, his hands squeezing it so hard that Ben thought it would *pop* right out of his fingers and tumble to the ground.

Even from a distance, and the fact that his small frame was cloaked under an oversized jacket, Ben could see subtle tremors shudder through the boy's shoulders. Emotions spent, the boy sat in silence.

Ben couldn't breathe. His chest was heavy with the burden of the boy's words. He knew the lives of the homeless on the streets were twisted with horrific backstories, many the results of their own poor choices and some with regrettable circumstances that put them there, but he'd never concerned himself with their troubles.

But this boy was the raw form of the results of humanity's carelessness, the offspring of one broken from the cruel hand of destruction.

"I'm Ben. What's your name, boy?"

"Aden," he said, barely above a whisper. "My name is Aden."

9

*B*en was kind of surprised to see the boy back again. He was sitting down on the same crate, his face lifted as he watched the sky. Apparently, the boy hadn't heard Ben come out yet, so he was able to watch him for a moment. His expression was thoughtful and reflective as he gazed upward, and Ben wondered what things were going through the boy's mind. Aden must have finally sensed Ben's presence because his eyes dropped to where Ben stood at the bottom of the steps. He shifted and sat up taller.

"Good to see you, Aden," Ben called out. Ben felt the weight of the bag he held that contained his dinner, judging how far it would go to feed them both.

"Hey, Ben." Aden gave a little wave.

Ben walked over to another crate by the back wall and hefted it to his shoulder with one hand, balancing the thermos and a paper sack in the other. He made his way to where Aden was and set the crate down across from him before depositing the thermos at Aden's feet. Then, he lowered himself onto the crate and rested the food sack on his knees.

"Help yourself," he said, nodding toward the thermos. "Sorry, it's hot chocolate again. I haven't been to the store yet to buy coffee. Shoulda just brought some from home."

Aden reached for the canister. "It's fine. I don't really like coffee anyway."

They sat in comfortable silence as Ben opened the sack and offered one of the two slices of cold pepperoni pizza to Aden, taking the other for himself. He also handed over the small bag of pretzels he'd packed, shoving the empty bag down under his feet.

"How was your day today?" Ben immediately chided himself. *What kind of day do you think the kid had, Ben? It's not like he had a lot of choices...*

Aden didn't seem to mind the question. He was savoring the pizza, chewing every bite slowly and pulling off pepperonis to pop in his mouth. Ben wished he'd just given the boy both of the slices of pizza.

"I had an interesting day," Aden told him. "Want to hear about it?"

"Well...sure! I'm all ears." Ben said, feeling encouraged at the boy's willingness to share..

"I was walking by this apartment building and saw this little girl throw a woman down the steps. She landed right in front of me; her arms and legs were sprawled out in different directions and her head was kind of twisted funny. And the woman was wearing a bathing suit—which was kinda weird," Aden shrugged as if he had just told Ben nothing more earth-shattering than that the price of apples was going up.

The news hit Ben like a jolt of electricity. He sat up and scooted to the edge of the crate.

"*What?!* Where was this? Did you call for help? Was the woman still alive?" Ben couldn't spit the questions out fast enough.

Aden held up a hand to stop Ben. His face was a mask of serious concentration.

"I don't think the woman was alive, but the girl that pushed her did come down to pick her up."

Ben's jaw hung open. *What was going on here?* He jerked his head around, as if expecting someone to walk by so he could get their attention to have them check into this.

"Dear Lord, son. You *saw* all this?! How old was this 'girl' you are talking about? She *picked* this woman up—this woman who you don't even know was still alive—and did *what* with her? What were *you* doing during all this? Why didn't you go for help or something?" Ben's voice rose in panic.

Then…Aden smiled.

Smiled.

"Ready for this?" Aden was snickering now. Ben was convinced he was sitting across from a sociopath and wondered if he could get his belt off fast enough to hog-tie this kid until the police arrived.

"It was a doll, Ben. A Barbie doll." Aden busted out in laughter. "You should see your face!" Aden must have *really* noticed his face at this point and the fact that Ben was not smiling because his laughter tapered off to a giggle before it stopped altogether. He cleared his throat.

"Sorry, Ben. I was just kidding. I mean, I really did see a little girl throw her Barbie down the steps today but I just thought it would be funny to make a story out of it."

Ben blinked, then shook his head slowly, his breathing slowing back to normal, before he broke out into a soft chuckle himself.

"Well, I'll be. You sure had me there, son. Almost gave me a heart attack." He reached up to wipe at the thin layer of sweat that had formed on his forehead.

"I like to make up stories," Aden told him. "Usually, they are fairy tales or funny stories. That one was mean. I'm…sorry."

Ben reached over and gave Aden a playful punch on the arm. "It's alright, boy. You had me there but it's funny now. You have quite an imagination! I'd love to hear more of these stories you come up with but you better warn me next time that it's just a *story*, deal?"

Aden grinned. "Deal."

10

*A*den had been coming by the bakery for several weeks now. Ben told him that his break normally began around 8:30 p.m. weeknights, so Aden headed over after the 7:45 p.m. showing started at the AMC Broadstreet 7 theater. Aden would sit and watch the crowds lined up outside the theater. He didn't get why women went to watch a movie in tight dresses and spiked heels they could barely walk in. *I guess girls just like to have a reason to get dressed up*, he thought.

Meeting Ben every night gave Aden something to look forward to. It became a comfortable ritual for the two of them. Ben made it a habit to make an extra sandwich for Aden, learning that he like extra mayonnaise and hated Swiss cheese, or he would set aside day-old pastries that were marked to be thrown away.

Ben had even gone as far as to give up his extra strong black coffee he loved to drink during his break and started drinking hot chocolate instead because Aden preferred it. He'd made sure to stock up on an industrial-sized box of individual packets—with marshmallows, like the boy liked—so they wouldn't run out for a while.

One night, Ben had filled the thermos with black coffee just to test the waters with Aden.

"Yuck, Ben, this isn't hot chocolate!" Aden complained after he'd taken a big chug of the bitter coffee from the thermos cup. "How can you stand this nasty stuff?" He spit the coffee into the bushes behind him.

Ben laughed at Aden's reaction.

"Aw, now, son, just trying to make a man outta you. I guess I could've sweetened it with sugar and some cream. You're lucky. I make it three times stronger when I drink it for myself."

Aden glared at him and made a gagging sound in his throat.

"That just ain't right, Ben," he complained.

When Aden came by the next night, he and Ben sat and chatted about Ben's childhood growing up with sisters and how Ben's boss, Eddie, who owned Angelo's Bakery, flirted with the female customers when his wife wasn't around.

When Ben handed him a cup full of dark, steamy liquid, Aden lifted one eyebrow and peered cautiously down into the drink.

"It's hot chocolate—I promise," Ben said with a smirk. Aden took a timid sip and smiled.

"They had a new litter of puppies in that pet shop on Chestnut Street today," Aden announced. "I played with them through the window. They were the cutest thing." Aden pulled a tissue from his jacket pocket and wiped chocolate from his chin. "You ever have a dog, Ben?"

"Sure enough," Ben answered, warming to the subject. "I had more dogs growing up than I can count on both hands. I don't think there was ever a time in my early years that I *didn't* have a dog."

Aden continued. "Well, I always stop at this one corner where there's this street performer. He knows how to play a fiddle and even a harmonica. Anyhow, he has this little dog that sits by his feet—and this dog is *ugly* too," Aden stuck his tongue out and made a face. "And when the man plays really high notes on the harmonica, the dog starts howling, real low at first, until he just rears back and yowls up a storm. It makes everyone bust out laughing when he does that."

Ben chuckled. "See, that's the thing. People aren't comin' out there to hear fancy fiddle music playin' as much as they're comin' to see that little dog. Animals just have a way of touchin' people's hearts and openin' their pocketbooks. His owner knows it too—smart man."

Aden nodded, then glanced up at Ben. "When you were my age, what kinds of things did you like to do, Ben?"

Ben rubbed a finger across his chin, considering the question.

"Well...I can't say I had a lot of options being that our place was far from town and we didn't always have a lot of time for just goofin' around. But I did have a buddy who would borrow his pa's truck and a few of us would shoot jackrabbits with our shotguns from the bed of the truck for fun. Back then, it wasn't nothin' for young boys to run around with guns. We learned young how to be responsible and safe with them. Not like teenagers these days." Ben snorted.

"Anyhow, sometimes in the evenings after supper, me and my pa would sit at the table and listen to baseball games on an old radio we had set up in the kitchen. It was one of the only things we had in common: a love for the game. He even took me to see a game or two when I was growin' up. Those were real special moments for me." Ben smiled at the memory. "You know who the Phillies are, son?"

"A baseball team, Ben. I'm not that dumb," Aden rolled his eyes.

Ben went on. "The Phillies were, and still are, my favorite

baseball team. My pa was a Brooklyn Dodgers fan himself but he listened to all the games just for the fun of it. Like any team, the Phillies have had their good and bad seasons. In fact, I recall back in '82, the Phillies played a hundred and sixty-two games and won eighty-nine of them. Two years before that, in '80, they had ninety-one wins and seventy-one losses. They were in first position that year."

Aden was sure Ben couldn't miss the glazed-over look in his eyes as he chattered on about baseball stats.

"Anyhow," he said, " every team has got their good and bad years, but a true fan sticks with their team through thick and thin." Ben shrugged, letting the subject drop.

"I guess you couldn't call yourself a fan if you didn't," Aden said, grabbing another ham sandwich from the bag. Ben had started making it a habit to pack a few extra sandwiches and other snacks for Aden so he could stash them in his backpack for later.

Ben only had ten minutes before his break was over and today was Friday. He was off on the weekends and Aden wouldn't be back until Monday night.

"Got any new stories, kid?" Ben asked. Aden peeled the plastic wrapping away from the sandwich and tore off a man-size bite, chewing thoughtfully.

"Nah, I'm not feeling it tonight. All that baseball talk made me tired." Aden stretched and stood to grab his bags from the ground. "I'm going to go sit and read in the bookstore for a little while. They don't close for another hour or two." Aden loved to go to the bookstore and the library, where he could find a quiet corner to read books that he picked from the shelves.

Ben stood with him.

"Probably better head in a little early anyway," he said. "I gotta stop by the little boys' room real quick."

Aden watched Ben reach into his back pocket for his wallet.

"How about a few bucks to buy yourself a candy bar while you're there?" he asked, pulling out a five-dollar bill and holding it out to Aden.

Aden looked at the money and thought about it, but only for a second. He shook his head.

"No, Ben. I don't want it."

Ben pushed the money back down and slipped the wallet into his back pocket. He gave Aden a nod.

"Alright, son. You be safe out there."

11

When Aden showed up Monday night, Ben was already outside working on breaking down a large stack of boxes into a neat, flat pile. He looked up when he heard Aden approaching.

"Hey, Ben! Whatcha doing?"

Ben looked over the top of a large cardboard box he wrestled with. He pushed his full weight against it until it flattened to the ground.

"You're just in time, boy!" Ben smiled broadly, tossing the flattened box near the stack by the wall. He pulled a large handkerchief from his back pocket and mopped his brow.

Aden was excited. "Really?! For what?"

Ben made a dramatic show of sweeping his arms toward the stack of unfinished boxes. "To help me break these boxes down for pickup tomorrow." Ben pointed over at the porch. "Throw your stuff up there."

Seeing the reluctant look on Aden's face, "Oh, come on now, it'll just take a few minutes; then we'll sit and eat."

Aden grumbled under his breath as he walked over and tossed

his stuff onto the porch. Kicking at a chunk of broken glass on the ground, he shuffled back over to where Ben sliced through the packaging tape on the boxes with a utility knife. When he finished cutting the tape on a box, he handed it to Aden and showed him how to flatten the box and make neat piles that Ben would tie up with string later.

Aden muddled through the work at first, his stack of boxes starting to pile up. Ben slowed his pace, allowing him to catch up. They worked quietly together for several minutes before Aden spoke up. "Do you like working here, Ben? I mean, like, do you ever get tired of cleaning and fixing things all the time? Seems like your job isn't super exciting."

Ben's answer was gruff as he gave Aden a sideways glance. "Well, to answer your question honestly, son, I don't think work has to be something that you *like*, it's just something that you *do*. My pa used to tell me that working hard is what keeps a man alive; that when a man stops workin' he might as well lie down and die."

Aden stared at Ben liked he'd just landed from another planet. "Sheesh, Ben, that's a little dramatic. What's the point in living if we have to work all the time just to be happy?"

Ben heaved the last box Aden's way before standing up and stretching.

"*Pshaw,*" Ben huffed. "See here, son. Work isn't just about doing something physical with your hands—although that's important too—but it's about always trying to make the world just a little bit better. Work might mean you have to put effort into makin' a relationship survive. It can also be in the form of trying real hard to keep your mouth shut when you want to tell someone off. Work means progress toward somethin' positive. It's the opposite of sitting around and doing *nothin'* and not even trying. I don't claim to be a religious man myself, but I'm pretty sure my granny used to quote the Holy Bible when she said somethin' about idleness being the devil's workshop."

Aden reached for another box. He was getting faster at this. "That's deep, Ben. Kind of creepy though."

Aden made quick work of the last few boxes while Ben chattered on about unimportant things like the weather and other topics he paid no attention to, then stacked them neatly on the last pile they'd created against the back wall. Turning to Ben, who now sat on the porch waiting for him to catch up, Aden planted his fists on his hips and asked, "Do you think the Bible says anything against us stopping and eating now?"

Ben reached down and grabbed a wadded ball of discarded tape from the ground and hurled it at Aden, who ducked just as it sailed past his head.

"Let's go eat, boy," Ben said, tousling Aden's hair as he passed him and headed to the porch to grab the food. "I guess you earned it tonight."

BEN HAD BEEN ROLLING the idea around in his head for a few days now. He loved to watch Aden come to life when he was telling Ben his stories. It was during those moments that Aden was transported to his rightful place as a young boy: free from the weight of the world, bubbling with energy and childish antics—happy. Aden had grown comfortable enough with Ben that, whenever Ben teased or grumbled, Aden gave it right back to him.

Aden never volunteered any details about his mother or why he chose to scrape out a survival on the streets when he could allow someone to place him somewhere safer. Ben came to care about the quiet, mischievous young man with the expressive eyes that held a hint of sadness in their depths. Aden had swept into Ben's life as a sparrow fluttering to find a place to build its nest.

Ben tried to tempt Aden to open up by sharing some of his own childhood memories, but it was like skipping a pebble on the water and waiting for the ripples to reach the other side—how much Aden wanted to share was entirely in his control.

"Aden, I got an idea!" Ben said one night after one of Aden's stories made him laugh so hard it gave him the hiccups. "I got one of those pocket recorder things at home I could bring. You can tell your stories and I'll record you. Then, I'll go home and write them out in a notebook from your recording. All your stories written down in a book...imagine that. Shoot, maybe you could submit them to a magazine or somethin' and become a famous writer someday!"

Ben was wound up with the idea of the project and, after presenting it to Aden, looked to him to share in his excitement. Aden stared at Ben, his head cocked to the side, eyebrows scrunched together as he considered Ben's offer. After a moment, his face smoothed as his enthusiasm caught up with Ben's.

"Well, alright...let's do it! It kinda sounds cool, I think. We could fill up a whole notebook and... Hey! You could draw the pictures for the stories—like a professional illustrator! Of course"—he gnawed on his bottom lip—"I couldn't pay you or anything until people started buying my book..." His elation deflated as the enormity of the task settled over him.

Ben put his hands up to interrupt. "Ain't happenin', son. I can't even draw me a stick person without it lookin' like you handed a pencil to a one-year-old. I got me a good imagination but it all stays up in my head." He tapped an index finger against his forehead for emphasis. "Can't never get down on paper what I see in my mind. Better leave drawings out of it for now."

Ben's comical reply seemed to settle Aden's anxiousness. He laughed before tilting back the cup to drain the last of the now-tepid chocolate and handing it back to Ben, who screwed it back onto the top of the thermos. Aden shifted on the crate and tucked his legs against him for warmth.

"Do you have a family at home, Ben?" Aden asked.

It was an innocent question but Ben felt the breath go out of him. It took him a second to absorb the shock of the unexpected inquiry. It was a predictable question that everyone tends to get around to eventually but, somehow, it made Ben almost *angry*—at least that's what he thought he was feeling at the moment. A thousand sparks flew around inside his mind as reason frantically sought to seize and tame them.

Family. Home.

Ben choked on the words that formed but never made it past his throat. Aden watched him intently, waiting for his reply, a flicker of uncertainty in his round eyes. Ben shook his head. It was the best attempt he could make to answer the boy. Aden's pebble thrown on the water sunk like a lead marble into the abyss of Ben's thoughts, never making a single ripple on the surface.

BEN LAY in bed that night staring up into the darkness. He hadn't meant to make Aden feel bad. His past just wasn't something he let himself think about very often and he didn't have a ready answer to give the boy. The story of what was once his family was a brief novella at best. Their small unit of three was a short-lived dream that had come and gone before he'd known what he had. For every good memory there were bad ones that erased them.

Ben had tried hard to be a loving father to Jeremy and made an honest attempt at being a good husband, but the booze always got in the way. Even after fourteen years of being sober, the demon showed up unexpectedly, sitting on his shoulder, invading his thoughts and tempting him. Ben would conquer the demon in an upswing of self-confidence and resolve, only to wake up a blubbering mess of wrinkled clothes and vomit a few days later and realize he'd undone everything he'd tried to make better.

One Friday night, when Ben stayed out all night drinking again, Emma had taken Jeremy, who was eight at the time, to make a better life. He didn't blame her—not then, not now. When he'd swaggered in late the next morning after waking up sprawled across the front seat of his car in the tavern's parking lot, he found the note she had left him.

Maybe it was his best friend, Jake, and a new employer being willing to give Ben another chance that kick-started his recovery. Or perhaps it was the reality of his devastating loss that finally sunk in after being sober for a few days. Either way, it was a bittersweet unfolding of a new turn in the road for him and no one to share it with.

Tears trickled down Ben's face as he continued to stare into the empty darkness above him. Shadows danced across the ceiling, mocking him, reminding him how alone he was in the world. He could feel his palms get clammy and a burning start deep in his belly.

If he didn't get control, he'd be drowning in a bottle of whiskey before he could stop himself.

12

*A*den brought Ben a surprise this time. Ben could tell right away Aden was excited about something by the way he was pacing back and forth with his hands jammed down in his coat pockets, first looking up at the trees, then down at the ground, then at the door Ben had just stepped out of, one eyebrow cocked as he watched Aden's antics with growing interest. A big smile was plastered on the boy's face as Ben made his way down the steps.

"Boy, you lookin' like you just won the state spelling bee or something," Ben said, looking him up and down. Ben sauntered over to his crate, dragging it closer to Aden's with his foot, and plopped down. The thermos was placed between his feet on the ground and a paper bag set down near Aden, who had seated himself on the very edge of his crate and was focused on unzipping the front of his backpack.

Aden glanced at the bag on the ground next to him, ignoring it, then over to the thermos at Ben's feet. He thrust an arm down into his backpack as he mumbled, "That thermos is new."

Ben started to explain that he figured it was time to replace the old dented one but shrugged off the unnecessary explanation. Aden didn't look like he cared about that right now.

"Ta-da!" Aden announced as he held up a small white box wrapped in cellophane, a frayed pink ribbon dangling from one corner. "I found this box of chocolates today! It hasn't even been opened!" He frowned at the drooping pink ribbon. "Guess the ribbon got torn up a little," he said as he pulled it off the corner of the box and dropped it into the opening of his backpack. "Anyhow, I thought we could celebrate our birthdays!" Aden's face was a mask of excitement and wonder. Ben leaned forward to peek at Aden's treasure, his anticipation building.

"Well," Ben said, "this is about as good a party as one could have! I don't know that I've ever eaten expensive chocolates out of a fancy box before. 'Course it ain't my birthday or nothin'—is it yours?" Ben asked.

Aden's brows puckered in concentration as he worked the lid off the box and set it down on the ground next to him. "Who cares?" he shrugged, "We can celebrate a birthday whenever we want, right?"

Ben reached down to retrieve the thermos and unscrewed the lid. He poured the first cup of chocolate and inhaled the warmth of the steam as he watched Aden. The boy held the open candy box in his lap and was staring down at the decorated mounds, each encased in a delicate white paper cup.

"Well, whatcha waiting for, boy? Serve us up those fancy birthday chocolates." He motioned to the brown bag. "You got a bologna sandwich in there too."

They spent the next few minutes of their time together taking small bites of chocolate—it just felt like you should eat special chocolates in small appreciative bites instead of gobbling them in one messy gulp—and passing the hot chocolate cup back and forth between them. Ben wasn't a fan of chocolate (licorice was more to his liking) but he closed his eyes in mock delight as he sampled his piece just to make the experience fun for Aden. Aden was taking forever to finish his second piece, nibbling around the edges and turning the chocolate over to inspect it like it was a rare gemstone in the hands of a collector.

Ben could tell this was a special moment for Aden after always having to eat cast-off food out of the trash. Ben wondered if the boy had ever had a box of chocolates to himself before. *And, here he is, sharin' this box with me.*

Aden must have felt Ben's eyes on him because he hurried to pop the rest of the chocolate piece into his mouth and licked his lips. He reached for the box lid and pressed it down firmly.

"We can eat a little each night," Aden announced, the resiliency in his voice suggesting that he wouldn't give in to the temptation to sample another piece before tomorrow night.

"Guess it's my turn for a little contribution to our birthday party," Ben said. His hand slid to one of the side pockets of his wool jacket and Aden watched him struggle to pull something out. Ben tugged out a small, black box and set it down on his knee.

"It's a pocket recorder, like I was tellin' you about," Ben explained. "I just put fresh batteries in it this afternoon 'fore I left the house." Aden stared blankly at him—the significance of the moment lost on the boy.

"We can start recording your stories for me to write down."

Aden's face lit up as he remembered Ben's idea about recording his stories. He leaned forward and poked a timid finger toward the device resting on Ben's knee, then drew it back like he thought it might snap at him. He frowned.

"I've never seen a recorder so small like that. My mom had a bigger one like it in the closet. She used to record songs off the radio when she was a kid," he said.

"Yeah, well, same idea here," Ben said. "You just start talkin' and I'll push the button to record you. You have a story ready to share?"

Elbows planted on his knees, Aden rested his chin on his palms as he thought about a story to share. He picked at the gravel on the ground with the tip of his shoe for a moment before sitting up and announcing,

"Sure, I have one. It's not real long or anything, but I like it." He reached over to push down the box of chocolates still poking up out of his backpack and zipped the bag closed.

Ben waited patiently while Aden pulled the bologna sandwich from the crumpled bag at his feet and carefully pulled the cellophane halfway down to hold the sandwich without his bare hands touching it. Aden wiggled to make himself more comfortable on the plastic crate and brought the sandwich to his mouth for a bite. Ben was getting ready to complain that they didn't have all night to do this, when Aden swallowed and began his first story.

Ben pushed the *RECORD* button on the device.

"Okay, so, there was this old lady that lived on a farm just outside of a big city," Aden began, then faltered. "I mean...I guess she doesn't have to be *old*..." Ben waved an impatient hand for Aden to go on. "Well, anyhow, she never went to the city because she didn't like crowds and all the crazy people that lived there. She liked to do things the old-fashioned way because that's all she knew. She washed her clothes every week in a big washtub and hung them to dry on an old rope she had tied between two gigantic trees at the back of her farm. After the clothes dried for a few hours, she would go back outside, take them down, and throw them in a big basket she carried with her."

"One day, the old lady noticed that there was a pair of men's pants on the rope." Aden became more animated as he tore another bite from the sandwich and continued the story between chewing. "The old lady lived alone so, naturally, she only expected for *her* clothes to be drying outside. She thought that somebody was playing a joke on her. She looked around to see if there was anyone around but didn't see one soul for miles—and she could see pretty far out there on that flat farm land. Anyways, she took the strange pants down and tossed them into her basket, figuring she would throw them out later if no one came to confess their prank. Then, she figured that maybe somebody thought she had a husband who needed the pants and had donated them to her. She really didn't know *what* to think at this point. She just shrugged and continued gathering the rest of her clothes off the line. That was when she noticed that one of her skirts was missing!"

Aden started giggling, clearly aware of the ending of the story before Ben did, then steadied himself with a big breath and continued. "Now, the poor old lady was really confused! *What is going on here?* she thought, shaking her head and looking around. She stood there, totally confused, before she finally gave up and went into the house. Then, a few days later, when she went to get her dry clothes again, there was her missing skirt hanging on the rope! But now one of her other skirts was missing!" Aden was laughing harder now—head thrown back, his sandwich forgotten.

Ben chuckled too but wasn't quite sure where the story was going yet. "Go on now. This is gettin' good," he urged.

Aden leaned toward Ben, forgetting the black box on Ben's knee as he got into the story, his voice lowering to build suspense. "She had never believed in ghosts before but started worrying that maybe there was such a thing when she heard a knock on her door a few days later."

Ben leaned in toward Aden. He half expected a drum roll to come from somewhere to complement the intense moment.

"The old lady answered the door and a man was standing there and he was wearing…" Aden's body shook with all the giggling he was doing as he worked to spit out the last words, "Her missing skirt!" He started laughing so hard that he almost dropped the forgotten sandwich in the dirt.

Ben was laughing too even though he didn't know the punchline yet. It was enough just imagining a man standing in the old lady's doorway wearing a woman's skirt. Or, maybe it was hearing Aden's uncontrolled giggling that tickled Ben. "This I gotta hear," he prompted.

"Well," Aden started again after getting a grip on himself. "The man explained that he was a traveler and had wanted to wash his dirty pants in the river that was near the old lady's property. But he didn't have anything to wear while they dried. He told her that he had borrowed one of her skirts to wear while his pants were drying and figured he would come back after dark to get his pants back. But when he came back later that night, everything was gone— including his pants!"

Ben threw his head back and broke out into a hearty laugh. He kept one hand on the recorder, though, so it didn't slip off.

"The traveler told the old lady that he wore the skirt for another day or two, hiding in the woods, hoping that his pants would show up back on the line," Aden said. "But, by then, the skirt he was wearing was filthy and needed to be washed too. He washed it and exchanged it for another skirt that was dry, since his pants were still missing. 'I'm sorry, ma'am,' he told her, 'I got to go into the city and I can't be wearing a skirt. Can I have my'"—Aden and Ben were both laughing hard now and wiping tears from their eyes —"'pants back?'"

Aden covered his mouth with one hand as he laughed, while the other hand still held the now-drooping sandwich. He noticed it then and stopped laughing long enough to take another bite.

Ben punched a finger on the *STOP* button, shaking his head and chuckling. "Where'd ya get that story, boy? I'd like to actually see some vagabond walkin' around in a skirt lookin' for his pants," he said, still snickering. He tucked the recorder back into his jacket pocket and retrieved the thermos cup from the ground.

Screwing the cup back on the thermos, Ben reached down to collect wrappers and napkins scattered at their feet. He was pretty sure it was way past time to be done with his break.

Aden shrugged into his backpack and reached for his sleeping bag. "I just made it up," he said. "I think of all kinds of things when I'm waiting to fall asleep at night. Nothing better to do, I guess."

Ben shook his head and smiled. "Well, I'm gonna have me another good laugh when I listen to this and copy it down." Suddenly, Ben grew somber, all frivolity dissipated as he considered his next words. "Where you sleepin' tonight, boy?" His gray eyes were serious as stared at Aden.

Aden shrugged and looked away. As he stood up, the sleeping bag made a *swishing* sound against his thigh.

"I'm good, Ben. Honest." He shrugged again and offered his hand for a high-five. Ben's hand met his in the air.

Ben worried that he'd asked too soon, broken an unspoken rule between them to never bring up Aden's existence outside of their little world at the back of the bakery.

Aden looked at the ground, then back up to Ben, a forced smile fixed on his face.

"I'm good."

13

*A*den sat hunched on the ground, his back pressed against the jagged edge of the entryway corner, the uneven bricks digging into his right shoulder blade where the backpack had shifted. His legs were trembling and he could feel the dampness from a layer of sweat that was forming above his upper lip.

Four boys stood over him, blocking any escape. He'd been warming himself inside the sheltered entryway of the bookstore he always visited, browsing through a discarded newspaper to pass the time until he would meet Ben, when they stepped out of the shadows. A narrow alley was sandwiched between the bookstore and a multistory apartment building. It was from this dark alley that the boys had emerged and come up on Aden without warning.

Aden stared up at them, silently praying that they would move on and leave him alone. Across the street, an angry tomcat crouched under a light post, howling and spitting at an intruder lurking in the shadows. His high-pitched warnings were answered by equally aggressive growls and hisses. Between the raging felines and the wall of unfriendly faces towering over him, the whole scene was unfolding like an ominous forecast of evil intentions.

By the way the boys glared down at him, Aden had no doubt in his mind that evil was on their agenda tonight.

The boy at the front was the biggest of the group and seemed to be the leader. His loose-fitting tactical black khaki pants, black-and-white checkered Vans, and red zip-up hoodie were a stark contrast against the backdrop of the drab filth of the neighborhood. Most people who were up to no good wore dark colors to blend in with the shadowed buildings and soot-covered concrete walls surrounding them. But the somber boy standing in front of him seemed determined to stand out.

A bulky gray knit cap was jammed down over his ears. A narrow cascade of black hair that had escaped the cap draped lazily over one eye. Two of the other boys were dressed in all black from head to toe, both wearing black knit beanies, while the last boy, the smallest, was dressed in blue jeans and a striped flannel shirt that looked to be three sizes too big on him. He wore a San Francisco Giants baseball cap turned backwards on his head and was thrusting his chin up and down in a nervous, energetic cadence.

Aden's eyes drifted over each of the boys' faces, his heart thudding like a bass drum against his shirt. Their features would be forever engraved in his memory after this night, he knew. But Aden didn't move. He didn't think he could even if he wanted to. It felt like his joints had all locked in place.

The leader acted first, darting in so fast that Aden never saw it coming. Snatching the newspaper out of his hands—a chunk of a corner still clasped in Aden's closed fingers—the boy threw it down on the sidewalk.

"Whaddya doin', kid, looking in the *Lost and Found* section for your puppy?" the boy sneered into Aden's face. "You're a little young to be runnin' away from home. You mad at your granny or somethin'?"

His comrades snickered as the smaller, nervous-looking one with the Giants cap moved forward out of the shadows and slid in close to the leader's side. Before Aden could respond, the small boy grabbed a fistful of Aden's jacket hood and ripped him off the steps. Aden heard the tearing of fabric and felt his elbow jam against the wall corner, sending a sharp pain through his lower arm.

"No, *please*, just leave me alone," Aden whimpered. He tried to swing his arms up to defend himself, but the bulk of the load on his back weighed him down.

With the other boys joining in, they dragged him into the alley and shoved him down next to the brick wall of the apartment building. His sleeping bag had rolled off as they dragged him. The smallest boy reached for him again, giving him another violent shove and tearing off his backpack with several jerking motions. Aden felt like his shoulder was being torn out of its socket. Panic coursed through his body in icy waves. He felt like his throat was full of sand, trapping his screams in its depths. He was disoriented, shell-shocked, frozen with terror.

Aden managed to crawl closer to the wall and press himself against it, curling his body into a ball. He didn't remember hitting his head but felt throbbing pain on the left side of his skull. He watched one of the boys wearing all black unzip his backpack and dump its few contents out on the ground. The boy kicked Aden's clothes, books, and other belongings around, even stomping on the small box of chocolates Aden and Ben had shared the night before.

The second boy in all black jogged over and kicked the box lid against a metal trash bin near the opposite wall, the soft *thump* echoing in the narrow alley, while the other boys stood around laughing and rooting the two boys on. Aden watched in a petrified stupor as they molested his meager possessions. After the brief distraction of entertainment, the boys turned and moved in unison toward Aden.

A shadow blocked Aden's view as the pair of black-clad legs with the Vans appeared in front of him. "We ain't never seen you 'round here before, kid," the voice snarled, his menacing tone strangely harmonizing with the two tomcats still going at it across the street. "You shoulda stayed home with your momma." Aden knew the voice without looking up: It was the largest boy—the leader.

The first blow came from where the boy with the baseball cap stood. Aden saw the foot coming toward his face and tried to block the force with his hands.

He pressed harder against the wall behind him, sinking his body further into the ground to soften the blow, but it was pointless. The forceful kick made contact with Aden's left eyebrow—a thousand brilliant lights suddenly filling his vision. His head jerked back and slammed against the brick wall. He heard a dull *thud* shudder through his skull mere seconds before the pain registered.

Aden didn't remember much after that, other than the muted grunts that escaped his lips as his body was battered with an onslaught of fists and feet, the pain from the impact not fully registering in his brain. He felt the crunch of gravel against his ear as he tried to curl into a tight ball to protect his body from the beating.

Boiling waves of nausea turned and twisted in his stomach. The rolling mass rose in his chest before the flow of hot bile projected from his swollen lips. He had no idea how long it was before the blackness came—when his body no longer registered the pain.

BEN CHECKED the time on his watch again. *8:55 p.m.*

Aden usually showed up right on time, a little early even, for Ben's break at 8:30, but there was no sign of the boy. He needed to head back in soon or Mia would wonder where he was. But he was worried. It wasn't like the boy had anyplace else to be and Ben knew Aden looked forward to what was probably the only solid meal the kid got on most days. There had to be a good reason he hadn't showed. Ben couldn't ignore the creeping dread that the reason wasn't one he wanted to hear.

The sky was a magnificent canopy above Ben. A blanket of stars covered the night sky while dappled clouds drifted in front of the half-moon, blocking it from Ben's view. The display was peaceful, calm—the polar opposite of what Ben was feeling at the moment. He'd never taken much time to think about God, but figured this might be a good time to slip in a prayer.

"I believe you're up there, God, and you're seein' much more than I can see. If you don't mind, watch over the boy, wherever he is. He's been through enough in life."

Just as the last words were uttered, the clouds parted, allowing the moon to cast its warm glow over the empty lot where Ben sat talking to God. He hoped it was a good sign.

"Gotta go," he mumbled, pushing off of the porch wall. He reached down and scooped up the thermos and bag at his feet, almost dropping them in his distraction, and shifted the notebook tucked under his jacket to secure it. He stared down at the bag in his hand.

Better leave it here in case he shows up. Don't want him going hungry the rest of the night because he missed me.

Ben left the bag on the top porch step, hoping Aden would see it.

He was in no hurry as he rested his hand on the door handle and looked around again. Part of him was hoping that Aden would come running around the corner, claiming that he'd been on an adventure somewhere and had lost track of time. He doubted Aden had any real *adventures* that were so exciting that he would miss meeting him, but Ben was struggling to make sense of the boy's absence.

Did the police pick him up, or worse, some pervert? Ben bit his lip in worry, glancing over at the empty crate Aden always occupied. *He's got that big old clock down there at city hall. It's not like he didn't know the time.*

The Philadelphia City Hall clock tower—a regal French Second Empire-style timekeeper, towering five hundred and forty-eight feet over the city—featured four clock faces, one of which faced Broad Street, one of Philly's main thoroughfares. Anyone within blocks of the tower had access to the time.

"Where are you at, boy?" Ben shook his head once more at the hazy night sky and pried the heavy door open.

He hesitated briefly before the door swung closed and latched behind him.

"ADEN, son, wake up. I made your favorite: blueberry pancakes with whipped butter and honey," his mother whispered. Aden's senses nudged him to respond. A faint, sweet smell mixed with a rich spicy scent that he couldn't identify drifted into his nostrils. He loved blueberry pancakes more than anything in the world but that's not what stirred him.

It was her voice that called to him—reaching through the fog of his dreams, stirring a deep yearning in his heart. Her touch dainty as a fairy's, as delicate fingers brushed the hair back from his eyes and gently tucked it behind his ear. Soothing, comforting...he felt himself drifting back to sleep.

"You know what today is?" she asked, her breath tickling his ear. He couldn't remember what today was. "It's your birthday, son," she offered. Her small hand rubbed his shoulder in a slow, rhythmic back-and-forth motion, like the ebb and flow of the sea against the shoreline.

He felt the heat from her hand seep through the thin material that covered him. It warmed his skin against the morning chill that had settled over his weary body. He felt so tired...

His birthday.

They always spent the whole day together on his birthday. They would snuggle on the couch and read books or work on a puzzle on the coffee table. He remembered her sitting and listening to him read pages and pages from his joke book, indulging him with a smile or a shake of her head in response to goofy riddles that weren't even that funny.

They would order pizza for dinner and each enjoy their own pint of their favorite ice cream—his was chocolate peanut butter— for dessert. At bedtime, like most nights that he was lucky enough to have her home, she would sit on the edge of his cot and listen while he told her stories that were birthed from his lively imagination.

One night, he told her a story about a dragon that attacked pirates, another about a little girl who kept magic feathers in her purse that she dropped on mean people to make them become kind. Another time, it was about a king who invited his whole kingdom (a small one, thankfully) to live in his palace.

His stories tended to have a hero or heroine that helped others in need or came to someone's rescue because it made Aden feel happy. He always tried to weave a funny twist into his tales just to make his mom smile. How he loved her smile... If he was particularly creative, he could get her to laugh out loud.

"Wake up, Aden..." Her voice called again to him, breaking through the fog of his memories. His eyes remained closed but he pictured her pale skin and long brown hair that flowed in waves down her back. He imagined her beautiful green eyes that carried a hint of sadness, yet glowed with love when she looked at her son.

"Momma," he whispered.

14

*A*den's eyes jerked open. He tried to focus but indistinguishable images danced in his vision and he felt dizzy. He closed his eyes and tried to open them again. This time, he made out a dark shadow in front of him but could only focus one of his eyes—the other was swollen shut. He heard labored breathing. *Is that me?* He felt so disoriented.

Then, the shadow in front of him moved. He squinted with his good eye and more details came into focus. A woman was crouched in front of him. Her head seemed remarkably large and disproportionate. Aden blinked again and the woman became more clear. She was an older woman with dark brown skin. She wore a fur cap on her head and there was a wild panicked look on her face. The woman reached out to nudge Aden's shoulder.

His body jolted from the pain.

"No!" he whispered. "Don't touch me…"

"Are you alright, kid?" She placed a hand to her chest. "I was so scared—I thought you were dead." She leaned in to inspect him a little closer. The woman's breath smelled like stale cigarettes and Aden's stomach tightened with a wave of nausea.

Kneeling close to him, the woman blocked his view, but he could make out colored patches of a medley of shoes and boots and knew that a small crowd was forming behind her.

"I've got to... get up. I need to get out of here," he croaked.

Aden reached for the woman's arm and latched on. He leaned against her as he tried to sit up. Shards of pain exploded throughout his body. He was sure he was going to black out. Tears threatened to come but he fought them back, their salty moisture stinging his swollen eye. He refused to cry with all these people staring at him. Aden couldn't seem to clear his head. He felt like he was drifting in a dense fog, confused, and trapped.

"I can't stay here," he said aloud—but it was really to himself he spoke.

Aden shifted his head to use his good eye to search for a place to escape to. A narrow door in the side of the apartment building caught his eye. Using the woman to lean on for stability, he tried to stand. His legs wobbled under him and he landed hard on his backside.

"Sit still, honey," the woman said, "Help is on the way." She tried to hold him down with a firm hand on his shoulder, but Aden resisted.

There was a distant wail of sirens that grew louder as they neared the scene. Aden felt a sudden rush of adrenaline. Rolling to his knees, he gripped the woman's heavy jacket and used it to propel himself to a standing position. He swayed but stayed on his feet this time.

Taking shallow breaths through the pain and nausea that engulfed his body, Aden steadied himself for a moment before shuffling toward the door—away from the gawking crowd and the fast-approaching sirens.

"Honey, you're hurt," the woman called out, standing and

holding out a hand to him. "You need to wait for the ambulance." A man in a business suit stepped from the crowd. "Hey, kid, you need help. You need to go to the hospital," he said. Other voices joined the chorus, beckoning for Aden to wait.

Aden struggled to quicken his steps, his ears tuned to any footsteps following.

"I...I live here," he croaked out. Every step was excruciatingly painful and he knew he was limping badly. "I'm...I'm okay. I just wanna go home." He didn't wait for an answer or give them a chance to stop him.

God, please let the door be unlocked.

Aden wanted to lean his tortured body against the door and give in to the pain, but fear drove him past it. They were right. He was sure he needed to go to the hospital but he couldn't take that chance.

By some miracle, the door was unlocked when Aden's shaky hand gripped the knob. With a sharp pull that made Aden gasp in pain, the door swung open. Aden pushed through and entered a dimly lit hallway with stairs leading to the top floors. Under the stairwell, Aden noticed another door and veered toward it.

It was an old supply closet that looked like it hadn't been used in years. There wasn't even a doorknob—just an empty hole where it should have been. Aden curled his fingers into the hole and pulled the door toward him.

The tiny closet was empty except for a few old beer cans and dust balls scattered on the floor. Hoping no one would come looking for him, Aden dragged himself in, pulling the door closed behind him, and slid down the closet wall to the grimy floor. His breathing was labored as he worked to tuck himself into a ball against the corner.

He knew his head was a bloody mess. Something felt sticky on the back of his scalp and his nostrils were packed with crust. Licking his lips, Aden tasted something metallic and coppery.

I'm going to be okay, he told himself. *I'm going to be fine...*

Drowsiness settled over him. He could feel open cuts and sore spots all over his body, but he didn't care. He didn't want to think about anything about tonight—not the hoard of curious bystanders in the alley, not the agony torturing every inch of his body, and he especially couldn't bear to picture the faces of the boys who brutally abused him just for the fun of it. He hated them, hated his mother for leaving him out here, hated the people staring down at him with pity...

He didn't want to fight all the emotions and pain entangled in his mind right now. All he wanted was to be left alone. Nestling his head into the closet corner, he gave in to the pain and exhaustion.

15

"Sorry I'm late, Mia." Ben poked his head around the corner while he hung up his jacket in the hall supply closet. They've got Fifth Street all blocked off for repairs. Had to go three blocks outta my way to get here." Mia peeked at him through the other side of the glass display case she was wiping down.

"No worries, Ben. Business has been slow. Maybe all the traffic being redirected has discouraged customers from dropping in." She gave the case a few more swipes with the cloth before throwing the rag over her shoulder and walking over to where Ben leaned against the counter. She pointed at a white cardboard box behind him.

"I pulled some goodies left over from this morning. There's a few bagels and donuts and a couple of brownies, I think. Give 'em to that young man when he comes by tonight," she said, pulling the damp rag from her shoulder and tossing it into an old paint bucket on the floor reserved for rags and aprons that needed laundering.

"Aden," Ben said softly.

Mia looked back at him. "Huh?"

Ben shrugged. "Oh, the boy—his name is Aden."

Mia washed her hands at the sink. "Aden...that's a nice name. Does he live close by here? Doesn't his family wonder where the kid goes at night?"

Ben snapped two paper towels from the holder on the wall next to him and handed them to Mia to dry her hands with. He chose to ignore her questions.

"Thing is, Aden hasn't been comin' by the past few days. I'm a little worried about him," Ben said.

Mia looked up from drying her hands. "Oh? Maybe he's sick?" Eyebrows raised, she teased, "Or maybe he's tired of hanging out with an old man." Her face softened. "Think about it, Ben. He's a young boy. Why wouldn't he be hanging out with friends instead of you?"

Mia didn't know Aden had no friends—and no home, for that matter—but Ben wasn't about to share all that. He didn't feel that he had the right to tell that part of Aden's story.

The bell above the door tinkled as a middle-aged man with two small boys walked in. Mia threw the paper in the trash bin and adjusted her apron as she went to wait on them. She gave Ben a playful punch on the arm as she passed him. "He'll be back, Ben. If for nothing else, for all those sweets you keep his belly full with."

Ben grinned and turned toward the kitchen to get started on his work. As he washed up the baking pans and mixing bowls, his mind drifted back to Aden. He couldn't help but worry. Mia didn't know that Aden pretty much had nothing better to do than *hang out* with an old man most nights. *I'm the only friend he's got right now, even if I wouldn't be his first choice for company,* he thought, reaching up to turn the water off.

Ben continued to fret as he swept, puffs of flour swirling from the floor and tickling his nostrils.

Should I go look for him? he thought. *No, I wouldn't even know where to start.*

Ben ran through scenarios in his mind as he pushed the neat pile of spilled sugar and flour he'd made onto the dustpan.

Maybe the police or child protective services picked him up and he's getting the help he needs. Maybe his mother found him and brought him home. He shook his head. *Aden would be better off without her.* Ben stood up suddenly, broom dangling in one hand, with a sobering thought.

Oh, God, I hope he wasn't lured into some trucker's rig and is headed to God-knows-where, or picked up by a pimp...

He couldn't stand here thinking about this. Mia would be calling him to help up front soon and he wasn't finished back here yet. Ben quickly brushed the rest of the pile onto the dustpan and dumped it in the trash.

*a*den didn't know much about broken bones but he didn't think he had any. After spending the rest of the night and most of the next day cramped inside the tiny supply closet, he knew he needed to come up with a plan. Someone was sure to discover him here.

When he tried to stand, his head spun wildly and his legs buckled under him. He had to lean against the wall for almost five minutes before the dizziness passed and he was strong enough to push open the closet door. He knew he should just slide back to the floor and forget the whole idea, but he was mad with thirst and he badly needed to go to the bathroom.

Aden crept into the dark hallway. He had no idea what time of day it was. He waited to be sure he didn't hear anyone coming and turned the knob on the outside door. He was grateful to see that it was dark outside. His heart pounded as he peeked around to see if the boys had come back to look for him. There was no one in the alley as far as he could tell.

Moving slowly, Aden slid behind a trash bin to relieve himself, then picked his way through a few bags sitting at the top of the bin, looking for food. He could only reach whatever bags were close to the top because there was no way he could haul himself over the edge to reach for more. His head was pounding and his ribs screamed in pain with every small movement. He still could barely see out of his swollen eye. He found nothing to eat but did find a half-empty bottle of soda that he guzzled down.

His movements were awkward. Aden bit on his bottom lip to keep from crying out and had to stop several times to lean against a wall to rest. He was scared, peering cautiously over his shoulder with his good eye several times, thankful no one was around. He was sensitive to every noise: the sound of children playing from an open apartment window above him and thinking he heard a rat skitter by near the trash bin. He stayed toward the back of the alley to avoid the streetlights.

There was no sign of his backpack but he did find his sleeping bag, which had rolled under an empty bin near the alley entrance. After several tries at getting down on his hands and knees and another minute stretching out his arm enough to touch it, Aden was finally able to retrieve the bag. He'd reopened a wound on his head in the process but he was beyond caring at this point.

Aden wouldn't be caught outside at night again in this part of town. With the sleeping bag clutched close to body, he made his way back to the supply closet, hungry and in pain, but safe for now.

———

BEN WAS THROWING out the dirty mop water when he spotted Aden. He was sitting on the ground under a canopy of trees by the edge of the loading dock. Ben pushed the empty bucket off to the side of the porch and made his way down the steps. Aden didn't look up as he approached. Ben slowed his pace.

The boy was hunched over, poking around in the dirt with a small branch, oblivious to Ben's presence. It was his silence, or maybe just raw instinct, that alerted Ben that something was wrong.

"Aden?" Ben whispered. He stopped a few feet from Aden, waiting for the boy to acknowledge his presence.

Maybe he's daydreaming and didn't hear me come up, Ben thought. *I don't want to scare him out of his skin just walkin' up on him.*

He waited.

"Hey, Ben," came Aden's faint reply, his eyes fixed on the stick he held.

Ben held his ground—unmoving. It was like looking at a whipped dog. Any wrong move might cause him to bolt for the bushes.

"You sure are a sight for sore eyes, boy," Ben said, testing the waters with a few timid steps. Something didn't feel right. "Thought you mighta found someplace serving fried chicken and green beans and stuck around there for a while—not that I'd blame ya."

Silence.

Ben moved closer until he had reached the crate across from the boy. He settled himself on the crate and faced him, waiting. With his neck stuffed down in his jacket and the hood pulled over his head, Aden resembled an old turtle, sunken and hibernating in its shell. His jeans were torn at one knee and the left sleeve of his jacket was covered in something crusty and dark red.

Blood? Ben inched forward. A stench that smelled like stale sweat drifted from him. Ben's eyes traveled over the boy, searching for any other disturbing evidence. He noted several deep scratches across the top of his hands. Ben's gaze took in the area around

Aden. The familiar sleeping bag was tucked against his side but he didn't see the backpack.

Aden pushed the hood from his head and looked up.

He didn't mean to, but Ben gasped when he saw Aden's face. It took a moment to reign in his shock before he released his breath in a slow whistle.

Aden's left eye was a deep violet color and there were various faded bruises on one cheek and on his jaw. An angry-looking wound curved from under his pale hairline and met with the dark hues of his violet-shaded eye. His bottom lip drooped and was slightly puffy. But what broke Ben's heart the most was the boy's eyes: they were lifeless and aged, like his very soul had drained from his body.

"Who did this, son?" Ben asked, his voice shaking with emotion.

"Some boys." Aden shrugged, dropping his eyes back to the ground.

Ben's chest filled with rage, but he kept his voice under control. "How'd you clean those cuts up?"

"I didn't for a day or two. I just hung out inside this building, sleeping a lot. When I felt a little better, I snuck into the bathroom at a gas station and cleaned up as much as I could. I lost my backpack, so I didn't have any other clothes to change into or anything," Aden said.

Ben was at a loss for words—his own anger and pain threatening to strangle him. It was bound to happen, Ben knew. He was actually surprised that getting jumped, or worse, had taken this long to occur.

At such a young age, Aden was practically a flashing neon sign for pedophiles, sex traffickers, gangs...you name it. How he had managed to hide himself from plain view in a city that never sleeps was beyond Ben's understanding. Aden should have had medical attention—probably still needed it.

How had the boy dragged himself somewhere and taken care of himself those first few days?

They sat in silence. The boy was obviously struggling with his own anger and shame right now, not to mention the pain from taking a beating from a bunch of street thugs. Nothing Ben could say would erase any of that.

It wasn't the most eloquent approach, but Ben was desperate to offer something.

"Why didn't you go grab some lady's skirt off a clothesline or somethin'?" Ben grinned, even though Aden wasn't even looking his way.

Aden glanced up at Ben and gave him a half-smile before turning his attention back to the stick.

"Ain't no way I'd ever be caught running around in a woman's skirt, Ben."

*B*en and Aden gradually returned to their nightly routine, but Ben could see that Aden was disconnected and skittish, like an abused dog when you reach out to pet it. The boy's bruises had faded and his limp was gone but a shadow lingered over the boy that made Ben's heart ache for him.

Ben questioned him about where he was staying, although he already knew the boy wouldn't give him an exact location or anything. Ben had never understood why he wouldn't tell him where he stayed at night, but he'd never pressed Aden about it.

Aden assured Ben that he'd found a safer place to hole up at night that was closer to Angelo's.

"I still want to come see you but I don't want to have to go far in the dark," Aden said.

Although Ben could probably predict what the response would be, he swallowed his reluctance and offered anyway.

"You can stay with me for a few days, son, until we can get something else figured out for you. I don't like seein' you out there alone like this." Ben knew Aden couldn't live with him and Jake because the boy might be classified as a runaway and Ben didn't want to get involved with something illegal. Or Ben might be obligated by law to report a minor living in his house. For all he knew, he might already be breaking the law by not turning Aden over to the authorities.

Looking livelier than Ben had seen him in days, Aden's head shot up and he glared at him. "No, Ben, I've told you before, I'm fine. Quit bugging me about it," he growled. "*Please,*" he softened, realizing he'd come across a little gruff.

Ben studied the ground at his feet and nodded.

"Understood."

ONE AFTERNOON, while he was getting ready for work, Ben tucked the recorder and notebook into his bag before leaving the house in hopes of coaxing Aden to tell one of his stories. Ben had already copied down Aden's first story in the book and thought he would show the boy what he'd written to give him a little encouragement.

On his way to work, Ben decided to drop by Walmart and purchase another backpack for Aden. He looked for a green one but it was the middle of the school year and backpacks weren't hot items right now. He doubted Aden cared, since the boy had been toting around a plastic grocery bag the past few weeks. Ben had no idea what he carried but did notice he had on a different shirt one night under his jacket.

"Well, looky here, got you a new shirt on..." Ben said, tugging on the bright red material poking out of Aden's jacket.

"I found it in a bag of clothes someone left in their driveway. I figured they had put it out for the trash anyway," Aden told him.

Finally, at the bottom of a pile of dusty totes and bags, Ben found two canvas backpacks, one blue and the other—*wonder of wonders*—green with a brown suede-like bottom and several external pockets. He tugged the green one from the bin and tossed it into his cart.

He wandered down the office supply aisle and picked out two small notebooks and a three-pack of colored pens for Aden so he would have something to do when he got bored. While he was at it, Ben decided to grab some new socks and a pair of jeans that looked like they might fit Aden. Then, he spied an endcap display full of wool beanie caps and threw a youth-sized one in his cart.

In the checkout line, Ben grabbed a few candy bars and bottles of water to top things off. He got the feeling that the boy didn't want any kind of charity—other than a snack or a sandwich Ben shared with him, and only if Ben was eating too—but he figured he'd worry about that later.

As he drove, Ben thought about Aden's situation. He was at a loss on how to help the boy. He knew from talks with Aden that he was afraid of the police picking him up. He didn't trust them, which Ben assumed had been instilled in him from a past experience or by someone. He already knew that living with him was out of the question. Two bachelors harboring an abandoned minor was asking for trouble.

But he knew that doing *nothing* for Aden was just as wrong.

Aden showed up right on time. He even gave Ben that smile that had been hidden over the past several weeks. Ben smiled back as he shifted the load of the backpack, thermos, and food bag between two hands and walked over to where Aden sat. Aden eyed the backpack with curiosity but didn't voice his thoughts. After sitting down, Ben unloaded his burden on the ground in front of him while Aden pulled a sleeve of crackers from his jacket pocket.

"Gonna have us another party, boy?" Ben asked, eyeing the

crackers. "I hope you brought some cheese for those crackers. Ain't nothin' like sharp cheddar to partner up with crackers."

Aden grinned and held out the cracker sleeve.

"Well, I provided the crackers. You bring the cheese next time." Ben tugged out a cracker and stuffed it into his mouth.

They talked for a few minutes before Ben pulled out a pocketknife from his back pocket to cut off a tag from the backpack. Grabbing the bag by one of its straps, Ben swung it down in front of Aden.

"Got a little somethin' for ya today at the store. Don't want to hear no fussing from you about it either. Fact, we ain't even gonna talk about it." Ben held his hands up to discourage any protests before they came.

Aden set the crackers down on a rock and reached for the backpack, holding it in front of him to inspect it before settling it on his lap. He started to say something but Ben had made it clear that the subject was closed. After a moment, he did anyway.

"Thank you…" Aden mumbled, staring down at the backpack with an awed expression, running a hand slowly down its side.

It was dark green with two open side pockets and a large one on the front with a zipper that had a black pull tab. The bottom was light brown and made out of a softer material. Aden ran a finger over it and felt its softness. He even leaned in to smell the newness of it.

Ben watched as Aden squeezed the sides and felt the bulk inside. As if reading his mind, Ben offered, "Look inside. I picked up a few things I thought you could use." He thrust his chin toward the brown paper bag on the ground. "Got a sandwich in that bag too —roast beef and provolone." Ben stood up and stretched, sparing Aden the need to respond.

Aden pushed the backpack to the ground between his knees and unzipped the larger section. He pulled out a stiff new pair of jeans first and looked up at Ben, who had sat back down and busied himself unwrapping a sandwich.

Without taking his eyes off of his task, Ben said, "Let me know if they don't fit. I can exchange 'em." Aden rolled the jeans up and pushed them against his chest as he reached in and pulled out socks, water bottles, and a gray knit beanie.

He was running out of room on his lap but didn't want to put everything down on the dirt. He peeked inside the backpack and shuffled things around with his hand instead. After a moment, he pulled out a plain blue spiral notebook.

"What's this for?" he asked, holding up the book for Ben, who was now watching Aden. His gray eyes peered over at the book.

"For you to write stuff down when an idea pops into that little head of yours or maybe you can draw pictures of interesting stuff you see." Ben looked down at his watch and scooped the thermos onto his lap. After filling the cup, he handed the steaming drink to Aden.

"Drink up. Break's over. I gotta go."

Aden pushed the notebook back into the backpack and reached for the cup. He tipped it, taking a large gulp, and swallowed hard. Ben could tell the boy had probably burned his tongue on the hot liquid but wouldn't admit it.

Ben stood and stretched again before reaching for the cup. He screwed it back in place on the thermos and gave Aden's shoulder a pat before heading into the bakery. He didn't offer any more words —he knew none were needed. Before he reached the bottom of the first porch step, he heard a timid voice behind him.

"Thanks, Ben."

18

*B*right orange construction cones outlined the back half of the lot where Aden and Ben sat every night. Aden stepped closer and noticed that the concrete was broken up and piled in several medium-sized heaps around the area and some kind of heavy equipment machine was parked stoically near the edge of the property.

Aden wasn't sure what to do. He usually sat on his crate to wait for Ben, but that area was demolished and the crate nowhere in sight. For all he knew, it might even be buried under one of the piles strewn about the property. He decided to stand and wait by the back porch.

He didn't have to wait long. The back door opened a moment later and Ben walked out, hauling his trusty thermos and a plastic bag. He also had a mysterious yellow cloth draped over his arm.

"Evenin', Aden," Ben nodded, setting his load down on the back porch before reaching back to shove the door closed. Then, he picked up the yellow cloth from the ground—which looked to Aden to be a large towel—and spread it neatly across the edge of the porch.

"Gonna have to sit up here tonight," Ben said, jutting his chin in the direction of the orange cones just in case Aden hadn't noticed. "Guess one of them tree roots busted into a water pipe or somethin'. They came out this morning to dig it up."

Aden hesitated. He didn't like sitting out in the open and the porch was the brightest spot out there. He much preferred the darker area at the back of the lot, where anyone walking up wouldn't notice them right away. Seeing that Ben had everything all set up on the porch already, Aden had no choice but to join him.

"Uh, alright, I guess…" Aden mumbled, setting his bags down on the bottom step and walking to where Ben had already seated himself on the towel.

"What's the towel for?" Aden asked.

Ben patted the empty spot next to him. "Concrete gets mighty chilly. You'll thank me for laying this towel down first."

After unwrapping their bean and cheese burritos, which Ben proudly announced that he had made himself that morning, Ben told Aden about a fishing trip he and Jake would be going on in a few weeks.

"I get a few days of vacation every year. I usually like to spend it getting outside of Philly, experiencing a little nature firsthand. Anyhow, I'll be gone for the whole weekend."

"Okay, Ben. Got it," Aden said.

"I'll remind you before I go. You want me to tell Mia to save you a few treats that she can bring out for ya?"

"No, thanks, Ben. I'll be fine. I don't want Mia doing that," Aden told him. He didn't want the extra attention and he'd never even spoken to Mia before. *I'll just have to figure out something else to do while Ben's gone.* He decided to change the subject.

"I've never been fishing before," Aden told him. "But I've seen those fishing shows they have on TV. It looks super boring."

Ben arched back, a shocked look on his face.

"Ain't never been fishing!? Well, that's a cryin' shame right there, son. I'm sorry to hear that." Ben paused, considering his hasty words. "No...no," he mumbled, "I guess you might have never been fishin' before... Well, my pa took me fishing from the moment I could hold the pole upright. I was probably around four years old. It was one of our favorite things to do together—my pa was always workin' and I didn't get to spend a lot of time with him." Ben smiled over at Aden. "You know, I might just have to take you fishin' myself."

Aden shrugged. "I don't know, Ben. I still think it seems boring."

Aden heard a *harrumph* from Ben.

"Well," Aden grinned. "It *does*."

19

"I started that notebook of your stories," Ben told him the next night. "Brought it to show you one night but…" He trailed off. "Anyhow, I was wonderin' if you got another story you wanna share? I brought the recorder." He pulled it out of his jacket pocket. "Already told Mia I was gonna take a few extra minutes for break."

Aden's mouth was full of a blueberry muffin Ben had brought him. They'd had to sit on the yellow towel on the back porch again since the lot was still tore up, but Aden hadn't minded as much. In fact, he seemed quite relaxed, swinging his legs as they dangled off the porch.

Ben was relieved that the boy was opening up again. He wasn't as withdrawn and skittish as he'd been after his ordeal with the boys in the alley, but there were some nights when he preferred to just sit and wasn't in the mood for conversation. Ben never pressured him.

Aden swallowed and jammed the last chunk of muffin in his mouth before answering.

"I forgot about that notebook," he said. "Um…let me think."

Aden considered for a moment as he gazed up to the canopy of bare tree branches above them.

"Well"—Aden licked his lips and tucked a strand of hair behind his ear—"this one is actually a dream I had a few nights ago, but I can sort of fill in the details of what I can't remember. It's sad, though." He glanced to Ben.

"Okay, I can handle sad," Ben answered. "I'm ready." He set the recorder on his knee and pushed the *play* button.

Aden licked the muffin crumbs from his lips and began.

"There was this little brown rabbit that lived near a large open area with no trees in the middle of the woods."

"Clearing," Ben said.

"What?" Aden stopped, clearly irritated at the interruption.

"It's called a *clearing*," Ben continued. "Anyhow, go on."

Aden rolled his eyes. "Really, Ben?" he grumbled. He glanced over at the recorder. "Don't write that part down."

"Anyway…the *clearing*," he started again, "was a beautiful place with all kinds of colorful flowers scattered all over it. It was the middle of summer when everything was blooming and there was plenty to eat. Every afternoon, the animals came there to play together. The little rabbit went there every day too. His favorite thing to eat was this tiny little yellow flower—I don't know the name of it—and he would spend his mornings chasing his rabbit friends around and looking for that flower. His family came too but just stayed at the edge of the trees to watch the young rabbits play in the open space. They didn't like adventure like he did."

"One day, the little rabbit was bored with playing and decided to do a little exploring on the other side where he noticed a thick, grassy spot. He thought that maybe he might find a whole patch of those yellow flowers that he loved. He and his friends had been chasing each other when the little rabbit crept off away from the group to the patch of tall grass to explore. He didn't find any yellow flowers, but the high grass was fun to jump around in. He was enjoying himself and didn't realize how long he'd been gone. Suddenly, he heard birds screeching and a loud thundering noise near the edge of the forest. He hopped to an opening in the dense grass to look out and saw four lionesses running around, attacking all the animals in the, uh…*clearing.*" Aden shot Ben a look.

"The scared little rabbit saw one lioness with a young raccoon, one of the rabbit's friends, in her powerful jaws, shaking it violently back and forth like she was playing with it. A red fox ran through the middle of the clearing with two smaller females chasing it. The poor fox was panting from the effort of trying to outrun them but they were on him in less than a few seconds. The little rabbit stayed low and still in the tall grass, whimpering—if rabbits even make noise—not sure what to do. He started to creep forward, thinking he should do *something,* when he noticed a dust cloud on the opposite side where his family had been earlier. He froze."

"There was nothing he could do. He shook with terror and crouched in the grass until the lionesses had finished slaughtering the animals that had been caught out in the open. It was hours later and close to dark before the little rabbit was brave enough to crawl out of the grass and make his way to where his family was.

He tried not to look at all the torn bodies of his friends and the other creatures thrown all over the clearing like shredded ragdolls. The little rabbit was looking toward the edge of trees, making his way to his family. He found them; their bodies tangled in the brush at the forest edge. They were gone. Just scattered piles of bloody fur and bones…" Aden's voice trailed off. "I haven't really thought of an ending for it yet," he finished, shrugging.

Ben stared at Aden in shock and horror. The boy looked pale, detached—as if he had somehow disappeared into his own story. The tale was depressing and gruesome. Ben had to adjust his face, softening his shocked expression into a frown, so Aden wouldn't notice how disturbed he was.

"Whew, that's…well, that's a sad one, Aden, just like you said. Especially about that poor rabbit's family and all."

"Yeah." Aden's voice sounded hollow. "It *is* kinda sad but I guess the little rabbit shouldn't have wandered off like that."

"Probably better he did," Ben answered. "Else he woulda been killed right along with all the other poor creatures. At least he lived."

Aden turned to Ben, his eyes haunted. "I think he would have preferred to die with his family than be left alone in the world." Aden turned away. He reached for a water bottle from his backpack.

Ben's eyes dropped to his lap. He had forgotten to turn the recorder off.

20

*B*en listened to the recording later that night, planning to transcribe Aden's story into the notebook. Instead of writing though, he simply listened to the story again and their brief conversation afterward before tossing the recorder onto the end table and leaning back in the recliner.

He was failing Aden. Clearly, the boy was hurting, missing belonging to a family, and needing the security of a home and a normal life. Ben was torn about what to do. He knew the boy couldn't remain on the streets. He'd already been attacked and it could have ended much worse than it did. Ben knew it was only a matter of time before predators got their hands on the boy and abused him.

He couldn't continue to live with himself knowing that the boy was in constant danger. He also knew that Aden would never forgive him if he contacted the authorities about him. The boy would feel that Ben had betrayed him and, right now, Ben was the only person Aden still trusted in the world.

Ben heard Jake's truck pull into the garage and the back door open a few minutes later. He waited for Jake to unpack his lunch box and heard him hang his keys on the hook by the stove. Jake's habits were predictable and it was only a matter of another five minutes or so before he walked in with a mug of coffee and his boots dangling from one hand. Jake raised his mug in a toast as he moved to sit on the end of the couch, his boots tossed unceremoniously on the rug at his feet.

"What's up, Ben?" Jake nodded, kicking his feet up onto the coffee table.

"Nothin' much. Just sittin' for a spell before I head off to bed." Ben yawned. He hadn't realized how tired he really was until just now.

Jake took a big gulp from his mug and leaned over to set it on the table next to his feet. He leaned his head back against the couch pillow. "Yeah, I hear you. It was actually quiet at the shop today. How's things at Angelo's? Eddie still growling at everybody these days?"

Ben chuckled. "I'm sure he is but I don't see him much. Don't mind that one bit, either." Jake joined him in a laugh. The two of them had shared many chats about Ben's grumpy boss over the years.

Well, I guess it's now or never...

Ben cleared his throat and pulled the recliner handle at the bottom of the chair to raise it to a sitting position. "You remember I was tellin' you about that boy that drops by to chat with me on my break sometimes?"

Jake considered it for a moment, then nodded, his head lifting off the cushion as he looked over to Ben. "Oh, yeah, I do. He still comin' around?"

"Yeah, he is. Nice boy. Sad thing is, he's..." Ben hesitated. "He's homeless." He let the revelation hang in the air for a moment while he studied Jake's reaction.

The crease that formed on Jake's forehead gave Ben second thoughts about where this was going. "That right?" he asked. "Where does he stay? Does he belong to a gang or something? How old is this kid?"

Ben wondered if he should have just kept his mouth shut but knew he could trust Jake to help him work through a solution.

"Well, I don't really know where he stays—here and there, I guess. Keeps to himself, except for stoppin' by the bakery in the evenings." Ben paused. "Thing is, he's only twelve." Ben knew that admission would definitely elicit a response. He wasn't disappointed.

Jake almost knocked his coffee cup to the ground when he sat up and jerked his feet off the table. Leaning forward, he pinned Ben with a hard stare. "You serious, Ben? He's just a young boy, for crying out loud! Did he run away from home or somethin'?"

Ben licked his lips, stalling. "Shoot, Jake. Don't you think I've been carryin' this around with me, trying to figure out what to do? His own momma shoved a backpack on the boy almost a year ago and left him on the steps of a homeless shelter."

"Thing is, the kid never even went in the building. I know he's a sittin' duck for whatever street scum comes along and has already taken a beating from some rough street boys. I also know I'm his only friend in the world and that he would rather die than be picked up by the police. Makes out like he's more scared of them than whatever comes after him on the streets."

As Ben talked, Jake melted back into the cushions, arms folded firmly across his chest, a frown etched across his face. He looked at Ben like a disappointed teacher who had just caught his star pupil cheating on a test. Jake didn't say a word. Ben had no idea what was going through his mind at this point but he knew Jake didn't approve.

Ben continued, "Anyhow, I know I couldn't bring him here. If child protective services found out we had a minor living at our place and we hadn't reported it, well…we don't need that kind of trouble."

The words poured out of Ben. After all these months of agonizing over what to do about Aden, it felt good to talk it out with his friend. He held up a hand to stay any interruptions from Jake. He figured he should just spew everything out before he lost his steam.

"Anyhow, Jake, I made a decision. I'm gonna call someone tomorrow. Check into things and get the boy some help." Ben quieted. He'd run out of things to say—had even surprised himself by providing his own resolution. However, he felt it necessary to add one last detail.

"His name is Aden."

Jake hadn't interrupted Ben during his confession, but the frown he wore deepened into a scowl. He just stared, one eyebrow cocked, while Ben had poured his heart out across the coffee table.

Not knowing what to do with the awkward silence, Ben studied the nicks and scratches on the edge of the wood table, as if seeing them for the first time. Years of abuse from glasses and keys dragged carelessly across its surface had left it dull and unsightly. The marred surface reminded him of his own life and how he'd carry scars on his own heart forever. He didn't want that for Aden.

Ben heard Jake sigh. His voice broke through the fog of Ben's thoughts. Leaning toward Ben, the frown now abated into a sad smile. Jake addressed Ben as a father would a son.

"It's the right thing, Ben. By looking at you right now, I'm thinking that you don't agree with that, but it's still right. You know you couldn't live with yourself if something really bad happened to the kid."

Ben knew he was right. It was what needed to be done months ago but hadn't because Ben chose to ignore his conscience.

"Worse part is," Ben said, "only time I see Aden is when he comes by on my break. The boy knows he can depend on me for a little food and a friendly chat."

He huffed in frustration and ran his fingers through his hair. "What am I gonna do, have the cops snatch him when he shows up like I planned an ambush or somethin'? He'd feel like I betrayed him…and, well, he'd be right." Ben met Jake's eyes. The more Ben talked about it, the more the whole idea stressed him out.

He reminded himself he was doing it to *help* Aden. Maybe the boy would look back later in life and be grateful that Ben had done something. Ben had serious doubts that would happen.

Jake gave Ben a look of compassion that only a true friend could give.

"Take it from me, Ben. You're doing the best thing." Jake said. Ben felt like laying his head on the table and weeping.

If only I could believe that, he thought.

en was up earlier than normal, even though he'd been at the bakery last night long after midnight helping Mia finish up a big order. He started a pot of strong coffee and popped two pieces of wheat bread into the toaster. *Don't know why Jake is always pushing me to eat healthy. Why can't we get some white, or better yet, sourdough bread in this house?* Ben jammed the knob down on the machine.

The toaster was an ancient model and dented like an old junkyard car, but still had plenty of life left in it. Only thing was, the timer in it was broken, so you had to keep an eye on the toast through the slits on top, pulling the plug from the wall when the bread was the shade of brown you liked.

Ben looked out of the dingy kitchen window while he waited for his toast and coffee. The clouds were dark and hung low in the sky, matching Ben's mood this morning.

He had already looked up the number for the Philadelphia Department of Human Services and had left a message. The office didn't open until 9:00 a.m. and it was barely 7:30. The recording on the answering machine informed him that, if he was calling with an emergency, he should hang up and call 911. There was a long recital of extensions he could choose from before Ben was instructed to leave a message.

The dread he felt after hanging up the phone seeped into his gut and coiled into a nest of fire that didn't sit well in his empty stomach. It wasn't until he heard a soft crackling sound that he remembered his bread was still in the toaster. Jerking the cord out of the wall, he rescued the toast before it charred to a crisp.

The house was quiet as he ate breakfast. *Too quiet.* It felt like the walls had eyes and were glaring at him, silently chastising him for deceiving his young friend. Ben squeezed his eyes shut, trying hard to block them out, thinking instead of Aden—so young and vulnerable in a big, scary world. Images flooded his mind: Aden curled up and shivering under a bench, the swollen purple eye, blood on his torn jeans, the giddy excitement when the boy shared the box of chocolates he'd found.

He thought back to when he'd met Aden outside of Angelo's Bakery that first night: a frightened boy in the middle of a crime-ridden city where adults didn't even dare venture to be outside after dark. The last vision his mind conjured up was an image of Aden's little rabbit, traumatized by an unspeakable horror that left the innocent creature orphaned and vulnerable.

Ben opened his eyes and stared down into the dark pool at the bottom of his coffee cup.

I am doing this for Aden.

A WOMAN with a pleasant voice called about an hour later, identifying herself as Mrs. Anderson. She was with the Department of Human Services and was returning a call from Mr. Ben Morgan.

Ben hadn't expected a call back so soon, especially from an office of the government. It hit him then that he hadn't even rehearsed what he would say first.

Ben almost chickened out and hung up on her, but held his ground. He mumbled through a brief explanation of his contact with a young boy who was homeless. He shared how the boy had made it a habit to drop by his work in the evenings and that he tried to make sure he always had food on hand to share because he didn't know how often the boy had access to a decent meal. Ben asked the woman what could be done and how he could help.

"There is a hotline number that you can call but I can go ahead and get things rolling," Mrs. Anderson said. "We typically send out a police officer to investigate initially. The boy could be a runaway and his family may be looking for him or he may be lying to you to gain your sympathy and get a free handout. Either way, you made a wise decision in contacting us."

Why is that line starting to sound so familiar? Ben thought.

Ben doubted that a kid with a decent home would go looking for free handouts, but he kept his mouth shut.

"You say that you have no proof that he doesn't just go home at night?" she asked.

"No," Ben said, "I don't have *proof,* so to speak, but the boy carries a backpack and a small sleeping bag and pretty much has the same dirty clothes on most days 'cept for a shirt change here and there. He also don't look like he's had a haircut for months. It's pretty obvious that he don't bathe often either and the little food that I share with him is awfully appreciated—you know what I mean? I see lots of homeless folks and this boy seems to fit that description pretty clear to me."

Ben wasn't sure why he needed to justify his concerns but

maybe this was the normal questioning process these folks put everyone through. Either way, irritation gnawed at his gut.

"Yes, sir, that's fine," Mrs. Anderson said. "Do you know the boy's name or any other information about him?" Ben could hear papers shuffling in the background. "We'll need to check on a missing person's report as well," she added as an afterthought.

"Aden. That's the boy's name," Ben answered. "Don't know any last name. I think he is around twelve or so."

"Alright, Mr. Morgan. You've been very helpful. Let me give you my direct number. Are you expecting Aden to show this evening?"

"Yes, ma'am. He comes most nights."

"Here's what I need from you then. When Aden shows up at Angelo's, give me a call and I will arrange for an officer to stop by and check on the situation. Meanwhile, I'll make some calls on my end and see if anything comes up about the young man."

Ben jotted down Mrs. Anderson's number and gave her the address to Angelo's as well as a physical description of Aden before hanging up.

Carrying his plate over to the trash can, Ben scraped his meager half-burnt toast breakfast into it. He'd lost his appetite.

*a*den sat on a patch of grass in the park watching joggers glide by on the path in front of him.

Two young women jogging together passed first, looking like young gazelles bounding their way to a grazing party in the mountains, while a middle-aged man passing by minutes later lumbered along clumsily. His labored breathing and sweaty, red face made Aden wonder why people put themselves through all that torture just to stay healthy.

When he became bored with people-watching, he wandered over to the South Philadelphia Library on Broad Street. He loved to lose himself in the ocean of books that were at his disposal whenever the whim hit him to drop by. He especially enjoyed browsing the young adult section, pulling random books off shelves and reading descriptions on covers to see if any caught his interest. A small collection of books was already filling his arms.

Aden could get lost in the hundreds of tidy rows of multicolored book covers and computer monitors lined up neatly along the walls. Besides the thousands of books he could devour for hours, Aden loved the huge, overstuffed patterned chairs scattered in random nooks and crannies throughout the building that provided privacy from curious eyes.

It was to one of these chairs in a far corner that Aden retreated with his stack of books clutched securely against his chest. He had been careful to avoid drawing attention to himself when he'd come in. A kid wandering around a public building on an obvious school day was bound to stick out. *Then again, how many kids skipped school to come to the library?*

Aden's feet didn't even touch the ground when he sat all the way into the overstuffed chair. They dangled carelessly off the edge as he adjusted the pile on his lap and leaned over the side to shrug off his backpack and sleeping bag onto the ground. He felt like Goldilocks trying out Papa Bear's chair.

Cracking open a book from the top of the stack, Aden began to read as he settled deeper into the chair cushion. It was a book about the Spartans from ancient Greece and how they were a people completely dedicated to war and physical superiority. He was awed with how boys were sent away to military school when they were only seven years old. Aden couldn't imagine a little kid leaving his family and everything he knew to go off to live with strangers.

Well, he thought, *I guess all their friends would be going too so they wouldn't really be alone. It might actually be fun hanging out with friends all day—if I had any friends.* Aden read on for a few more chapters and, although he was intrigued by the disciplined, exciting life of the Spartans and their ruthless attacks on the Athenians, his mind started to wander.

Aden had never had a real friend. His mom had a few friends with kids who dropped by their apartment once in a while. Most of the time, the kids were either shy and just stared at Aden or were annoying pests who touched his stuff and left everything a mess.

One afternoon, his mother announced that a friend and her little girl were coming over. She said they needed a place to stay for a few days.

"Listen," his mom instructed him, "Ang and I have to work tonight, so you be nice to her little girl for me, okay? Can you do that for me?"

"How old is the girl?" Aden cringed. *I hope she's not a terror who screams for her mom all night.*

"I don't have any idea, Aden. I think she might be around five." At the time, Aden was eight. "Her name is Milly—short for Melissa, I think."

Aden rolled his eyes. *Five? Great, she's going to cry for her mom all night.*

"Fine... I guess we can watch TV and I can show her how to play Spades," he said.

His mom snickered. "Well, Spades may be a little complicated for a five-year-old, but I know you'll make it fun either way." She leaned over and kissed him on the forehead before heading to the kitchen to make lunch.

Later that night, after his mom and Ang left for work, Aden led Milly to the living room, balancing a big plastic bowl of popcorn in one hand and two juice boxes in the other. He set the snacks on the carpet and scooped up the TV remote.

"What do you like to watch on TV?" he asked.

The tiny girl just stared at him.

Flipping through several channels, which were limited to mostly news and sitcoms at night, Aden glanced over to see if she showed interest in anything.

Milly sat cross-legged on the floor next to him, looking down at a ragged stuffed dog she held in her lap. At least that's what he *thought* it was. The clump of fake fur on her lap was filthy. It had four legs and a stout body. It also had a long snout like a dog with a button sewed onto the end of it. One ear was missing and tiny puffs of wispy white stuffing peeked through a small hole where the ear had torn off.

Milly cradled the bedraggled creature against her, a thin willowy arm stretched around its middle. She pushed her thumb from her free hand into her mouth and sucked noisily. Other than the rhythmic movement in her cheeks from the thumb-sucking, Aden thought she looked like a miniature ice statue by the way sat trance-like, hardly ever blinking her eyes.

Aden turned the TV off.

"Do you want me to read you a book?" he asked.

One small shoulder lifted in a faint shrug. It was enough of an invitation to prompt Aden to walk over to a set of shelves in the corner and pull a few books out.

He sat back down on the rug with two books, old favorites his mother used to read to him: *Bear Snores On* and *Where the Wild Things Are*. He held them up in front of Milly, one in each hand.

"Which first?" he said.

Milly shifted her eyes to the books in front of her. She pointed to *Where the Wild Things Are*.

"I don't like monsters," she mumbled around the thumb planted in her mouth.

He read *Bear Snores On*.

Milly's thumb slid from her mouth as she wrapped both hands around the stuffed animal, pulling its matted head up under her chin as her eyes skimmed the pages of the book Aden held up for her. He even faked a really loud sneeze when the bear let out a sneeze in the story and thought he heard a muffled giggle. Aden paused occasionally to ask her if she could name the little creatures that he pointed out in the book. A tiny elf voice answered, "Rabbit…skunk (which was really a badger, but Aden let it go) …bird…"

Her replies were barely above a squeak, but at least he had her attention.

After looking at a few picture books Aden dug out of a box from the hall closet, he spent the rest of the evening showing her his bottle cap collection and drawing pictures on scratch paper and asking her to guess what he drew.

When she yawned and her small fist reached up to rub her eyes, he announced it was time to go brush her teeth and get ready for bed.

"I don't have a *toofbrush*," she told him.

"Well," he said with a shrug, "you can't use mine. You're just gonna have to skip that tonight." Aden told her to grab her sleep clothes and follow him. He led the way to the bathroom and waited until she went in and closed the door.

While she changed, Aden grabbed the pile of books from the living room floor and stacked them on the coffee table near the couch. Milly had brought her own blanket—a thick throw adorned with cute puppies all over it. There were no extra pillows, so he gave her his. He could live without it for a night or two.

Milly came out of the bathroom dressed in her pajamas—also decorated with puppies—and made her way to pick up her stuffed dog-bear-creature from the chair where she'd left it. Aden patted the pillow on the couch.

"Here ya go. Best bed in the house."

Crawling up onto the couch, she rested her head on his pillow. Her thumb was already back in her mouth.

Handing her the puppy blanket, Aden motioned to the books on the table in front of her. "I left the books here if you want to look at them. I put the monster book there too. You should look at it. I used to love that book and the monsters in it are actually friendly. Besides, monsters aren't real anyway."

"Yes, they are," she said, her words muffled by the wet slurping of the thumb in her mouth.

"Nah, they aren't. It's just your imagination."

Her eyes drooped and the thumb-sucking slowed. As Aden turned to leave, Milly looked up at him with a serious expression on her angelic face. She plucked the thumb out of her mouth. Her voice was so soft and timid, Aden had to bend down closer to hear her.

"Uh, huh. They *are* real. Sometimes, they follow my mommy home and come into our house."

Suddenly, Aden understood. He nodded and patted her cheek.

He'd seen those kinds of monsters too.

When Aden walked out of the living room, he left the light on.

ADEN'S EYES FLEW OPEN. He felt disoriented and confused, his mouth pasty and dry. Panic thudded in his chest at the unfamiliar surroundings. It took a few moments for his mind to register that he'd fallen asleep in the library chair. Jerking upright, he looked around, scanning for anything out of the ordinary—not that he would know what would be *out of the ordinary*. There was no one in sight.

He had no idea how long he'd been sleeping in the chair. Someone may have already noticed him and made a call to report a kid skipping school. There was a large window to his right. A quick glance told him that the sun had crept lower in the sky and it was now late afternoon.

The books piled on his lap had slid sideways into the crack of the chair cushion. He righted them and pressed them against his chest as he scooted to the end of the chair. Setting them on the floor, Aden reached for his backpack and slung it over his shoulder, then reached for the strap of the sleeping bag and hefted it onto his back.

At this point, it didn't matter if someone noticed him because it was after school hours and he blended in with the other library patrons mingling around.

Passing through the sliding glass front doors, a wall of cold air hit Aden like a tidal wave crashing over him. The warmth that had engulfed him during the past few hours was sucked from his body in a matter of seconds.

It's going to be another miserable night, Aden thought as he pulled his jacket hood over his head and jammed his hands deep into his pockets.

Hot chocolate was going to be a real treat tonight.

he clock on the wall read 8:23 p.m.

Ben had been a wreck all evening. Mia even asked him if he was sick after he burned his arm on an open oven door and knocked over a large bowl of confectioner's sugar, sending a layer of white snow over half the kitchen and leaving Mia coughing in a cloud of powdery haze. Ben apologized as he helped her clean the mess and reassured her that he wasn't sick.

"I'm just distracted today, I guess," he told her.

"Well, you need to be *distracted* somewhere outside the kitchen, Ben. Go do something harmless like wiping down the bathroom or rolling coins from the register drawer," she told him, giving him a friendly shove out of the way.

Ben didn't know if he could go through with this. He hadn't really thought it through completely. How would he know when Aden had arrived? I mean, he knew to expect him a little after 8:00 p.m., but he needed to know for sure before he made the phone call.

There was no window on the back wall, so it wasn't like he could look out to see if he'd shown up. Ben would have to stick his head out the door and *that* would be obvious. He couldn't very well call Mrs. Anderson while he was sitting right *next* to Aden. What would he do when the police showed up?

I need to tell Mrs. Anderson to make sure the officer makes it sound like he just got an anonymous call from...someone else. Ben tried to organize a plan.

This is getting worse by the minute.

Ditching the whole idea became a serious consideration for Ben. He had to give himself a quick pep talk as a reminder that, in the long run, this decision was for Aden's benefit. The boy couldn't keep living on the dangerous streets, fending for himself, not attending school, and a hundred other reasons this intervention was necessary. Ben knew that he couldn't continue sleeping at night with the burden of this knowledge weighing like a mountain-sized boulder on his chest.

Ben glanced at the time again—8:30 p.m. He knew he was stalling. Before he could change his mind, Ben reached for the phone and dialed the number scrawled on the card that he'd fished out of his shirt pocket.

"This is Paula Anderson. How can I help you?"

"Uh, this is Ben...Ben Morgan. We spoke this morning about... uh, a homeless boy—not sure if you remember...."

"Yes, Mr. Morgan, I know who you are," she interrupted. "Is Aden there now?"

"Yes, he is," Ben lied, assuming that he would be. "I was wonderin' if you could tell the officer that you send to, you know, make it sound like somebody else called so it ain't so obvious... you know? I mean, I don't want..."

"Of course, Mr. Morgan. I understand. We can keep it discreet. An officer should arrive in less than twenty minutes. Please try to keep Aden there with you. You need to know, Mr. Morgan, that if

Aden tries to run, the officer will pursue him. This is for Aden's safety. He is a minor that is considered to be in a dangerous situation. The officer will detain Aden and escort him to my office, where I will be waiting. I'll take things from there, Mr. Morgan. We'll make sure Aden gets the help he needs."

Ben heard her explanation. He knew it was a necessary part of the process, but anxiety threaded its way into his chest. His heart thumped recklessly and he had to take several deep breaths to keep panic from taking over.

His voice felt like it was disembodied from the rest of him as he mumbled a reply and ended the call. The call only took three minutes, but he was already emotionally drained.

Time was running out—for his evening break and also for Aden.

ADEN SAT HUNCHED on the overturned crate. Ben had located a few more crates for them to sit on after theirs was broken up when the lot was being repaired. *At least this one is sturdier than the last one.* Aden huddled deeper into his coat, trying to keep warm and scribbling pictures in his notebook while he waited for Ben. *What was taking so long?*

After scanning the back door of the bakery for the tenth time, an unsettling thought struck him. *What if Ben was sick today and didn't come to work?* Aden chewed his bottom lip, worrying. *Maybe he just had something to finish up for Mia.*

He had a good story to share with Ben tonight that he thought up that afternoon. After he'd left the library, Aden had a few hours on his hands until he would be meeting Ben and had wandered to the park to people-watch and work on his new story.

The story was probably birthed from a muddled combination of the books Aden had browsed through this afternoon in the library. Still, he'd put together what he thought was a great tale and wanted Ben to get this one on his recorder while it was fresh on Aden's mind.

Plus, to be honest, he was hoping Ben had packed something extra special tonight because he was starving.

Before leaving the park, Aden had poked around several trash bins and didn't find anything to eat besides a slimy green salad in a mangled plastic container that made him gag just looking at it. He threw it back into the can. Near another bin just outside of the courthouse, he'd watched a pretty Asian lady with her hair pulled into a neat bun, wearing an expensive-looking red trench coat and black high heels, eat an apple and drink a bottle of juice she'd pulled from a nylon bag next to her.

She sat alone on a low cement wall by the courthouse steps. Aden stayed back and leaned against a tree, acting like he was waiting for someone. When she was done, the woman zipped her bag closed and stood to toss her half-eaten apple and what looked like a half-full bottle of orange juice into the trash before settling her purse and nylon bag on her shoulder and hurrying into the courthouse, her heels clacking their way up the steps.

She's probably a lawyer on break and had to hurry back to an important court case, Aden thought, heading toward the can where the woman had tossed her leftovers. Glancing around for onlookers, Aden reached in and snatched the apple and juice bottle. He took his treasures behind the wall where the woman had sat and sunk his teeth into the juicy apple.

But that was hours ago. *I could eat a horse right now.* On cue, Aden's stomach gave a loud rumble and he looked again at the back door. *Nothing.*

Just as he slid his notebook and pen back into his backpack, Aden heard the back door groan as Ben emerged wearing his gray wool jacket, his thermos swinging faithfully at his side, and a familiar brown bag tucked under his arm. Aden grinned. *Finally.*

Aden watched him take each step carefully, judging each one as he descended on it. Ben didn't bother to look up as he lumbered over to where Aden sat. He usually wore a lopsided smile permanently fixed on his face when he came out, but not tonight. Aden watched with curiosity as Ben approached.

He must have had a bad day, he thought. "Hi, Ben," he called.

24

*B*en was quiet as he seated himself and placed the thermos on the ground. Only then did he look up at Aden as he handed him the brown bag of food.

"How ya doin', kid?" Ben said.

Aden was already unrolling the top of the bag to check out what Ben had packed. He pulled out a snack-sized bag of potato chips.

"You know that old man I was telling you about that plays the harmonica with his dog in front of that diner?" Aden said, tearing open the bag and shoving chips into his mouth.

"Yeah...he still there?" Ben asked. He bent down to tie his shoelace, avoiding Aden's eyes.

Aden told him how the dog howled along with the old man's harmonica-playing again tonight. He said that people would laugh at the pint-sized dog while they dropped money into a coffee can next to the man. Aden went on about how the dog was smaller than the coffee can.

"He's so dorky-looking, Ben, that it almost makes him cute. He has this underbite..." Aden demonstrated by pushing his lower teeth up over his top lip, "...that looks hilarious when he howls.

You gotta see him," he said, exchanging the empty chip bag for a hoagie wrapped in white paper. Unrolling the hoagie, he peeked under the top piece of bread.

"Yes! Pickles!" he exclaimed.

"I was laughing so hard," he continued. "Someone had brought the dog a little sweater—I guess since it's so cold outside— poor thing, and he almost looked embarrassed to be wearing it! I mean, can a dog even care about stuff like that? He looked humiliated and practically hid under the old man's legs!" Aden giggled.

"No, I don't think dogs care one bit about what they look like," Ben muttered, "but I bet that poor fella is howlin' cause that harmonica hurts his little ears."

Ben was only half-listening as Aden rambled on. Even with the chill in the air, he was sweating under his coat. His nerves were on edge and every sound made his stomach jump. The bakery—along with most of the businesses in this part of town— was closed at this time of night, so there wasn't a lot of traffic going by.

It should be any time now, he thought.

You couldn't see car headlights very well from the back of the building, so Ben's nerves were on hyperalert at every flicker of light as he strained to listen for the sound of tires on gravel.

Ben knew he needed to say something else before Aden got suspicious. He was never this quiet and Aden was sure to notice.

"I also suspect when that dog realizes how warm and toasty he feels with that sweater on, he won't be complain' much," he said, reaching for the thermos. He didn't trust himself to look at Aden right now.

Aden shrugged. "Yeah. The way the poor thing shivers all the time, you think he would appreciate it."

"Anyhow, I went to the library today and they have these huge stuffed chairs. It was like sitting on a throne or something. It was so cozy…" Aden paused.

A tall shadow emerged from around the corner of the back of the building. Aden stiffened, his words dissolving into nothingness. For a moment, Ben worried that it might be a thug or someone else instead… His back was to the building but he knew by looking at Aden's face that it was probably the police officer.

Ben had expected them to drive around to the loading dock, but they had obviously decided to walk back here instead. *Maybe so that Aden would have no warning?*

Ben was paralyzed with dread as the officer moved in closer.

Eyes wide, his hoagie suspended in the air, Aden sat frozen as he watched the officer approach.

"Evening, folks."

Ben heard the voice, and knew now that it was a male officer, but his eyes stayed glued on Aden. *What have I done? I can still back out, cover this up somehow, pull the cop aside and tell him that it was all a misunderstanding…*

The officer's boots made a crunching sound on the gravel that echoed against the concrete wall of the building. Ben felt sick.

He turned and stood at the same time, facing the officer.

"Evenin', sir," Ben nodded. "How can I help you?"

The officer looked from Aden to Ben before returning the nod. He was young, probably somewhere in his early thirties, with light brown skin and wavy jet-black hair that reflected the floodlight above him. His eyes were dark and intense, a perfect complement to the dark uniform and menacing duty belt he wore, but his bright smile helped to soften the overall sinister look.

"I'm Officer Renhart with the Philadelphia Police Department." Pointing over to Aden, he asked, "This boy with you, sir?"

Ben glanced back at Aden. His cheeks were flushed and there

was a wild look in his eyes as he sat hypnotized by the officer's presence.

"Um...yeah, he's...a friend of mine," Ben stumbled. *Please don't run, Aden.* He turned back to the officer, but the officer's full attention was on Aden.

The officer addressed Aden directly. "How old are you, son? You live around here?"

Except for lowering the hoagie to his lap, Aden hadn't moved. He didn't answer.

"Son?" the officer prompted.

ADEN TRIED TO SPEAK, he really did, but the words lodged tight in his throat and he had to swallow several times before he could answer.

"I live a few blocks away," his voice squeaked. He pointed over his shoulder to no area in particular. "I'm twelve...uh...sir," he added.

The officer stepped closer and stood near Ben, who also turned to face Aden. Aden's eyes shifted from one face to the other.

He was starting to panic. He could feel a frosty tingle climb up his spine and his lips suddenly felt heavy and numb. The large man, one hand resting close to the gun at his hip, was like a wall of a looming storm bearing down on him. Aden wanted to cry but everything had plugged up inside him, leaving him shaking with anxiety.

"Do your parents know you're here?" the officer continued. "You're a little young to be out this time of the night," he said. "I think I better run you home and make sure everything is okay." His hand beckoned for Aden to follow him.

Aden started to answer but the sound came out sounding more like a hiccup.

Ben hadn't said a word. His eyes were locked on the ground and he looked like he was about to cry himself.

When Aden didn't respond, the officer moved in and held his hand out for Aden. "Come on, son. Let's get you home."

Aden looked at Ben who had now lifted his eyes and met his gaze. He blinked once, twice…nothing more.

Say something, Ben…Tell him that…I'm with you, that I'm your nephew…anything.

Aden's look begged for Ben to help—to intervene—but he didn't. Ben simply stared at Aden, another slow blink…his soft gray eyes reflecting an emotion that Aden couldn't discern—that logic defied—but that steadily made its way into Aden's conscience until he *knew*.

Ben did this.

25

*R*un! Every instinct within him screamed. So, he did.
Again.

Like so many other times since that first day at the shelter—always running. It was an exhausting existence to live in.

The sandwich tumbled to the ground as Aden leapt off the crate. Tripping over his backpack, he scrambled toward the dark shadows of a row of shrubs at the back edge of the property. He thought he heard someone call his name but the only voice that registered was the one that warned him to flee.

Over the months, Aden's survival instinct had become fine-tuned. Finding places to camouflage himself and hide from people had become second nature, so it was natural that he would dive for the dense brush. He was much smaller than the stocky man and, he figured, naturally faster without the extra weight of the officer's duty equipment and heavy boots.

He was wrong.

Aden hadn't made it ten feet before the officer was on him, strong hands gripping his shoulders, pulling him backwards. It surprised Aden how fast the officer had caught up. Misjudging the officer's bulk as a disadvantage was Aden's first mistake. Fighting back was his second. He was no match for the brute strength and experience of the burly man. Aden's body twisted and writhed as he struggled to free himself from the officer's viselike grip. He could feel his heart pounding furiously in his chest.

"Settle down, son," the officer growled against Aden's ear. "I'm not going to hurt you."

Aden was sobbing now, pushing with all his might against the strength of the officer. But his grip held firm as he shuffled Aden across the lot toward the building. They had reached Ben, standing mutely in the same place he'd been since the officer had addressed Aden, his body a statue of grief as he watched the officer wrestle with Aden. Narrow rivers of tears coursed down his weathered face and his lips trembled like a dam holding back the flood of words he wanted to say.

But Aden wouldn't have heard them even if Ben had shouted them from tallest skyscraper in Philadelphia—he was so distraught. He felt like his chest was caving inward from the realization that Ben had turned against him. His crazed mind flew in a million directions, frantically grasping for reasons why Ben would want to hurt him.

All the physical effort he poured into fighting the officer flowed from the powerful emotions that coursed through him at being betrayed by the only person in this world left that Aden had allowed in—had trusted.

The officer struggled with Aden, almost falling on top of him when Aden suddenly lunged at Ben.

"*Why*, Ben?! I trusted you! I thought you were my friend," Aden spat out through the tears and snot dribbling down his lips. He was pushed to the ground and straddled as he heard the *tinkling* sound of cuffs being pulled from the officer's belt.

"Son, I don't want to have to use these…"

Aden stilled.

"No…no…please," Aden whimpered, defeated. "I'll walk. Don't chain my hands." He was breathing hard and trying to swallow the sticky saliva pooled in his mouth. His body shuddered from the exertion of the last few minutes. He was sure he was going to pass out. The experience was already so horrific that he couldn't imagine his hands being locked behind his back on top of it all.

"We'll try this one more time, son," the officer said, panting himself, his voice oddly tender. "I'm gonna stand you up and you can choose to walk to my car or I will carry you there. I'm not here to hurt you. I'm here to protect you and you are making it harder than it has to be. Understand?"

"Yes…yes, sir," Aden sniffed. There was no fight left in him as the officer helped him stand. Aden noticed another bakery employee standing on the porch outside the back door. She was a stout, short woman with dark hair plastered tightly against her head in a large bun. Her eyes were wide with shock, one hand cupped over her mouth as she watched the scene before her. Aden turned his face away.

Mia. She probably knew too…

The officer nudged him forward gently. Aden hung his head, his sobs quieting to watery sniffles while he submitted to the guidance of the officer's hand. He dared not look up at Ben. He sensed him nearby but every part of Aden rejected giving Ben the satisfaction of seeing the pain in his eyes.

A soft cry came from beside him. Ben's voice was strained as he reached out to Aden.

"I *am* your friend, Aden," Ben whispered, stretching out a timid hand, grazing Aden's jacket sleeve with his touch. Aden refused to acknowledge him.

Ben tried again.

"I wanted to help, Aden…I know you don't understand…" His words trailed off into silence.

Aden lifted his eyes and stared straight into Ben's face. "Go away!" Aden growled, starting to sob again. "I *hate* you, Ben! I *hate* you!"

The officer gave a soft tug on his arm. Aden jerked his arm away and started walking—Aden leading the officer now more than the other way around as they made their way to the waiting patrol car.

26

The city lights swept past in a blur as Aden leaned his forehead against the window in the back of the patrol car. He wrapped his arms tight against his chest. The world looked so different from this perspective. It made Aden dizzy with the sights and sounds changing so rapidly outside: cars roaring past with blaring horns and pounding radios, marquee signs blinking neon colors, people pouring out over sidewalks and dodging vehicles. It was an endless blur of confusion and color that left Aden feeling small inside the tight space of the backseat.

Tears welled in his eyes again as he thought of what his mother must have felt trapped in this same place, with a metal barricade between her and the front seat—a rolling prison.

Mom, where are you? Aden thought. *You're supposed to be protecting me.*

Aden reached up to wipe the tears from his cheeks and dried his hand on his pants. A quiet acceptance of his fate washed over him. As the turbulence in his heart calmed, he understood what he was feeling, and it was what he had expected to feel: *Relief.*

Whatever life handed him at this point would be out of his

hands now. He was tired of running, of wondering where his next meal would come from, where to hide so he can sleep at night. Aden was weary of it all.

But what if things only got worse? he thought. *Where do I go from here? To live with strangers? Juvenile hall? Don't horrible kids go to those places?* Aden thought of the boys in the alley.

All because of Ben...

I wanted to help, Ben had said. Aden had no idea where the officer was taking him, no clue where he would end up tonight, but he was sure being locked in a cell or whatever they planned to do with him was not what he considered *helping* at all.

Aden's fear turned to bitterness as he thought of Ben's deceit. Ben had made him feel like he was, well, almost family. *Almost,* Aden thought, *like a son.* And Aden had never known his real father, only the revolving door of men his mother brought home that left a bitter taste in his mouth just thinking about it.

Some of the men showed up drunk with vile tempers and his mother would scream at them to leave when they got rough and bullied her. Aden wanted to protect his mother, but knew he was no match for them. Instead, he hid in the closet and jammed his fingers into his ears to block everything out. It made him feel small and weak and he vowed he would never treat a woman that way.

Aden's lips quivered as he studied the city lights blurring past his window.

Mom...we should be together, Aden spoke to her in his mind, imagining that he was somehow connected to her wherever she was tonight. *I don't need Ben. He's a liar and no better than those jerks you let in our apartment.*

An angry realization swept over Aden. *It's not just Ben. You failed me too, Mom. I wouldn't have been forced into this situation if you hadn't pushed me out of your life and left me alone. I can't trust anyone...not after this...not ever.*

Aden's face was damp with tears again. His shoulders trembled as the grief overcame him. Surrendering to the grief and frustration, he crumpled like a broken doll against the car door.

THEY RODE for a long time in silence. Aden had gotten control of his emotions after his meltdown, the only evidence being the stiff tears and mucus that had dried on his face. He hadn't bothered to wipe them away. The only sounds left in the vehicle came from the dispatch radio echoing inside the squad car.

"What's your name, son?" the officer asked, penetrating the silence.

Aden noticed that they were getting off the freeway. There was less traffic on the streets here and, turning on the first street from the off-ramp, they drove near a cluster of tall office buildings.

His eyes met the officer's in the rearview mirror. He remembered when Ben had asked that question the second night Aden had showed up at the bakery. He hadn't planned to ever share anything personal with anyone, but something about Ben had drawn him in and he'd allowed a small door to his heart to be opened. Ben tiptoed his way through that opening and a friendship had grown. It was because he'd let his guard down that his heart was broken now.

"I'm Aden," he mumbled, turning back to the window.

"Where do you live?"

I don't know why he's asking me this stuff. I'm sure Ben already told him everything about me.

"I don't live anywhere. I'm taking care of myself right now." He almost said "until I find my mom" but stopped himself.

A low whistle came from the front seat.

"It's a rough place on the streets, Aden. Where's your family?"

Aden couldn't answer that question even if he had wanted to because the only family he'd known his whole life was his mom and he had no idea where *she* even was. He shrugged as the officer eyed him through the mirror.

When Aden didn't reply, the officer turned his eyes back to the road and left him alone.

They were on a quiet street full of tall office buildings, most of which had unlit windows and locked gates in front of the doorways. Aden spotted several shadows huddled in dark corners, blankets drawn up over them to protect them from the elements. The helpless offspring of the streets, spewed out from the mainstream of society to spend their days and nights foraging out some kind of existence.

Like me, Aden thought bitterly, *and I was doing fine until tonight.*

Aden leaned forward to look out the front window.

"Where are we going?"

"I'm taking you to meet someone at Human Services," the officer told him. "Her name is Paula. She's a social worker. Real nice lady—you'll like her. Paula will get you a good meal and find you a warm place to sleep tonight. Everything's gonna be alright, kid."

They pulled into a covered parking area below a towering building with columns of windows that climbed its sides all the way to the sky. Aden remembered watching a few cop shows on TV and he'd seen plenty of bad guys taken "down to the station," but none of them looked like this place. Aden didn't know what to make of it.

What does a social worker do anyway? He slid back into the seat.

They rode in a small parking garage elevator that smelled like puke and stale cigarettes to the ground floor and made their way through a set of glass double doors, down a long hallway, and into a small waiting room that made Aden feel claustrophobic. The lights were a dim yellow and the temperature in the room almost rivaled the frosty temperature outside.

An older woman with short brown hair with hints of gray streaks glided out through a side door near the corner of the room. She wore black slacks and a pale blue sweater over a white tank top. A wide smile was on her face as she swept into the room with an energy too cheerful considering the late hour. Aden stood stiffly at attention in the center of the room. He felt like a soldier waiting for an inspection.

"Thank you, Officer Renhart," she smiled brightly at the officer. Then, she moved toward Aden.

"Hello, Aden. Please, have a seat right here," she said pleasantly, pointing to a chair next to her. Aden walked over and sat in a chair on the far side of the room instead.

Following him, she sat down on the edge of the coffee table in front of Aden and crossed her legs. Pinning him with her deep brown eyes, she leaned forward and reached out to shake his hand. Aden offered a weak handshake before jerking his hand back.

"I'm Paula, Aden," she told him. "I'm a social worker here at the Department of Human Services. Are you hungry? We have some leftover cheese pizza in the refrigerator and a few cans of Coke, if you're interested." She clasped her hands together and rested them comfortably on her lap as if she had all the time in the world.

Aden found himself backing up against the chair, not sure what to make of Paula. He broke away from her stare and studied the carpet instead. She seemed harmless enough but he wasn't about to let his guard down. He wouldn't forget that lesson again. However, his body responded to the offer of food since he hadn't even eaten half of the hoagie Ben had brought him. He also needed to go to the bathroom.

"I guess so," he said and shrugged, putting on a brave face. "But I need to use the bathroom first."

"You got it." Paula stood so abruptly that Aden jumped in his seat. Fortunately, she hadn't noticed as she turned to lead him back toward the door she'd come through. "Follow me. There's a bathroom on the way to the lounge." Turning toward the officer, she said, "I'll just need you to fill out a few forms for me." Officer Renhart nodded and followed them down the hall.

27

hile Paula finished up paperwork with the officer and made phone calls, Aden gulped down three pieces of pizza and drank two cans of Coke. He was just finishing his second can when Paula swept into the lounge with a clipboard and several papers under her arm.

Pulling a metal folding chair over from the corner of the room, she tossed her clipboard and papers on the table and sat across from Aden. After asking questions about when and where he'd last seen his mother, where they had lived (Aden didn't know the address), other family Aden had (which was none that he knew of), his last name (he refused to tell her), and a battery of other questions he could barely answer, Paula set her pen down and leaned back.

"Good enough for tonight, Aden. It's late and I know you're probably tired. I'm going to drive you to stay with a family for a few days while we try to locate your mother. The Pearsons are a very nice couple with a little boy of their own. I've already called them, so they're expecting us. It's only for a few days until we get some things figured out. Okay?" Paula said.

Aden felt overwhelmed. *What if it's not okay with me? What happens then?* His voice screamed in his head but to Paula he nodded weakly.

The adrenal rush that had accumulated throughout the night was settling along with all the food he'd just eaten. Exhaustion made his muscles feel heavy and clumsy but his nerves were still on hyper-alert for any new danger he might face. He didn't want to be taken somewhere else with more strangers, being forced to go along with whatever they had planned for him. Not once had anyone bothered to ask him what *he* wanted, how *he* felt with all of this.

"What will happen in a few days?" he asked.

Paula stood. She reached to rest her hand on his shoulder but Aden shrank away from her. She withdrew her hand and reached for the paperwork on the table.

"I don't know the answer to that question yet, Aden. But, you and I have a bit of a drive ahead of us so we need to get on the road. We'll get it figured out. I promise. Okay?"

As THEY DROVE, Paula explained that the Pearsons were a young couple who lived just outside of Philadelphia in a town called King of Prussia. She chatted about growing up on a farm in Lancaster, Pennsylvania, and about her five siblings, of which she was the oldest.

"My family never understood why I wanted to move to the big city." She smiled over to Aden, the reflection of the passing streetlights dancing across her face. "My siblings all stuck around to help on the farm but I wanted more excitement in my life than cleaning out horse stalls for the rest of my life."

Aden didn't even pretend to be listening. He disconnected as he observed the scenery changing outside of his window. He could sense that the woman was trying to make him feel comfortable but he was too distracted to care at the moment. He watched as the cluttered city streets he'd grown up with opened up to yawning empty spaces and landscape dotted with sprawling trees and houses that were as big as castles to Aden. It all felt so foreign.

He had never been outside of Philly and the quiet stillness of the world beyond it, along with the thousands of stars dancing in the wide-open sky, made him feel like the heavens were collapsing down on him. The smattering of stars Aden normally observed from the city were just tiny clusters of light drowned out by the domineering neon lights of billboards and marquees compared to what he was seeing now.

Meandering their way down an endless gravel driveway, Aden noticed a dim light up ahead. As they drew closer, Aden saw that it was a light glowing from the front porch of a tidy stone house that looked like it was transported straight out of an eighteenth-century village.

The stone exterior of the house was painted white with patches of red-colored rocks peeking out between the layers of white stone. Two rectangular windows framed in red wood weathered with age hung on either side of a large door faded to the same red as the window frames. Some sort of an overhang jutted out from the roof and slanted downward over the doorway, supported by two narrow wood beams that looked as if they could be pushed over with a firm shove. A large window rested on the A-frame roof with a chimney perched behind it, covered with the same stone as the house.

The landscape looked like scenes Aden had only observed on postcards or in nature documentaries he'd watched. He'd spent the majority of his young life closed behind walls of concrete with a limited selection of drab shades of colors, surrounded by trees and shrubbery that blended into one another as if someone had walked through the streets with a large paintbrush and given the city a brief swipe of a few shades of green and then called it a day.

The scene that opened up in front of Aden was serene, unencumbered with the sharp angles and suffocating closeness of tall concrete buildings. In the city, everything was hard: bars and chains on doors, metal poles and signs, heavy steel cars lining the streets, reinforced walls—even the faces of the people who passed you on the street.

Even though it was late at night, the moon and stars bathed the land with a sea of light. Aden spied remnant patches of snow tucked between clusters of pink flowers that spread over the land in no particular order. They seemed out of place in wintertime, when Aden was used to seeing bare branches and sparse, dry leaves.

The quaint house stood alone at the top of a slight rise with a few animal pens erected close to the house. A worn shed was nestled under a regal tree that had probably seen more seasons than anyone Aden had ever met.

Paula maneuvered her car into an open gravel area at the back of the house. She drew up beside a sturdy, dark blue truck and shifted the car into park.

"Ready, Aden?" Paula asked, turning off the engine and cracking open her door.

Ready for what? Aden thought. *I haven't been ready for anything that's happened tonight...*

"Not really," Aden mumbled under his breath. Paula wouldn't have heard him anyway because she was already standing behind the car waiting.

As they walked up a tidy path lined with red stones toward the porch, it dawned on Aden that he had nothing with him but the clothes he wore. His backpack and sleeping bag had been left behind at Angelo's. He assumed Ben had picked up his things, though Aden was sure he would never see them again.

A weathered wooden door opened to reveal a mountain of a man who filled most of the wide doorway. He had a head full of dark wiry hair that connected to a shaggy reddish beard that covered most of the bottom half of his face. A white T-shirt peeked out from under a brown-and-blue plaid shirt. Thick hands were jammed down into faded jeans as the man waited for them to approach.

Aden was taken aback by the man's formidable size and gruff appearance. He wasn't sure what he had expected—*a man in a sports coat and suit pants?*

Was this Mr. Pearson? He stared up at the man in morbid fear. *I can't stay here. I can't...*

Aden had to stop himself from turning around and racing back to the car.

As Aden and Paula mounted the porch steps, the man stepped forward to greet them with a cheery smile, transforming his face from a rough mountain man into a friendly giant.

He spoke with an unhurried, easy drawl. "Evening, Paula. Hey there, Aden."

Aden was surprised that the giant knew his name but remembered Paula's call to the Pearsons earlier.

"Hello, Cray. How are you this evening?" Paula answered. Aden noted that she used the man's first name. *How many kids does Paula bring to stay here?* Aden worried. Paula turned back to Aden and ushered him forward.

"Aden, this is Mr. Pearson."

Mr. Pearson reached out to shake Aden's hand but Aden turned away, averting his eyes to the briefcase draped over Paula's shoulder.

"Come on in." Mr. Pearson drew his hand back and waved toward the open doorway. Angela saw you pull up and went to get some coffee brewing. Aden, you can set your things over there." He gestured to a wooden bench in the entryway. Aden saw the fleeting look of embarrassment on his face when the man noticed that Aden's hands were empty.

"Well…not a problem," he corrected. "We'll get you fixed up with something."

He led them into a large kitchen with more cabinets lining the walls than Aden had ever seen in one room. The kitchen was bathed in white and robin blue with bright floral rugs and a colorful collection of ceramic birds gracing the shelves lining one wall. A large wooden table stood as a focal point in the middle of the kitchen and was covered with soft blue floral mats with a huge bowl of fresh fruit arranged in the center.

A woman, whom Aden assumed was Mrs. Pearson, was pulling down coffee mugs from a cabinet that towered above her tiny frame. Setting the mugs down on the counter, she turned to greet them.

"Hello there!" she chimed. "Hi, Paula…Aden," she said, walking over to him, "I'm Angela." Aden was glad she didn't try to hug him or shake his hand. He was getting sick of meeting new people tonight and everyone touching him.

"Hi," he managed.

Paula had set her briefcase down on the table and was retrieving papers from it. She turned to Angela just as Angela started to say something else to him. He was more than happy to have her attention turn to Paula.

"I have a few papers for you and Cray to sign, Angela," Paula said. "I'll be on my way after that. I'm sure this young man could do with a warm bed and a good night's rest." She gave a thumbs-up to Aden before turning back to Angela. "Do you have everything you need tonight?" At a nod from Angela, she continued, "I'll drop by with some other things Aden might need tomorrow afternoon. We can talk more then."

Angela moved back toward the counter. "Are you sure you wouldn't like a cup of coffee or anything before your long drive back?" she asked.

"No, thank you, Angela. I really do need to head out," Paula told her.

Angela waved Aden over to a chair at the table. "Have a seat, hon. How about you? Would you like a drink or something?"

Aden shook his head.

What I really want is to crawl under the table and be left alone.

He sat down.

After signing papers and discussing details that Aden paid no attention to, Paula walked over and crouched down in front of him.

"I'm going to head out now, Aden." She spoke softly, so that only Aden could hear. "Angela and Cray are wonderful people and you'll love their little boy, Blake. Angela has something you can wear tonight and she can wash the clothes you have on until tomorrow when I bring some fresh things for you, okay? Get some sleep and I'll be back to check on you tomorrow."

Paula stood, looking him over carefully. "Of course, I'll have to guess on sizes unless you know what size you wear—around a ten, twelve in boy's?" she guessed.

Aden shrugged. He didn't really care either way at this point.

"I don't know," he answered.

It was sinking in that he was going to stay in this house with strangers out in the middle of nowhere. He felt panic rising in him again. This whole night had been like a scene from the book, *A*

Series of Unfortunate Events. His night felt like one trouble after another tumbling together into one gigantic nightmare.

When Paula turned to leave, Aden pushed off his chair.

"I don't want to stay here. My mom…I want to wait… somewhere else, until…until you find her." His gaze shot around the room for an escape route, his hands balled into fists as he fought off the terror gripping his body. He took a step forward, not sure which way to go but knowing that he had to do *something.*

All three adults turned to look at him, but it was Paula who stepped forward. He didn't even feel her reach for his hand. She was quiet for a moment while she waited for him to calm himself.

"It's going to be alright, Aden." Each word was spoken with purpose—slow and careful—as if Paula was hand-feeding each word to him so Aden could digest them.

"I am going to do everything in my power to find your mother. You have to trust me—trust the Pearsons—for a few days until we have some answers." Paula lined her eyes to Aden's so he didn't miss her next words. "We all want what is best for you, Aden. I give you my word."

28

*T*he drive to John F. Kennedy Boulevard where Ben planned to drop off paperwork at the social security office was at least a twenty-minute drive, and that was on a good traffic day. Ben left the radio off and savored the silence as he took in the sights of downtown Philly.

At a corner bus stop, a group of people stood waiting, leaving small pockets of space between themselves as if they were avoiding any possibility of conversation between them. As far as Ben could tell from their stony faces, their efforts were successful.

As he searched for a parking space, Ben scanned over the men and women sitting on sidewalks—some leaned up against walls or propped against poles at street corners, all of them looking aimless and forsaken.

The homeless. Permanent fixtures on the landscape of the city that Ben had grown to love. Nameless people he had never really noticed before. Oh, he'd *seen* them, but Ben was discovering that seeing is not really the same as taking *notice*.

Ben nudged his car into a curbside spot and eased his door open into traffic as he stepped out. He was reaching into his front pocket for some change to feed the parking meter when he noticed an old woman sitting on the brick planter just outside the front entrance to the building.

Her shoulders were hunched forward until her upper body formed an almost-perfect "C" shape that ended where one bony leg crossed lazily over the other. She pushed a cigarette between her lips and took a long drag as she watched people walking by on the sidewalk with a dull expression. A drab olive-green duffle bag with a broken zipper lay at her feet, clothing and other odds and ends spilling out of it. Ben assumed everything she owned was probably in that bag.

After adding several quarters to the parking meter, Ben walked down to a silver trailer parked near the street corner and got in line behind a middle-aged man holding a spunky terrier with spiky brown tufts of fur framing its face, its small body wiggling impatiently in the man's arms. Ben waiting while the man finished his order and stepped aside.

"Yes, I'd like two beef hot dogs and a large coffee," he told the stocky teenager with the stiff white paper cap that stared down at him from the window. While he waited, Ben smiled over at the man and his dog. The man didn't offer a smile back, but the dog's tail wagged excitedly as he studied Ben.

Dog's friendlier than his owner, that's for sure, he thought just as the man's order was called and he pushed past Ben.

After he was handed his order, Ben grabbed packets of ketchup, mustard, relish, a few packs of sugar, and napkins before walking back over to the woman still seated on the wall. Ben was glad to see that the cigarette was gone. He couldn't stomach the smell of cigarette smoke. The woman looked up at him when he stood over her and held the food out.

"Well...thank you, sir." A wide, toothless smile spread across her wrinkled face as she reached for the gift with trembling hands. Ben leaned in closer to make it easier on her.

"No problem, ma'am. You have a nice day."

As Ben pulled at the glass door heading into the social security office, a heaviness washed over him. Instead of feeling at peace about helping the desolate woman, all that filled his mind was the last look on Aden's face when he'd stared back at Ben that night: hatred.

BEN HAD BEEN LOOKING for his umbrella all morning when he remembered that he'd last seen it in the trunk of his car. The first thing he noticed, though, when he opened the trunk wasn't his umbrella. It was the green backpack. Ben stared down at the crumpled backpack and swallowed a lump in his throat. *Aden's backpack.*

Ben had forgotten that he'd thrown the backpack and Aden's tattered sleeping bag into his trunk when he realized they'd been left behind the night Aden had been picked up.

Picked up, he thought with bitterness, *more like practically dragged by that cop to the squad car.*

The cop had locked Aden in the backseat of his car and come back over to inform Ben that he would drop by the next day to take a statement from him. Ben couldn't remember if he had even answered the man. Mia had slipped back inside after she'd walked out and seen Aden being taken away.

Everything was a blur from that night. Ben remembered sitting on the porch steps for over an hour with his head in his hands, too distraught to move. He thought Mia had checked on him once, but she didn't disturb him.

He had been meaning to call Mrs. Anderson and ask her what to do with Aden's things but forgot about them being in his trunk. What he had *really* wanted to do was call to check up on Aden and see how he was doing. He worried every day about how the boy was getting along and where they had sent him. *Did they find his mother?*

Ben didn't open the backpack—it felt too personal. He felt like he would be invading what little privacy the boy had. He mulled over how he could return Aden's meager belongings to him. Having them back might bring a small measure of comfort to the boy.

When Mrs. Anderson dropped by Angelo's a few days later to ask Ben a few more questions, he hurried her to the back office where they could talk privately.

"How's the boy?" Ben asked as he pushed the door closed.

Mrs. Anderson lowered herself onto the edge of Eddie's rolling desk chair.

"He's doing as well as can be expected right now, which is more than I can say about my end," she said, releasing a heavy sigh.

"We're having a hard time locating Aden's family," she told him. "I was hoping you might remember anything else that Aden shared with you that might be helpful in any way. I can't get him to open up to me. He's either hiding something or he just doesn't have any information to share."

Ben stood and fiddled with a pen from the desk while he tried to think, but was already shaking his head before he even answered.

"Well, Mrs. Anderson, Aden never shared much with me neither about his life before. I honestly don't believe there was much to tell anyway," Ben said. "I only heard him talk a little bit about his momma and about them livin' in an upstairs apartment or something. I got the impression that the boy didn't get out and experience much. Well...that is, until he was forced out on his own like he was."

"That's kind of what I figured." Paula sat watching Ben flick at the pen for a moment before he pulled his hand back and stuck it in his front pocket. She stood, pushing the rolling chair neatly back under the desk.

"Please," she said, "call me Paula. I really appreciate your help, Ben. If you think of anything else that might be useful, don't hesitate to give me a call." She reached into her purse and pulled out a business card. "I know you have my number already, but keep this on you just in case."

Ben considered asking about Aden's whereabouts but Paula beat him to it.

"We've placed Aden with a very nice family temporarily while we get things sorted out. He's safe and is being well taken care of. We have you to thank for that."

"Thank you, ma'am—Paula—I'm sorely needin' to hear that encouragement right now," Ben stuck out his hand to grasp Paula's in a firm shake. "Also, I have...the boy's things, just a backpack and whatnot that he left behind. I'm thinkin' he might want it and all."

"Yes, of course," Paula said, her voice brightening. "I'm heading out of town for a few days but will be checking on Aden when I return. I can arrange to pick his things up from you and make sure he gets them. Meanwhile, my goal is to find out who this young man belongs to and hold them accountable for placing him in this situation."

———

BEN KNEW he should be in bed already but his mind was still racing from his conversation with Paula and what she'd shared with him about Aden being placed with a family—a foster home.

He'd heard mostly positive things about families who foster children on both temporary and more permanent arrangements, but Ben had also read about some not-so-good foster homes in the news. He felt like Paula sincerely cared about the kids that she worked with and was sure she was careful about arranging the best possible placements for them.

Ben grabbed a soda from the refrigerator and made his way to the couch. He sunk his body down into the doughy cushions, not bothering to turn on any lights. The ambient light drifting in from the kitchen suited him just fine. His eyes scanned the shadowed room.

The walls were barren canvases. The lone bookshelf shoved in the corner bore only a stack of yellowed hunting magazines and an old alarm clock that hadn't worked in years as far as Ben knew. Other than the faded recliner across from him, a scarred coffee table and two mismatched end tables, the only other item of interest in the room was the lumpy, but comfortable, couch Ben was sitting on.

I guess two old bachelors don't care much for decorating.

Jake's wife, Kim, had died a few years before Ben moved in with him. He gave the room another pass. There were no photos on display anywhere. Jake and Kim had never had children, so there was no legacy to hallmark in photo frames. Ben wasn't sure why, but that depressed him. His thoughts drifted to his own grown son, Jeremy.

Jeremy was twenty-three now and Ben's heart ached from being shut out of his life. Ben was thirty-two when Jeremy was born; he hadn't been all that eager to have kids but knew Emma was feeling middle age bearing down on her. Ben was content with just drawing an honest paycheck every week. He had been a painter and sandblaster by trade and was employed at a local Philadelphia shipyard that paid well and offered a great benefit and retirement package.

Ben's idea of the good life had been coming home to Emma every night and spending weekends drinking with his buddies. One night, after an exhausting day of work and a night indulging in a steady flow of liquor, Ben ran his truck into the side of an unyielding oak tree. The accident shattered his lower leg and put twelve stitches in his forehead. The truck was demolished, but Ben lived to drink again.

The damage to his leg eventually healed but not to the satisfaction of his employer. The shipyard company wasn't willing to take chances with him clambering up the sides of ships and strolling across narrow beams. Ben was sent on his merry way with a pink slip and a handshake.

He started collecting a small disability check every month but joined the ranks of the unemployed for a season. His discouragement with feeling that he was "less of a man" because he couldn't provide for Emma drove him to drink even more. It was during this low point in his life, a time when Ben felt the least capable of becoming a father, that Jeremy made his appearance in the world.

Those early years with Jeremy were shining moments on the stage of Ben's life. When he wasn't working or—Ben hated to even think of it now—drowning himself in booze, he and Jeremy spent time sorting through Jeremy's baseball card collection, organizing and reorganizing them into a binder Ben had given him for his collection. They lived across the street from a park and Ben would pitch balls to Jeremy most afternoons after he came home from school.

Ben found another job doing part-time janitorial work for a local college in the evenings. The pay was barely enough to help pay the bills and Emma carried most of the financial weight for the family. This only added to the mounting frustration and distance between them, and Ben escaped as often as possible into a drunken stupor.

Emma's patience and, eventually, affection for Ben withered away like a dead, decaying tree until she finally stopped speaking to him and found more and more things for Jeremy to do that did not include his father: swimming lessons twice a week, joining the Cub Scouts, even a few months of karate lessons.

Jeremy's baseball cards were left untouched for weeks, which turned into months, until one night, when Ben came home after work, just as the sun was painting deep oranges and glowing yellows across the sky from behind the distant mountains, she and Jeremy were gone.

All that remained of them were a few scattered clothing items and a note taped on the bathroom mirror.

Ben looked down at the can gripped tightly in his hand. He hadn't even opened it yet. He stared vacantly at its circular aluminum top and the small looped pull tab. From this angle, you couldn't tell if it was a soda or a can of beer.

Ben set the unopened can down on the end table next to him. He noticed his hand was trembling when he drew it back. His eyes shot over to the wall clock. It was 1:48 a.m. The bars would be closing in less than fifteen minutes.

Thank God, Ben thought, balling his shaking hand into a fist. *I'd never make it before they closed.*

Ben leaned over to the lamp on the table and pulled the small chain dangling from under the shade. He hoped that more light in the room would chase away the dark thoughts that were invading his mind right now.

*a*den helped Cray drag a pile of dead branches they had cut down to a clearing at the back of the property, where Cray would burn them with other brush piles they had collected that morning. The Pearson's son, Blake, chased a surly, old hen who had wandered from the rest of the flock and won herself the attention of the rambunctious six-year-old.

Cray looked up as the hen passed near them, squawking and carrying on as she fled from Blake.

"Blake!" Cray hollered. "Best leave that hen alone or that bad-tempered rooster is gonna come after you!" He grinned over at Aden and mumbled, "I'm not kidding either. That rooster is meaner than a sleeping tomcat after someone dumped ice water on him. Crazy bird jumped on my back one day just for looking at him the wrong way."

Cray sent Aden to grab some twine from the shed. Aden was wary and found himself watching out carefully for the rooster. He didn't want to have any surprise meetings with him.

Aden had been with the Pearsons for a few weeks now and was still struggling to follow the household routines of waking early to get dressed for the day and help with chores before breakfast. He had never been an early riser at home with his mom and even living on the streets and waking when the city came to life, Aden never had anything pressing him to get up and start moving right away. He could sit and linger in the shadows while he watched people and figured out where he would forage for something to eat for breakfast.

Here at the Pearson's, everyone hit the floor running when the sun was barely up and were already chatting about the day's plans long before Aden had time to even wipe the sleep from his eyes.

It was bad enough having to watch his back for thugs on the street back in Philadelphia, now he had to worry about a rooster jumping him when he least expected it.

He hated it here. Sure, the Pearsons were nice enough and Blake was a sweet kid, but Aden didn't belong here. He was just a charity case thrown on the Pearson's doorstep and had never asked to be here. He had been doing just fine on his own.

And...Paula lied to me, he thought, anger beginning to boil in his gut. *She said it would only be for a few days.*

She had dropped by a few times to check on him and let him know that there was no real progress yet in finding any of his family, but Aden wondered if Paula was trying hard enough.

Then, she'd come by last week to tell Aden that they thought they may have a small lead in his mother's whereabouts. She said that a woman that the police had picked up on drug charges admitted to selling drugs to the women who worked the streets near Broad Street, in an area known as the *Badlands,* due to the prolific open-air drug markets and violence in the area.

"When they asked if she remembered running into a woman on the streets named Lauren," Paula told him, "she told the police that she thought she had and gave them a description of a thin woman with long dark hair and light-colored eyes. That's all she could tell them. The police interviewed a few people on the streets but came up with nothing."

Aden's heart stopped. *That was her. It had to be…*

Paula also shared that the police had pulled a rap sheet for a woman named Lauren, who matched the description but for whom they had no last name, but there was nothing to go off of from there either and they hadn't seen her on the streets for several months.

"We are putting all of our effort into searching for her, Aden. Until we find her, the Pearsons want you to stay as long as you need. They will even look into enrolling you in school this next fall.

Aden glared at her. *I won't be here next fall even if I have to crawl back to Philly.*

"Have you ever been to public school, Aden?" Paula asked him.

"I don't know what you mean by *public school,*" he said, "but I've never been to any kind of school at all. My mom taught me at home."

He didn't know any other kids to compare himself to, but Aden knew he was an excellent reader and that his mom had to keep buying harder math workbooks because they were all too easy for him. He didn't know what else the Pearsons and Paula expected from him and he didn't know why they were making such a big deal about it.

"That's okay, Aden. The school will do some testing so they will know where to place you in your classes. You would be in seventh or eighth grade, I believe," Paula said. "The Pearsons have even agreed to do some homeschooling with you first to help you catch up if you are too far behind for regular school right now."

Aden's heart was stone. It was all too much for him. He didn't want to be sent to a school with a bunch of other kids he didn't know. If the Pearsons wanted him to do schoolwork while he was here, then fine. But they couldn't force him to go to school against his will. He was just waiting for them to find his mom so he could go home and life could go back to what it was.

Aden had settled in his heart that his mother must have been desperate when she left him at the shelter. That she was overwhelmed and really hadn't wanted to do it. He was sure she regretted it now and had been searching for him but didn't know where to find him.

He held onto the hope that Paula would locate her or that someone that knew her would step forward with information and that he and his mom could go back to being a family again. He was sure he could be more help to her now and not such a burden. Another year or so and he could even get a job to help make things easier on his mom.

The idea of being forced to go to school kept him awake that night. Aden stared at the ceiling above his bed for hours, trying to figure a way out.

He considered running away. He knew he could go back to living on the streets even if he was miserable. He would have to go to a different part of the city, the police would know where to look for him now. He almost had a plan all worked out when it dawned on Aden that the Pearsons lived way out of the city limits and that he had no place to run from way out here. He knew how to survive on city streets but had no idea how to be homeless in the middle of farmlands and dense woodland.

Aden was emotionally spent and his body demanded sleep. As he drifted off, he tried to imagine a new story in his mind like he used to do to help him fall asleep. He visualized an enormous black dragon with glowing scales and fire in its nostrils appearing outside of his window and calling to him.

Come boy, climb onto my back and I'll fly you far away from here…wherever you want to go. Come…

But the dream faded as fast as it had appeared and was replaced by a real memory. One that was tangible and nudged at the corner of Aden's conscience as he drifted off to sleep. It was the memory of all of Aden's other stories. Bits and pieces of his imagination flowing back into his thoughts. Stories he'd created and shared—with Ben, who had written them down for him.

The notebook, Aden remembered. He wondered where it was now.

———————

he rain came down in a relentless torrent, sending waterfalls down Ben's car windshield and blurring his view of the road. The windshield wipers were making a valiant attempt at keeping up but only succeeded in swishing the rain aside before a fresh torrent blocked his vision again. The rubber on the wipers was half-shredded and next to useless. Ben had meant to replace the wipers months ago but kept putting it off. The weather had been mild and Ben didn't see the need for tackling the job just yet.

It was 2:30 in the morning and Ben had just left Angelo's. The streets of Philly were empty except for the occasional delivery and sanitation trucks. He reached over to crank up the heat, thankful that at least something was in working order in the old car. *Still cheaper than a girlfriend.*

He'd had to stay a little longer at the bakery tonight to unclog a sink in the kitchen. It needed to be done before Eddie and his wife, Louise, arrived to start firing up the ovens at 4:30 a.m.

Ben and Mia were off at midnight, but when one of the main sinks had clogged tonight, Ben was obligated to stay and fix it. Mia had stuck around for an extra hour to help Ben because she felt bad leaving him alone.

"Go on home, Mia," he scolded. "You ain't doing nothin' but making me nervous standing there starin' at me. Only one of us can be under this sink, anyway, and I'm the only one that knows what they're doing," he teased.

"Fine. Be stubborn. You smell like sewage anyway," she grumbled. "I'll let you lock up." Mia plucked her handbag from the wall hook by the back door with an exaggerated huff and let the door slam behind her. Ben just shook his head. *That's Mia for you,* he thought, *always so dramatic about everything.*

It was raining hard by the time Ben had locked up and jogged over to his car. He always parked across the street from the bakery in an abandoned lot because Eddie wanted the few parking spaces in front of the bakery to be for customers.

By the time Ben reached his car, jerked open the door, and slid into the seat, he was drenched all the way down to his tennis shoes. Mixed with the grime and dampness from sitting on the bakery floor covered in dirty backed-up sink water, he was sure Mia was right—he did stink.

It took a few minutes for the car heater to warm things up enough for Ben to stop shivering. Unfortunately, the windows fogged up from the moisture evaporating from Ben's body. *I'll just sit it out a few minutes*, he thought as he rested his head against the back of his seat and waited for the defroster to clear the windows.

Blinking to clear his eyes from the blanket of fatigue that had settled over them, Ben sat up and put the car in gear, pulling out of the lot and onto the empty street. He looked forward to indulging in a scalding-hot cup of tea and a steaming shower before crawling under his comforter and resting his old bones. He didn't mind the cold, even when the temperatures dipped below freezing, but he couldn't stand having wet clothes sticking to him.

I might not be so soppin' wet if I hadn't had to stand out in the rain and fuss with lockin' up that stupid back door. How many times have I told Eddie it needs to be replaced?

Eddie insisted that the door worked just fine and that he needed new equipment for the business before he bought a new door.

That's 'cause he never hauls the trash out in the middle of the night when it's freezing cold, Ben grumbled to himself.

The windows had cleared—at least on the inside—but, the rain was coming down in full sheets now. Ben slowed the vehicle until he could see better.

His fingers, stiff from the cold, trembled as he gripped the steering wheel and squinted through the rivets of water pouring down the windshield. The road in front of him was a blurry mirage as he maneuvered through the saturated roads.

"Yep, I always learn the hard way," Ben chided himself aloud. "Gonna buy new wipers first thing tomorrow." He squinted through the hazy windshield, the wipers squealing in protest against the glass as they fought against the abusive rain.

There was no warning. No premonition of imminent danger.

While the road was clear before him in one moment, in the next moment the car was filled with a flash of brilliant light that sliced through the curtain of water on the window of the passenger side, engulfing the car interior with such intense brightness that Ben's eyes closed tight in protest. He instinctively turned his head away from the blinding glare.

Oh, God…lightning? What…?

A deafening roar filled Ben's ears and rattled violently through his chest. Ben was trapped in a time warp as his mind registered danger but his body refused to respond. The roaring sound slowed to a low groan before escalating to a high-pitch screech piercing the air. Ben felt his body slam hard against the driver door. His head jerked sideways like a rag doll as it was flung against the door window. His hands instinctively flew up to his protect his face as his vision filled with vibrant sparkles of a million pieces of flying glass. The last thing he remembered was feeling the rain pouring down his cheek before everything was lost in a tunnel of darkness.

31

"*C*an you give me a piggy-*bat* ride, Aden? Please?"

Blake jumped and did somersaults on Aden's bed while he waited for Aden to finish buttoning his shirt. Cray planned to drive into town this morning to pick up parts for his fishing boat and promised to take Aden and Blake fishing after he made a few repairs on the boat. Aden had never been fishing before but Blake had gone with his father many times. It seemed like every hour Blake was reminding Aden about how much fun the trip was going to be.

"I know how to bait my own hook too, Aden. It's easy...I can show you how," Blake sang.

Aden wasn't sure if he was going to like fishing or not but Blake's excitement was contagious. Aden was starting to look forward to the trip himself with all that Blake was going on about it. There had to be something to it if a six-year-old got that hyped up over it.

"It's piggy*back*, Blake, not piggy-*bat*," Aden told him. "And stop jumping on the bed—I just finished making it."

Aden scooped Blake up in midair after a high jump and set him back on the ground. Grabbing his cap off the dresser behind him, he turned back to Blake, who was now hopping on one foot around the room.

"Alright," he said, bending down and offering his back to Blake. "Hop on."

"Yessss!" Blake ran over and scooted himself up onto Aden's back. Chubby arms reached up and circled his neck. It was becoming their daily ritual. Blake was always up before Aden and would creep down the hall to Aden's room and crack the door open to see if he was awake. Aden had developed a keen sense of hearing over the months of being homeless and even the slightest sound woke him. Sleeping had been a dangerous undertaking out on the streets. Keeping his ears in tune for danger was a vital tool to staying alive.

It had taken a week or two for Aden to adjust to sleeping under a roof in a real bed again. A *real* bed, with an actual headboard. When Aden was younger, he usually slept on the floor or the couch until his mom had gotten an old Coleman military cot from a neighbor who was moving out of state.

"It'll be like camping, Aden," she told him. "I used to love to build forts out of blankets and chairs when I was a kid."

Aden hadn't minded the cot because it was the first time he had anything that was close to having his own bed. Since it was portable, he had fun moving it to different rooms each night just for the adventure. Most of the time though, he kept the old cot set up in a corner of the living room. He was getting older and wanted more privacy and being alone in the living room made it feel like he had his own space.

Now, at the Pearson's, everything felt almost *too* quiet.

The constant background noise of car horns, barking dogs, music pulsating out of apartment windows—they had all blended together in a symphony of chaos that was the trademark of city life. Then there was the unique smell of the city. The air was permeated with a persistent odor of unwashed bodies and greasy food mixed with pungent drifts of vehicle exhaust and sewage. One couldn't discount the more pleasant aromas that also drifted over the city of fresh-brewed coffee from a cafe or the sweet smell of relish from the corner hot dog stands.

But Aden's favorite by far was the tantalizing scents that drifted out from the bakery where Ben worked. Aden's mouth watered just thinking about the deep-fried cannolis filled with creamy ricotta and the dense, moist blueberry scones that Ben saved for him from the leftovers at the end of the day.

Just thinking about Ben and the bakery made Aden's chest hurt. He drove his emotions back into the closet of his mind and slammed the door closed. He would rather feel hollow than to be tossed on an ocean of bitterness right now. When Cray whistled for the boys, Aden was ready.

"Quit squirming, Blake, you're choking me," Aden muttered.

THE SUN WAS CASTING its last glow over the treetops when they arrived home later that evening. They were covered in muck and smelled like a fish hatchery, but the threesome appeared happy as they teased and joked with one another. Cray was just pulling the truck around to the back of the house so they could unhitch the boat when they saw the familiar gray Honda pull out onto the main road from the driveway.

"That's Paula's car," Aden said. "Wonder why she was here." Concern and curiosity mixed with a surge of hope pulsed through Aden's body.

Did they find my mother? Had she come to tell him the good news but got tired of waiting for them to come home? Why would Paula have come all the way out here this time of the evening anyway? She always dropped by earlier in the day...

Aden barely waited for Cray to put the truck in *park* before jumping out of the cab. "I'll be right back," he told Cray and ran into the house to look for Angela. Cray must have understood Aden's sudden rush of adrenaline because he didn't stop him. Running through the back door into the kitchen, Aden spied Angela walking out of the laundry room with a basket of clothes.

"Hey, Aden," she paused, basket propped on her hip. "Paula was just here dropping something off for you. I put it on your bed." She smiled and walked over to set the heavy basket on the kitchen table.

"Oh, okay, thanks," Aden said, disappointment seeping into his chest. "Um, that's a long drive for her just to drop something off. Did she have any information or anything?" His eyes darted around the room as if expecting Paula to pop out of the next room or something.

Understanding crept into Angela's eyes. Her lips formed a sad smile.

"No, nothing about your mom yet, Aden. Paula was passing through the area and was just dropping by with your backpack. She said that she got it from a man named Ben a few days ago. He told her that it belonged to you."

Ben gave my stuff to Paula?

He didn't want to think about how Ben knew Paula. As far as the backpack went, there wasn't really anything in it that he cared about anymore. It was just full of a few old clothes, a couple of books, and other odds and ends of junk. He didn't know why Ben had even bothered.

Aden briefly wondered what happened to his sleeping bag, then dismissed it. He had no use for it either—at least he hoped that he would never need it again. He doubted Angela would let the filthy thing in the house anyway.

Aden turned away.

"I'm going outside to help Cray get the truck unloaded," he said.

"Wait...Aden," Angela called. "I know..."

Aden swung around to face her. "No, you *don't* know. Everyone keeps saying they don't know anything and expecting me to believe them! My mom didn't just fall off the face of the earth, Angela!" Aden was shaking with all the rage that he'd corralled and muzzled over the long weeks. "You and Cray...Paula, I don't know —*everyone*—is lying to me just because I'm a kid!"

Angela didn't speak or try to move. She let Aden spit his venom at her without interruption. Aden could see the concern weighing in Angela's eyes but, to him, it was just another stalling technique. He was sure she knew more than she was saying and he couldn't stand to be in the room with her right now.

Aden turned and jerked the back door open. He ran in the direction of the shed instead of over to where Cray and Blake were unloading the truck. Neither one of them looked his way and he was glad for it. A dark mood had settled over Aden, the excitement of the day deflating into a puddle of brooding that threatened to overwhelm him.

He searched for a place to be alone.

32

*B*lake dominated the conversation at the dinner table, telling stories about their day together, even sharing how Aden caught his first fish. "Mom, did you know that Aden never caught a fish before?" he said. "I taught him how! I helped him catch his first fish! Right, Aden?" Blake said, tugging on Aden's sleeve.

Angela and Cray smiled and shared in the boy's excitement. Then, their attention turned to Aden.

"You're quiet tonight, Aden," Cray said. Aden shrugged and glanced over at Angela, his look giving away his concern about whether or not Angela had told Cray about his outburst earlier. She kept her expression neutral.

"It was fun today," Aden said. He turned to Blake. "Thanks, Blake, for helping me catch that fish. Of course, a bunch of fish got away before I finally got the hang of it, but I had a good time." He turned to Cray. "Uh, thanks, Cray."

Blake didn't waste any time stepping back into the center of attention as he launched into more stories about their adventures that day. Cray added to Blake's stories but had to correct Blake a few times when his exaggeration got out of hand. Angela, however, was quiet and kept glancing over at Aden, trying to judge his emotional state.

She also wavered on whether she should tell him the other news that Paula had shared with her when she'd dropped by today. After his accusations earlier, she wasn't sure she—or Aden, for that matter—was ready for another storm burst.

"Did you find your backpack, Aden?" she said, testing the waters.

Aden nibbled on a corner of his cornbread. "No." He shrugged, avoiding her stare. "It's just a few clothes and stuff. I'll probably just toss it."

From Paula, Angela had an idea of what happened the night the police picked Aden up and a little of the relationship he had shared with Ben. She knew that Aden had been upset with Ben that night, so mentioning him right now could be a mistake, especially since Aden seemed out of sorts at the moment.

Whatever he's feeling, he may still want to know. She wrestled with the weight of the knowledge and whether it was the right time to share it or not.

Angela stood to grab the iced tea pitcher from the counter and walked over to fill Aden's glass. She kept her voice neutral so that it didn't appear like she was making a big production out of what she was about to say. She looked over at Cray for encouragement but he was focused on buttering a dinner roll. Blake had already run off to play in his room so it was just the three of them left in the kitchen.

Setting the pitcher down in the center of the table, Angela slid back onto her chair. She fumbled to find the right words to ease into the topic. She tried stalling by dabbing at some tea that had dripped onto the table with her napkin before crumpling the napkin into a ball in her fist.

Well, she thought, *here we go.*

"Aden, um, I didn't get a chance to mention to you something that Paula shared with me today...about Ben." She hurried to insert Ben's name so Aden wouldn't latch onto the wrong idea that she had kept something back about his mother. *He already believes we aren't telling him everything anyway,* she thought.

Aden looked up at the mention of Ben but dropped his eyes back to his plate when he noticed Angela looking at him.

"Yeah," he muttered, stabbing his fork into a mound of green beans on his plate. "What about him?"

Angela braced herself to deliver the rest of the message.

"Well, I'm not even sure if it matters to you, but Paula mentioned that Ben is in the hospital. I guess he was in a bad car accident a few days ago."

Aden's head jerked up, his full attention on Angela now as he stared wide-eyed at her. The forkful of green beans lowered back down to his plate.

"Ben's in the hospital?" he asked, shock registering on his face.

Angela hesitated, but finished with what she knew.

"Yes, Aden...he is," she continued. "Paula didn't know much about what happened. She got the news from his roommate, Jake, when she called to talk to Ben and he answered. The only thing he told her was that it was raining really hard as he was driving home from work and a truck slammed into him from the passenger side. I guess the traffic light was out from the storm and the truck driver claims he never even saw Ben until he hit him. Ben's car was totaled."

Her voice lowered. "Paula says he's in really bad shape."

33

*S*taring back down at his plate, Aden was silent. *Ben was hurt.* He didn't know what to think or how to respond. He didn't even know what he was *supposed* to be feeling right now. His heart was pounding and he felt like he was suddenly falling in empty space with no safety net under him. He knew he should say something, should answer Angela, but he just…couldn't.

Angela laid a hand on his shoulder. "I thought…Paula thought that, maybe, you'd want to know," she said. "I wanted to mention it earlier today but—"

Cray broke in. "Would you like to go see him, Aden?"

Aden felt the weight of Angela's hand on his shoulder. He looked up at Cray.

He didn't really have to think about it, the words tumbling out on their own as if Aden's voice had understood what his heart wanted before his mind had. "Yes…I mean, can I do that?" Aden asked.

Aden wasn't even sure *why* he asked to see Ben—why he *wanted* to see him. *But…Ben's hurt. How bad was he?* He didn't even know which way to steer his thoughts right now.

Will he...is he...going to die?

Aden felt like his chest was being crushed beneath a massive stone: disappointment, rage, defeat, revenge tumbled together with misery, heartache, grief, and fear. It was a combination like oil and water that, no matter how you threw them all together, they never blended in harmony. But a tiny sprout pushed its stubborn head above the turmoil inside of him and demanded to be noticed. He wanted....*needed*...to see Ben.

"Absolutely, Aden," Angela whispered, her hand drifting down from his shoulder to rest on his hand. "I'll call Paula in the morning and see if she can get the information about which hospital he's at and we'll plan to go." Looking to Cray she said, "You'd have to keep Blake when we do. Do you mind?"

"Not at all," Cray answered, "Just let me know and I'll take the time off," he nodded.

Suddenly, Philadelphia felt like a million miles away to Aden.

———————

ADEN SAT on the edge of the mattress and stared at the backpack sitting in the middle of his bed.

The backpack that Ben gave me.

He remembered the night Ben gave it to him and how overwhelmed with gratitude he felt for such kindness even though Ben hardly knew Aden. He tried to remember if he'd even thanked Ben for the gift.

Seeing it again stirred conflicting emotions in him. He couldn't deny that being at the Pearson's had lifted a weight off of him. A weight that he hadn't even realized he'd been carrying. Worrying about his mom working on the streets at night, the isolation of being alone in their little apartment with no real connection with the outside world, only to be brutally thrust out into that world with no experience.

He hadn't really thought about *home* in a long time, a very different kind of *home* than the Pearson's compared to what he'd known with his mom. Aden realized that being hungry on the streets wasn't the first time he'd felt hunger. How many nights had there been no food in the apartment and Aden had gone to bed dreaming about pizza and soda, a special treat he and his mom shared when money was good? Most days, Aden just got by with dry cereal with no milk and ramen noodles. It had never occurred to Aden until now that, even when there wasn't any food in the cupboards, there never seemed to be a shortage of wine in the refrigerator.

Maybe it was because Aden was seeing it from a different perspective that he felt a prick of anger in his gut.

The backpack blurred as Aden blinked back tears of frustration. The memory of his mother on the morning she left him assaulted his mind. She had pushed his backpack, the one that was torn off him by the mob of thugs in the alley, at him and told him to go inside the shelter. A homeless shelter. *For adults*, he huffed. It was as if his mom had taken the burden of caring for him off her own shoulders and shoved the burden on Aden.

Did she really think I was strong enough to face all that alone? A single tear slid down his nose and lodged against the corner of his bottom lip.

He didn't wipe it away. It was because of *her* that he had suffered. She was the reason for his tears. He'd been left alone in the world to fend for himself. His mother didn't know that he never went in the shelter but did she even have any idea of what they would have done with Aden? Where they would have sent him? Who he could have ended up with?

It was her fault that he'd suffered all those months, his body cramping with cold all those long nights curled up in that dumpy sleeping bag he'd found discarded, no pillow, and everything he owned—which was practically nothing—rolled up in a bag he bore on his back.

He should hate her. But… he couldn't. She was—would always be—a part of him. He was angry with her and thought she was a coward for not keeping him…but he loved her…he missed her.

And, right now, looking at the bag Angela had left for him on his bed and knowing that he should be angry with him too, Aden was also missing Ben. When he thought about Ben laying in a hospital bed, broken and shattered, possibly dying for all Aden knew, he could feel the layers of bitterness surrounding his heart begin to flutter apart like the petals of a wilted flower in the breeze.

You hurt me, Ben, but I think I understand…why you did it.

Aden thought back to that night at Angelo's and the look on Ben's face. His eyes had pleaded with Aden to understand, even though he couldn't see it through the anger and fear that night. All Aden could think of in that moment was that Ben had betrayed him. Aden still wrestled with the "why" of it all but he was tired of fighting the whole world: his mom, Ben, the Pearsons, Paula, the police…every person he met at every turn in his life.

There has to be someone I can trust.

Aden reached up and flicked away the tear still caught on his lip. His mom was the one who pushed him away, whatever her reasons. He didn't like being forced to stay here, to not have a say or make his own decisions, but he had to, begrudgingly, admit that they were all trying to help him in their own ways.

Aden reached out a timid hand to the backpack and drew it closer. He unzipped the larger section and peered inside. Aden drew back at the musty, foul smell that drifted out.

Whew! Did I walk around smelling like that?

He timidly pulled out a pair of jeans and a rolled up T-shirt and tossed them on the floor by his feet to be thrown away later.

I should just throw this whole thing away. I don't want any of this stuff.

Reaching inside once more, Aden tugged a torn pair of boxers and dirty socks out and added them to the pile on the floor before spying a book with a blue cover toward the bottom.

The notebook. Why was it in here?

He pulled it out and set it on the bed next to him.

Please, be okay, Ben.

Aden ran his finger down the cover, tracing the bends and crinkles on its surface from being stuffed in the bag. He reached to open the cover, then decided against it.

These are the stories Ben was writing down for me

My stories.

hoosh…whoosh…click. Whoosh…whoosh…click.
The rhythmic sound of the ventilator connected to the crumpled figure on the bed dominated the cramped room, drowning out the sound of birdsong in the trees outside the hospital window. The waxed floors reflected the muted sunlight peeking in from an opening in the window blinds.

A metal rolling tray was pushed into the corner, useless to the occupant of the room who lay motionless eight feet away. The bed stood parked behind a massive, faded blue curtain that was pulled across the center of the room for privacy, reducing the two sides of the room to the equivalent of two large closets.

Everything felt so sterile that Aden feared just walking through the door had dragged a host of fatal germs into Ben's room. He paused behind the heavy curtain, trying to adjust to the strong scent of disinfectant and something sour lingering in the air.

Taking a deep breath, he looked back at Angela, who remained in the doorway, allowing Aden to visit alone. She offered Aden a nod of encouragement. He turned back and moved part of the curtain aside with two fingers.

He could see the bottom portion of the bed with its raised rails and the lump under the sheets where Ben's feet lay. There was a soft beeping sound nearly drowned out by the low drum of the ventilator that echoed off the near-bare walls. Aden stepped forward and moved toward the foot of the bed.

It took a moment to register that there was a real person under the thin sheet. Ben's white-shrouded head appeared disembodied against the pillows propped under him. His pale skin looked pasty and almost blended into the white of the bandages that covered most of his head. His body sunk low into the crisp, white sheets that covered him.

The near-translucent patches of skin visible on Ben's swollen face were shaded in places with hues of blue and green. Aden could barely make out his eyes, sealed behind fluid-filled sacs, sparse dark eyelashes poking out from under the swelling. One hand rested on top of the sheets. Other than the IV tucked under a narrow bandage on top of his hand, it was the only part of Ben that Aden could see that looked, well…normal.

Aden was a stone as he watched Ben's chest rise and fall to the cadence of the machine that breathed life into his body.

The tears came unbidden and he hardly recognized they were there until he felt the wetness on his cheeks. He tried hard to connect *this* Ben—broken and withered on the bed—to the fun-loving man from the bakery with the deep, gray eyes that expressed volumes more than his words did.

Ben. The only true friend I've ever had. Aden sniffed.

Bolstered by the vision of the Ben he'd *known* instead of the unrecognizable figure who lay unmoving in front of him, Aden stepped closer to the bed.

He reached out hesitantly and rested his fingers on top of Ben's exposed hand, careful not to disturb the IV line. He'd never been close to anyone besides his mom and the intimacy of the moment felt awkward to Aden. He pushed a little closer to the bed and rested his elbow on the metal railing.

"Hey, Ben. It's me…Aden," he whispered, "They told me you were in an accident and were hurt real bad. Angela—um, that's the lady I'm staying with—brought me here to see you. Oh, and I got my backpack that you sent…thanks."

He wasn't sure if Ben could hear him but wanted to say everything he needed to while he was here in case—he didn't want to think of it—he never got the chance to later.

Many nights, when Aden lay tucked up against a building or huddled under a bench, he'd look up at the sky and talk to his mom, asking her where she was and why she had walked out of his life. He shared with her about how afraid he was and how he missed her. A part of him desperately needed to believe that they were somehow connected through some sort of telepathy or that the angels carried his words to her on the wind. That, somehow, she *heard* or *felt* him. But he'd grown wiser—cynical even—over the months and understood that it was just foolish dreaming. But he had talked to her anyway because it made him feel closer to her—had made him feel better somehow.

Standing here next to Ben, he had that opportunity. Maybe Ben couldn't hear him, but if there was any way he could, Aden was not going to miss that chance.

"I didn't want to see you for a while, Ben. I was really hurt and, I guess, angry because I felt like you had betrayed me," he said. "I didn't know what to think, you know what I mean? I thought…I thought that you didn't want me around anymore…just like my mom." Aden began to cry. A tear rolled off his chin and dripped onto his hand. The wetness seeped between his fingers onto Ben's.

There was no movement or response from Ben; the ventilator

and monitors attached to his body never broke rhythm or even stuttered as they performed their life-sustaining tasks. Aden was discouraged by Ben's lack of response to his agonizing confession but the nurse and Angela had both warned him that Ben would be unresponsive. They had both encouraged him to talk to Ben anyway because there was still a chance that Ben was able to hear him.

He couldn't stay long. *Just a few minutes*—the nurse had warned.

It was time to leave. Angela was waiting.

Aden had one more thing to say. He hoped with all his heart that Ben could hear it.

"It's okay, Ben. I understand better now. I...I *forgive* you," Aden said with a sob.

He reached up and gently touched the bandage on Ben's head. His emotions ran so deep, he wished he could bring Ben back to him with just his touch. That, somehow, his touch would have the power to heal Ben.

He hadn't realized until this moment how much he had missed the old man's laid-back, soft Southern drawl and easy smile. The little things he had taught Aden about the world that he had never experienced from his limited view of life from a third-floor apartment window in the middle of Philly.

Aden knew nothing about *normal* things people did, like road trips across the country, arguments with store clerks, cheating at card games, getting up for school every day, or having a best friend.

All these things Ben had let Aden experience through his eyes, from his own stories about his life growing up, during those brief chats sitting on overturned fruit crates in the back lot of a bakery. Other friends met in coffee shops or huddled up on couches to play video games, but Aden liked the humble little meeting place that he and Ben had constructed just fine.

Aden, too, had shared his own stories. Invented stories, concocted in his limited imagination that had been primarily fed through reruns on TV and the piles of books he and his mom picked up at the library every week or two. Aden had longed to experience the adventures that his mind dreamed up but had never had the opportunity.

The lonely nights hadn't changed much for him on the streets, even though people swarmed around him all times of the day, but at least he had felt safe in the apartment. *Except for the men that came home with her sometimes...*

Ben had made him forget his loneliness and had given Aden a tiny glimpse into what having a father might have been like for him.

"I gotta go, Ben," he whispered. "Angela says the hospital won't let us stay very long. But she said we could come back the day after tomorrow. I hope you got someone coming to keep you company, like your roommate—I forgot his name," he shrugged. "I don't really know how to pray or anything and I don't even know if there is a God even listening, but I'm going to pray for you every day. Okay, Ben?"

Aden touched Ben's hand one more time before saying his last goodbye. It was hard leaving. His feet were cemented to the floor and refused to move for several moments.

"Please wake up, Ben." Aden blinked away the fresh tears that threatened to fall and forced himself to back away from the bed. There was no movement from Ben, no sign that he even knew Aden was there, but Aden felt at peace. He'd found Ben again and had told him what he felt. That was enough for now.

35

*T*wo days later, the day Aden was due to visit, Ben woke up.

It was only for a few minutes, but it was enough for Ben to be vaguely aware of his surroundings. His head was foggy from the medication being pumped into his body and he was only able to open his eyes for a second before closing them again. He was aware of a chorus of beeping sounds near his head and a continual droning hum coming from the right side of his bed.

Ben panicked when he realized that a machine was controlling his breathing and that he was alone in a room he didn't recognize.

But the wild-eyed panic only lasted for a moment before the drugs coursing through him pushed him, mercifully, back into a lethargic state. As he sunk back into dreamless slumber, his last thoughts were of Jeremy. He never heard the nurse enter his room in response to an elevation in Ben's heart rate that had registered on her monitor in the nurse's station.

By the time she appeared at his bedside, Ben had drifted off again.

ADEN ARRIVED several hours later to find Ben just as he'd left him two days before. The swelling had gone down a little around Ben's eyes and the bandages around his head looked fresh. Aden pulled a stool over that had been left by the bathroom door and sat close to Ben's side. Angela had decided to wait down the hall for him, encouraging him to take as much time as he needed.

"The nurse said you have thirty minutes but if you want to leave sooner, we can," she said. Since Ben was sedated, Angela figured Aden might tire of talking to himself before the time was up.

Aden sat and quietly watched Ben. It was like seeing an apparition—one that Aden desperately wished would transform back into the *real* Ben.

A clear, plastic tube from the ventilator was fed down his throat with a strip of tape, which ran from one cheek to the other, securing the tubing in place. His mouth hung open in a soft oval shape and crust had formed around the edges of his lips where moisture had accumulated and dried in place. It was hard to tell that Ben was even alive, with no visible movement other than the rise and fall of his chest that was controlled by a machine connected to him. Aden wondered if he would ever hear Ben's voice again.

A female nurse walked into the room. Aden stood to move out of her way.

"You just stay right there, honey," she told him, patting Aden's shoulder before moving to the other side of the bed to check Ben's monitors.

"Hello, Mr. Morgan." Her voice was soothing as she adjusted a tube resting against Ben's cheek. "It's Trisha. I'm just going to check a few things and be on my way." The compassion and care in her voice reminded Aden of a young mother cooing over her baby. It comforted Aden to hear her talking to Ben.

Maybe Ben does hear me after all, he thought.

Trisha moved like a gentle fawn, making every effort not to disturb her fragile patient. Aden was mesmerized by her careful yet efficient movements as she pushed buttons and tugged on tubing to make sure it wasn't pinched and that everything was performing fluidly. Glancing over at Aden, she offered him a comforting smile.

"Can Ben hear us when we talk to him?" Aden asked.

Trisha moved to tuck the sheets back under Ben and adjusted his head on the pillow.

"I'm pretty sure he can, hon." Her voice was soft as she finished her task. "I don't know how much he understands with all the medication that he's on, but I think he knows you're here. You just keep on talkin' to him. It will be a comfort to him if does hear you." She winked at him. "I'm thinking it will be a comfort to you too."

She reached over and flipped a switch on one of Ben's monitors. "Tomorrow, the doctor is going to see if Ben is ready to be weaned off of the ventilator." She stared down at Ben as she spoke. "We'll start waking him up before they start the process. Hopefully, we will know more over the next few days. Meanwhile, you just keep on visiting and talking away to your heart's content."

Trisha walked around the side of the bed and patted Aden's shoulder once more on her way out of the room.

Aden had an idea. Angela said they could drop by to see Ben on their way to a dentist appointment on Friday. That was two days away.

If Ben was awake, it would be the perfect time to bring the notebook.

BEN GROANED as the nurse adjusted his position on the bed. He'd been weaned off of the ventilator for almost twenty-four hours and was no longer drifting along in the blissful world of sedation.

Although he'd been given meds to dull the pain, Ben still felt the searing burn in his side every time he took more than a shallow breath and the relentless throbbing in his head was worse than any hangover he'd ever experienced. Ben avoided opening his eyes because even the tiniest hints of light made it feel like shards of glass were being pressed into them.

He also felt nauseous at the smell of food. It started with the breakfast cart that arrived at his room this morning. When an orderly arrived at his room to deliver what would be his first real meal since being admitted to the hospital, his stomach tightened at the aroma of the mushy eggs and oatmeal and he shoved it away. Even the smell of the alcohol pads the nurse used sent bile up into his throat.

Every sound and smell was intensified. A friendly doctor, who didn't look a day over thirty, had dropped by and patiently explained that he'd been in a bad car accident and had a serious head injury, three broken ribs, multiple lacerations over his upper body, and had undergone an emergency surgery to stop the bleeding from a punctured kidney.

Ben blinked as he attempted to look up at the doctor but his head was killing him. He gave up and kept his eyes closed, nodding instead as the doctor spoke. Ben felt like they were talking about someone else. He had no clear memory of the accident and he was having a hard time grasping what the young man was trying to explain.

His thoughts were like scattered puzzle pieces in his brain—nothing seemed to fit together.

There were brief flashes of images that appeared in his head: a brilliant light illuminating the car interior, the smell of steamy sweat coming off of his body, rain beating against the windshield—that was the best he could conjure up. While the doctor talked, all Ben had wanted to do was slip back into the black abyss where he felt safe and couldn't feel the pain. Even now, as the nurse poked and prodded him, Ben just wanted to be left in peace.

He didn't know how long he'd been out this time when he heard his name being called.

"Ben?"

He heard the voice but was too exhausted to respond. He dismissed it as another ghost haunting his dreams as a result of all the drugs in his system. Every time he drifted off to sleep, memories—both good and bad—flicked across his mind's screen like someone flipping through TV channels. He wasn't sure what was real and what was just his imagination at this point.

Then, Ben felt a hand touch his.

"Ben, it's Aden."

I know that voice…

Ben's cheek twitched with involuntary spasms as he struggled to open his eyes. At first, Ben could only make out a shadowed form standing by the bed. Muted colors of red and blue floated in his vision. He turned his head toward the colors and tried to open his eyes wider. He could only manage narrow slits but it was enough for Ben to make out that the figure was a boy.

His heart quickened. He made an effort to lift his head but pain exploded through it with an electric jolt and he let it drop back against the pillow. In spite of the pain wracking his body and the fog in his head, Ben felt his chest swell with deep emotion. He didn't know if it was the resurrection of a long-forgotten hope or an overwhelming sadness that overcame him. He clung to hope.

"J...Jere..Jeremy?" His voice like a rusty door hinge after a long winter.

Ben could hear the boy breathing and felt a stirring next to him.

"No, Ben. It's...it's Aden. Do you know who I am? You don't remember me?" the boy asked. Ben's thoughts were too cloudy to catch the hint of sadness in the voice.

New images assaulted the shadows in Ben's mind: the back of an old building, a broken fruit crate on the ground, a metal coffee thermos...a boy's face, streaked with sooty tears and wide eyes filled with a thousand questions—all directed at him.

Aden.

Ben struggled once again to open his eyes again but invisible boulders pinned them down.

"Don't try to open your eyes, Ben. It's okay," Aden said. "I came to see you a few times but you weren't awake." A flood of words poured from him in a rush. "The nurse said they were going to wake you up yesterday and see how you would do. You seem to be doing real good too. I'm glad you can breathe without that awful machine. Wow, you really scared me, Ben. I didn't know...I just didn't know..."

The boy was speaking too fast. Ben struggled to stay in sync with what he was saying, but the connection was misfiring and Ben couldn't keep up. The boy sounded happy and nervous at the same time. Ben was overwhelmed. Yet, there was an excitement in the boy's voice that Ben recognized, a connection that drew him back to recent memories, moments shared between them.

The boy...Aden...

"Aden. It's you," Ben whispered. "You came."

"Yes!" Aden gasped. "You remember me! You're doing good, Ben!"

Aden kept saying how Ben was "doing good" like a teacher lavishing praise on an eager student. Ben's cracked lips formed into a lopsided grin.

"I brought something to share with you, Ben," Aden went on. "I know it's kinda soon. Let me just grab it real quick." Aden released his hand and Ben sensed his movement away from the bed.

There was a short grunt, then a soft *thud* of an object hitting the floor near the foot of the bed. Then, a rustling sound that Ben thought were papers or wrappers of some sort.

"Got it," Aden said, his voice closer to Ben now. Ben tried opening his eyes again, even managing a slight squint, but his vision was immediately flooded with the vibrant light above his bed and he shut them up tight again. The pain in his head was excruciating.

"You still awake, Ben?"

Ben was so tired, but his mind demanded this moment. He struggled to stay alert. This was the longest he'd been awake in days and he wasn't sure he could hold out much longer. But something in the deep recesses of his mind offered him a small dose of strength to go on. He lay very still on the bed to conserve his strength.

"Yes," he mumbled.

He had to rely on just listening to Aden's voice and try to interpret the sounds he heard. Something stiff leaned against Ben's arm and he heard the distinct sound of pages being turned.

"I brought the notebook, Ben. I can't believe you actually wrote my stories down here! I was gonna read them again because I don't even remember what stories I told you, but I decided to wait and read them to you so we could hear them again together. I thought that would be kinda cool. Right, Ben?"

Ben tried to answer him—he really tried. But all he could manage to do was nod his head, which he wasn't even sure he really did or had only imagined he had. He felt his body being sucked down into the sheets and the pain in his head had escalated until it was drowning out even the excitement of Aden being here with him.

He thought he heard the nurse come in and exchange whispered words with the boy. Muffled footsteps and cool hands that brushed his bare shoulder were all that he detected before the blackness overwhelmed him.

*A*ngela couldn't do it anymore.

Aden had resisted her all morning while she tried to work through a science lesson with him about atoms and molecules. She chose to ignore his dramatic sighing and frequent yawning, as well as the tapping of his pencil against the empty juice glass next to him. When he started kicking his toe against the table leg with an annoying *thud, thud, thud,* Angela slapped the textbook closed and threw herself back against the chair.

"*Really*, Aden?"

"I don't know why we have to break every single thing down to so many tiny pieces," Aden complained. "Does it really matter what everything is made of if we can't really see it anyway? It doesn't make any sense."

Angela leaned forward and propped her elbows on the table. She rested her chin in her cupped hands.

"Look, I know this can be boring, Aden. I wasn't a big fan of science when I was in school either. But it's a subject you can't avoid in life. Besides, it's important to know the building blocks of our world and who we are. You'll learn about other things later that you might think are cool, but you have to start with the basics first. Anyhow, this is what other seventh graders are learning this year and you have to be familiar with it before we enroll you in school."

"I'm not going to school," Aden growled, turning to look out the window.

Angela glared at the back of Aden's head but kept her mouth shut. She was sure he expected her to give him an instant scolding but she bit her tongue. Not that she needed to—she knew that her silence was speaking volumes across the table as it was. Curiosity evidently getting the best of him, Aden turned to look at her.

Angela's eyes bore into him like she was interrogating a murder suspect.

"I should've kept looking out the window," he mumbled, adding a dramatic eye roll.

"Are you afraid?" she asked, weary of tip-toeing around the obvious. She noticed how quiet the house felt and how the walls in the kitchen suddenly seemed to close in on them. She almost wished Blake would come trampling in right now with all his noisy, childish fanfare, and break the suffocating tension between them.

"No…" he said, eyes back on the window. "I just…I don't fit in with those other kids."

"You don't know that, Aden. You haven't even *tried* going to school yet," she challenged.

Aden turned to face her and, with sudden courage, matched her stubborn glare.

"Why am I going to go to school here when I would just be leaving anyway after they find my mom?" he asked. "There's no reason for me to go to school or even get comfortable here if I'm just hangin' around for a few more weeks." Aden huffed and turned away. "Don't get me wrong, Angela," he said. "You and Cray have been super cool with me and all, but I know that kids only came to stay in foster homes on a temporary basis. I mean…I get that you are trying to help troubled kids and that you are just trying to do your job, but I'm only here until you guys figure out what to do with me until I'm back with my mom."

Angela was furious.

"A *job*, Aden!? You think this is a *job* for me?" She trembled with anger. "If I wanted a *job*, I would put in my eight hours at the office and leave it all behind when I clocked out at the end of the day. No, Aden, being a *mother*—even a foster mother—is an honor that I *choose* to do twenty-four hours a day…every day. I don't *clock out* of my role as a mother at the end of a long day. I make myself available to you and Blake whenever you need me, because I *want* to. I would never give that kind of dedication to a *job*. Do you understand the difference, Aden?"

Aden wouldn't look at her.

"I don't need another mother. I already have one."

Angela almost choked holding back what she really wanted to say. *Yeah, right, you have a mother and where is she now?*

She had to get a grip on her emotions. Aden didn't need to see her lose control right now. *How can I make him understand? What if everything doesn't work out exactly like he has it all planned out in his mind?*

"What if they *don't* find your mom, Aden? What happens then?"

Each word weighed heavy on her tongue, transferring the burden carefully from her to him, as if feeding them to a baby bird, giving him time to absorb them.

The questions hung in the air between them, feeling more like accusations than honest inquiries. Angela saw that Aden was torn by her words. By the way his face crumpled as she watched him, she knew that, in some faraway recesses of his mind, the seed was there—had always been there—but that he'd refused to let it take root.

Angela voiced what she felt Aden was struggling with.

"Aden, honey, I know that this whole situation feels like you're beating your fists on closed doors. You want answers. You're tired of waiting for things to work out for you. I understand. But you need to know that there may be answers behind those doors that you might not want to accept."

The vulnerability she'd seen in Aden's face moments before was gone—his expression hardened to stone. Aden's voice was low and bitter as he pushed away from the table and stood.

"Well, I guess I better hold on to whatever little hope I have on this side of those doors, Angela. That's gotta be better than finding out that there was never any hope at all."

37

"*He threw the last gold coin into the well and watched it sink lower and lower into the muddy water until the last glow of light reflecting off of it was gone. Tiko watched the water's surface until the ripples from the coin's impact had settled and the muck floating on top of the water had melded together once again. He was satisfied. Sighing in relief, he picked up his walking stick and started home.*"

"The End." Aden snapped the notebook closed and tossed it onto the table next to the bed.

Ben had been resting his head back against a mound of pillows propped behind him, staring at the ceiling as he listened to Aden read the story he'd written. He frowned and turned his head to look at Aden, his forehead creased in puzzlement.

"Wait," he said, "you never did tell me before, but why did Tiko throw away that last gold coin? That seems to me to be wastin' a good thing when he coulda used it to buy his own land instead of slavin' for that scoundrel noble."

Aden gave Ben an annoyed look as if trying to explain the stock market to a toddler.

"*Because*, Ben. Look at all the trouble Tiko had already been through with those gold coins. He thought life was going to be easier after finding those coins but then everyone was trying to kill him and ended up stealing everything he had gained anyway."

"Besides, if the noble would have seen he had gold, he would have been suspicious of where Tiko got the gold and then Tiko would have had a whole lot more problems. He figured out that he was better off without it and that's why he got rid of the last coin. Think about it, Ben." Aden threw his hands up in the air for emphasis.

Hopping off the stool he'd been perched on for the past half hour, Aden bent down to stuff the notebook in his backpack on the floor. After an exaggerated yawn, he reached over and pulled the drawer open on Ben's nightstand. He peered in and frowned.

"I'm hungry. Got any snacks?" he asked, pushing the drawer closed and looking around the room.

"*Snacks?* Do you *really* think I got food hidin' in this room?" Ben gestured around the stuffy curtained-off portion of his hospital room. Pointing toward the nurse's station just outside his door, he said, "I only get to eat what *they* hand me on a tray, and it ain't nothin' you'd be interested in." Then, under his breath, he added, "Shoot, even Jake's nasty, dry barbeque chicken sounds appetizing about now."

Aden slipped back onto the stool. "Angela's picking me up in a few minutes anyway. Sometimes we stop for a milkshake. Peanut butter's my favorite." Aden drummed his fingers on the metal bar of the bed. "Angela tells me that I eat like a horse but she says she doesn't mind because I need more meat on my bones."

"Huh, milkshake..." Ben grumbled. "Rub it in, why don't ya."

Ben reached over and set his hand over Aden's drumming fingers to still them.

"I say she's right," Ben said, looking Aden over carefully. "You're lookin' better, son. You were just a skittish bag of bones showing up at the bakery most nights. You ate like a horse then, too."

Aden smiled and pulled at the waistband of his jeans to show Ben. "My pants are even getting a little tight," he said, laughing. "You want me to bring you something when I come on Friday?"

"Nah, I'm alright, boy," Ben said, adjusting the blanket around his waist. It had become twisted and was digging into his sore ribs. "How are things going with your foster family—the Pearsons, right?"

Aden shrugged and plucked at the sheets at the edge of Ben's bed. "Yeah, they're a nice family and I have a lot of fun with their little boy, Blake. He's six."

Aden didn't offer more than that. Ben watched him fix his eyes on a large plant in the corner. Its glossy leaves caught the light from the single window in the room and had mesmerized Aden. The plant was nestled in a sturdy, brown basket and had a large tag draped from a stem that read, *Get Well Soon, Eddie & Louise* in bold block letters.

Ben coughed softly to pull Aden's attention back. He guessed Aden wasn't going to volunteer any more details about the Pearsons.

"Well, glad to hear it, son. You know," Ben said, his voice growing serious, "the Pearsons must be some special people to drive you out here to see an old man a few times a week. Not to mention those milkshakes."

A sudden melancholy descended over Ben. It seemed to come out of nowhere and possess him. His face crumpled into its wrinkles, each crease deepening with dark shadows as Ben stared up at the blank TV screen mounted on the opposite wall.

"You remember me tellin' you before about my son, Jeremy?" His voice was soft and distant.

"Yeah, a couple times, I think. I don't remember you telling me much about him, though," Aden said.

"That first time you came into my hospital room, I thought... well, I hoped...you were Jeremy. Not that I wasn't happier than a lark that it was you when I figured it out," Ben hurried to interject. He shook his head at the memory. "Anyhow, I've been carrying around a lot of pain all these years. Pain—and guilt—over choices that I made that took Jeremy away from me."

"Yes, I remember you called me Jeremy when I walked in that day," Aden said, recalling how confused Ben had been. It had scared Aden to see him like that.

"I've had more time than I planned to sit here and think about how fragile life is and how I don't want to waste any more of it beating myself up over the past. I guess you showin' up at Angelo's was a good thing." Ben was looking intently at him now. "It wasn't just me doin' for you, son, but also you giving me something to care about outside of myself for once. Spending time with you, well...it kinda filled an empty hole inside of me that was left after Jeremy was taken away." He gave Aden's hand a squeeze.

"What I'm tryin' to say—and fumblin' all over myself tryin' to say it—is that it's time for me to move on from my past, maybe do a little healin' while I'm at it." Ben pressed down on Aden's hand, urgency in his voice. "I want those things for you too, Aden."

"You might feel justified in holdin' on to anger at your momma —shoot, even with me—but you're the one who suffers by holding all that self-righteous anger in, son. It's like your story 'bout Tiko and his gold coins—it'll just do you more harm than good in the end."

Aden was relieved to hear the rustle of the curtain behind him as Angela poked her head around it.

"Hey, Ben," she said, wiggling her fingers in greeting.

Ben nodded. "Morning, Angela."

"Ready to head out, Aden?" she asked.

Aden slid his hand from under Ben's and gave him a nod. "Thanks, Ben," he said. "I'll think about it."

Standing up and lifting his bag from the floor, he looked back and nodded to Angela before turning back to Ben.

"See you Friday," Aden said. "Call me if you want me to bring you something."

"I'll let ya know," Ben answered.

THE FAINT SCENT of Angela's fruity body spray lingered in the room after she and Aden left. Ben settled back into the crumpled nest of pillows and sheets and allowed his mind to drift back to Jeremy and his conversation with Aden.

He was surprised—and disappointed—to find himself thinking about a drink right now.

No. You're not going there, old man.

He'd made it all these years, working through the dull ache in his heart with a sober mind. It was time to stop hiding behind his failure and find his son. If he was rejected, it was still worth the opportunity that he'd been wasting all these years to tell Jeremy how he felt, how he'd missed him, and that he was sorry for his mistakes. It may not bring resolution or a restoration, but it would bring closure for Ben.

Yes, old man, he thought. *It's time.*

38

*C*ray and Angela had decided that Angela would continue to homeschool Aden for the time being. He was still resisting the idea of public school and became anxious when either one of them brought it up. During her weekly check-in, Angela talked with Paula about their concerns and the idea of sticking with homeschooling Aden for a while longer.

"Good idea, Angela, if you're up to it," Paula said. "Aden might need more time adjusting to a regular home life before he's forced to take on another new environment. It's probably more important to focus on Aden's emotional needs for stability first. I'm behind you one hundred percent."

"I don't want to rock the boat right now anyway," Angela continued. "He's really holding out on you finding his mom and him going back to live with her. He feels like everyone is dragging their feet—even lying to him about everything. He told me there's no point in being put in school when you might find his mom any day now."

"Actually...since you brought it up first, I do have some news to share." Paula's voice was hesitant. "There's been a possible lead in Aden's mother's whereabouts."

"Oh, really?" Angela said. The soft gasp in her voice caused Cray to look up from his laptop at the table where he'd been working. He raised his eyebrows in interest but Angela held up a finger for him to hold on.

"As you know, Aden has only been able to offer us a vague description of where the apartment he lived in was located. He said he and his mom had taken a bus across town before they got *separated*—as he called it. Of course, he claims they just lost track of each other somehow after that. He clammed up tight from that point on and wouldn't give us any more information—including his own last name."

"The police had started to canvass apartment buildings but the demographics of the city was proving too large to narrow down," Paula explained.

"Well, a few nights ago, they had a breakthrough. An elderly woman, who lives alone in an apartment building a few miles from where Aden was picked up, called the police when she heard someone trying to get into the door of an apartment across the hall from her," Paula explained.

"The woman reported that she knew that the apartment was vacant and that the landlord had changed the locks after the tenant who lived there had failed to pay the rent. According to the police, when they arrived, they saw no evidence of the door being tampered with but did lift some fingerprints from the doorknob. When they interviewed the elderly neighbor, she said that she had cracked her door open while she waited for the police to arrive and saw a woman trying to work a key into the door lock."

Angela heard a rustle of papers and assumed Paula was reading over some notes as she shared the information with Angela.

Paula continued, "The neighbor told the police that the key wasn't working and she thought the woman might be drunk and was trying to enter the wrong apartment. She was quoted as saying"—Paula cleared her throat and it was clear that she was reading directly from the report—"that 'the woman looked a lot like Lauren, the lady that lived in the apartment a while back with her boy. But, if that was Lauren, she looked real sick and was skinny as a broom handle.'

"Anyhow," Paula went on, "the police are comparing the fingerprints they lifted against ones they have on record for a woman named Lauren Tennison—whom they have reason to believe is Aden's mother—from her previous arrests for drugs and prostitution. The neighbor told the officers that the woman left before they arrived but didn't appear to get in a vehicle or anything. She thought she might have been on foot. The police are keeping an eye out and asking around on the street to see if they can locate any fresh leads."

"Yes, I remember Aden mentioning his mother's name was Lauren but, as you said, he wouldn't share a last name—even his own—if Aden even has the same last name. I'm guessing Lauren wasn't married..." Angela said. "Do you think this woman might be her?"

"Not sure, Angela, but we're hopeful. However, even if we find her," Paula continued, "Aden's mother would need to go through rehabilitation and counseling, not to mention court proceedings for Aden's abandonment, before we could move forward toward reuniting them. In fact, if she is looking at prison time, it could be an even more traumatic experience for Aden." There was an audible sigh from Paula as the heaviness of the situation fell over the conversation.

Angela moved to sit down in a chair near Cray, who had pushed his laptop to the side and now faced Angela. Concern etched his face as he waited patiently for Angela to fill him in on the conversation.

Angela pressed her fingertips against her forehead, feeling a headache coming on. She shrugged sadly at Cray, who leaned forward and lifted a hand, indicating his impatience with wanting to know what was going on. Angela nodded to Cray that they were almost done.

"Well…that's more than what the police have had to work with so far," she said. "Thank you for letting us know, Paula. Please keep us updated on anything new. We won't say anything to Aden just yet."

"I'll do that, Angela," Paula told her. "We hope to have some answers soon."

"What's going on?" Cray was on Angela as soon as the call ended.

She filled him in on the conversation with Paula and the potential lead that the police had on Aden's mother, whom Angela had just learned may be named Lauren *Tennison*. This was also the first hint they had at a possible last name for Aden.

When asked, Aden had refused to give his mother's or his last name to Paula, and she and Cray hadn't pushed the issue. Angela was sure Aden had his reasons for wanting to protect her and she believed he also wanted his mother to be found so…well, she just couldn't piece together the many "whys."

Cray held Angela's hand while she shared their conversation with him. When she was done, he lifted her chin with his finger and looked deep into her eyes.

"You're right. We won't say anything to Aden about this. It could lead to nothing and he'd be on an emotional roller coaster while we waited to hear back. No sense in putting him through all that." Cray stood and reached over to snap his laptop closed before tucking it under his arm and leaning down to kiss the top of her head.

When she heard the shower start in the bathroom a few minutes later, she rose to start lunch. She could hear Aden and Blake throwing a ball in the back yard, Aden hollering at Blake to watch the ball instead of looking around. She smiled at how heartwarming the scene sounded. Glancing at the clock, she stepped up her pace. The boys were sure to be bounding through the back door looking for food any time now.

As she layered roast beef and cheese on slices of homemade white bread, Angela thought about her conversation with Paula. She considered how Aden would react if he knew what Paula had shared with her. An oppressive grief pulled at her as she thought about all the boy had been through. Hope was his only lifeline during this fragile time in his life and she and Cray couldn't bring themselves to sever that fragile cord.

It's better to keep things simple, Angela surmised, *and just tell Aden that the authorities are still searching for his mother. That there was nothing new to tell, which was basically true at this point.* "Paula will keep us updated on any leads," was their standard answer whenever Aden asked if they'd heard any news about his mother's whereabouts.

No, she thought, pulling open the drawer for a knife to spread the mayonnaise, *there's no sense in breaking his heart when we have nothing to go on yet.*

39

*B*en was relieved to finally be home from the hospital and wearing his own pajamas, which consisted of a threadbare pair of black sweatpants and an old Rocky's Pizza T-shirt, instead of the hideous blue-and-white striped hospital gown with the open back that showed his rear end every time he turned over.

But, although being home beat a hospital stay any day, Ben was bored with sitting around the house all day.

At his appointment yesterday, the doctor informed him that he was making good progress and should be released to light duty at work by next week. Ben didn't think that would be a problem at the bakery except avoiding lifting heavy stuff for a while.

He had to admit that he and Jake had enjoyed the delicious meals that Mia had stocked their freezer with and wondered how he was ever going to go back to eating ho-hum generic brand turkey sandwiches and Stouffer's frozen lasagna that were his and Jake's go-to meals when neither of them had time to do the grocery shopping.

Ben planned to celebrate going back to work next week with a pit-stop by Pete's for an extra-toasted pastrami sandwich with a side of onion rings. The anticipation of it almost made him call Jake right now and beg him to stop at Pete's after work...

Since being released from the hospital, Aden had called to check on him a few times and told him that, when he was up to it, Angela and Cray wanted him to come over for dinner. "Plus," Aden said, "we need to work on our stories." Ben loved how Aden referred to the spiral notebook full of stories he'd transcribed from Aden's recordings as *our* stories. It made Ben feel like a valuable connection in the boy's life and—he had to admit—that was more important to Ben than he'd realized until recently.

Finding Jeremy had also become important to Ben recently as well.

It had taken a lot of rummaging through boxes of old files, but Ben had finally managed to dig up a phone number for his ex-wife's parents.

Emma had left no trace of her whereabouts, but Ben knew it was a safe bet that her parents had never left Pataskala, Ohio. Ben was convinced that no one ever left Ohio unless the military recruited them or they had lofty dreams of a better life where the grass looked greener. The tight-knit community sentiment appeared to run deep there and everyone seemed to feel strongly about keeping their roots firmly planted where they'd started. From what Emma had shared with him, most folks were content marrying their high school sweethearts and settling the next generation close by their friends and family.

Emma's parents probably live in the same house too, Ben thought. *If they're still alive, that is.*

Pataskala, a quaint suburb less than twenty miles outside of Columbus, Ohio was where Emma was born and raised. Everybody knew everyone and nothing notable was a secret: A prime example of small-town coziness and kinship at its best. Ben had been working over the summer as a welder's apprentice on a building project with his uncle's construction company when he first met Emma.

There wasn't a whole lot to keep him entertained during the long summer nights so he drove over to the Pataskala Street Fair one evening to check out the local excitement. It was there that he'd met Emma and, as they say, *the rest is history.*

EMMA'S FATHER had died seven years ago according to Penny—Emma's mother—when she and Ben spoke on the phone later that afternoon. Ben felt a strange stirring of nostalgia when she answered on the second ring, "This is Penny." She had answered the phone with that same salutation for as long as Ben had known her. Penny was a gentle, soft-spoken woman who had never made Ben feel like the loser that he knew he was back then. She was disappointed in how things had dissolved between Ben and Emma but had never voiced her opinion or taken sides.

Not like Emma's father, Dan, had. It was Dan who called Ben a week after Emma had taken Jeremy and left and boldly announced that *he* was the one who'd worked meticulously to help Emma oust Ben from their lives.

"If you care about your son," Dan told him one night when Ben attempted to call the house, "you'll stay away."

Dan continued to keep a vigilant post for years, protecting Emma and Jeremy's whereabouts from Ben. Now that Dan was gone, Ben hoped that he could persuade Penny to help him make contact with them again.

Well into her golden years, Ben guessed that she was lonely

because she stalled answering his request as she took advantage of her captive audience. Ben's ear was clammy with sweat against the phone as Penny caught him up about her life—the Methodist church she attended and all that she was involved with there, the knee replacement surgery she'd undergone three years prior, how Pataskala was growing and the traffic was getting so bad that it took her ten minutes to drive to the Kroger grocery store—until Ben caught her in the middle of a breath.

"Well, now, Penny, nothin' slowin' you down in life, that's for sure," he said, then rushed to continue before she started up again. "I don't want to keep you, so, um, would it be alright if I grab that number for Emma from you?"

Even though Jeremy was twenty-three now, Ben thought he should try to talk to Emma and get a feel for things before trying to contact Jeremy directly. Somehow, he just felt it was the right chain of command to follow in this situation…and he desperately wanted to do things *right* this time.

"Well, Ben, you know I'll need to ask Emma if it's okay for me to share her number first…" she said, a note of hesitancy in her voice.

"I understand, Penny. It's only right that you check with Emma first. You can always pass my number to her instead if she would prefer to call me." He had no way of knowing if Emma would bother calling or just change her number and wait for him to die so she could have peace.

Ben hadn't made any attempts to find her or Jeremy these past fifteen years. Not that his heart didn't ache to find them, it was just that he felt like he didn't have the right to. He figured he was doing them a favor all those years in "staying away," as Dan had suggested.

"I'll do that, Ben. She remarried a few years ago and I'm sure she will want to be careful…well, you know."

He wasn't sure what he'd been expecting. Of course she would have remarried. Most folks go on with their lives—most except for him, apparently. Ben was trapped in a time warp that ran movie reels of his past failures on replay every day of his existence. If she'd only remarried a few years ago, that meant that she most-likely raised Jeremy alone. Another knife of guilt twisted deep in his chest.

After ending the call, Ben flopped down onto the couch. Drawing his slipper-clad feet up on the cushions, he tucked a throw pillow under his head and closed his eyes against the torrent of emotions and tidal waves of memories assaulting him. He wasn't sure if the pounding in his head was a relapse from his head injury or old demons trying to claw their way back into his mind. He refused to acknowledge either one right now.

40

*S*he was just wrapping up another frustrating morning of homeschooling lessons with Aden at the kitchen table when Cray came in the back door, letting the heavy door bang against the wall as he worked to shove a loose arm into the sleeve of his jacket. The loud *Wham!* startled her and Aden. Their duo of taut faces glared at Cray in unison from their places at the table across the room.

Why is he staring at us with that stupid grin on his face? Angela stewed. As if she hadn't been agitated enough this morning. Cray had enjoyed the morning poking around outside where the hummingbirds flitted between the feeders hung in the oak tree off the porch and a soft breeze moved through the trees with a soft rustle. *The essence of relaxation...must be nice,* she thought.

Angela loved to sit out with her coffee in the mornings and soak in the sounds of nature. But, *noooo,* this morning she was trapped at the kitchen table with a brooding preteen, who had been grumbling and complaining before they'd even cracked a book open—actually, before he had even finished the eggs on his breakfast plate an hour ago.

Oh, joy, we still have three days left before the weekend too. She stared at Cray with annoyance.

The silly grin still plastered on his face, Cray mouthed *sorry* as he reached for the truck keys from a small row of hooks on the wall. The air was static with tension as Angela turned back to Aden, who had sunken lower in his chair, if that was even possible.

Reaching for the writing prompt worksheet that she'd been *trying* to work with Aden on, Angela made another attempt. Her voice strained, she told him, "Come on, Aden, this is *important*. It will only make your writing better." Angela sensed Cray still standing at the door, but her eyes were locked on Aden as she prodded him.

Aden's head rested in one hand propped on the table as he chewed on the end of his pencil dangling in the other. With a look that wavered between utter boredom and half-comatose, he stared at the single sheet of paper that Angela held in front of him.

"Don't you want to express your thoughts more clearly and make your writing more interesting?" she asked, punctuating every word with a shake of the paper as if the words could fling from the page into Aden's stubborn head. Finished with the scolding, she let the paper float down to the table between them and joined Aden in staring at the now lifeless page.

Angela heard the subtle *click* of the door latching closed and sensed Cray had remained on this side of it. Making his way to the battleground between Aden and Angela, Cray whistled softly.

Angela felt a warm hand on her shoulder. "Tag, I'm it," Cray announced with more cheer than necessary. "Ready for a break, Aden?" he asked. Aden lifted his head to stare up at Cray, which was a long way up being that Cray was not a small man. He rustled himself up in his chair, rubbed his eyes, and let out an overdramatic yawn that pricked at Angela's last nerve.

It was her turn to look up at her husband, her gaze transmitting a silent dialogue of appreciation and something akin to adoration. Angela's slight nod answered for them both.

Aden flicked the pencil down on the table and scooted his chair back.

"Yeah," he said. He looked to Angela for approval before he stood. All traces of the sulking boy from a minute ago suddenly erased.

She waved him off, shrugging in defeat.

"I'm just heading out to town to grab a part for the plow. Wanna come?" Cray asked.

Aden didn't need any more encouragement. "Let me grab my shoes," he said, halfway down the hall already. Cray leaned against the kitchen counter and folded his arms as he waited. He watched Angela gather a notebook and other supplies they'd been using into a neat little pile in the middle of the table. She stood and brushed past him.

Grabbing her favorite *I Love New Jersey* coffee mug off the counter—last year's birthday gift from her sister since Angela was born and raised in Jersey—she dumped the remnant of her cold coffee unceremoniously into the sink and rinsed the cup.

Her face brightened when she glanced over at the coffee machine and noticed that there were still several inches of black liquid gold in the carafe. Sliding down the counter to the prize, she emptied the last of the coffee into her mug. She grinned at Cray, who stood watching with amusement, and took a single noisy gulp of coffee.

"You rescued me just in time. I was ready to turn in my resignation as a homeschool teacher." She plopped down roughly into her chair, causing it to slide back a few inches.

"I rescued *you*? Maybe I was rescuing *Aden*." Cray walked over and tugged at a loose strand of hair resting against her cheek.

She batted his hand away.

"Oh, right, *exactly*," she huffed. "I think you and I will trade places next week. I'll take your job as a forest ranger for a few days and enjoy trail hikes, pick wildflowers, and spend the day testing my knowledge of animal tracks. *You* can stay home and try to teach English literature to a surly almost-thirteen-year-old," she grumbled. "I didn't really sign up for this, you know."

She studied her coffee, watching a few escaped grounds floating on its surface. "I agreed to be a foster mom and share my home and family with hurting kids. But I am *not* cut out to shape unyielding hormone-loaded teenagers into submissive, eager scholars. You know what I mean?" Angela looked up at Cray, expecting an ample dose of sympathy to appear on his face. Instead, Cray's expression was a mask of unveiled humor. Angela didn't share his amusement at the moment.

Cray's shoulders shook as he chuckled and pulled the coffee mug out of her hand, setting it down on the table. He reached down and pulled Angela into his arms.

"Come on, Ang," Cray cooed. "It's not like the boy is sneaking out at night and tagging all of the neighbors' barns with spray paint."

Angela pulled her head back to pin him with a hard stare. "Gee, Cray, that would be quite a trek if he was," she said, one eyebrow cocked, "since none of our neighbors live close enough for him to accomplish it."

Aden came running into the kitchen just as Cray was opening his mouth to answer. The moment lost, he pulled Angela in for a quick kiss instead before releasing her.

"Alright. Let's head out, then," he said to Aden, pulling his keys out of his pocket. Turning back to Angela, he added, "And, for the record, I've *never* picked wildflowers while on duty. They make me sneeze." He laughed and scooted out the door. Aden stood at the threshold zipping up his jacket, ready to follow.

Angela sat back down to enjoy her coffee. Glancing at the clock above the table, she sighed. "I have to head out in twenty minutes to get Blake from preschool anyway." She caught Aden's eye before he could escape. "We're back on this tomorrow, though. Deal, Aden?"

"Deal!" he called back, tugging the door closed behind him. Angela shook her head in wonder at the sudden attitude change in Aden. *They say girls are dramatic and emotional,* she huffed.

Angela's second cup of coffee was now cold. She groaned and walked over to the sink. "You owe me big time, Cray," she said, pouring it down the drain.

41

"Come on in, Paula."

Cray's voice was subdued as he ushered Paula into the living room where Angela sat, her hands twisted in a pink floral throw blanket bunched up on her lap. Cray made his way to sit next to his wife and reached for her hand. Angela worked one hand from under the soft blanket and tucked it under Cray's.

Normally relaxed and chatty, Paula sat silent and stiff on the edge of the lone recliner that faced the couch where Angela and Cray waited. Angela had already sent Blake off to his room to play and warned him to stay there until she called for him. She expected Blake wouldn't make an appearance any time soon with all the stimuli he was surrounded with at the moment. The toys in his room were normally organized in tidy boxes on shelves with handwritten labels for *colored pencils, puzzles, cars...* The rule was, after Blake finished playing with the contents of a box, he had to clean it up and place the box back on the shelf before he could exchange it for a different one.

After the phone call from Paula, Angela pulled out all the stops and had left Blake surrounded by three towers of boxes and instructions to keep himself busy and not disturb them unless it was an emergency. Judging by the look of glee on his face at the lapse of the rules, Blake would be engaged for at least a good hour or so.

Cray had come home early after Angela called him at work and told him that Paula had news about Aden's mother and was coming by around four o'clock to talk with Aden.

Paula also requested that Cray and Angela both be there. Angela didn't need to ask if she was bringing bad news: She sensed the tension in Paula's voice. Angela didn't give Cray much detail over the phone but it was enough for him to call in a replacement to cover the rest of his shift. He'd arrived barely ten minutes before Paula's gray Honda pulled up behind his truck in the driveway.

Angela told Aden that Paula was dropping by—which wasn't a big deal because she regularly came out to check on things—and had sent him to take a shower before Paula arrived. He'd stared at her like she had grown an extra head.

"Uh, can't I just shower before bed? That's what I usually do," he questioned. Angela insisted and he sauntered off with a bewildered look on his face. It was an impulsive request, she knew, and sure to stir his curiosity, but she didn't know what else to do. She was a bundle of nerves and needed to distract him while she waited for Cray and Paula. The last thing she wanted was for everyone to show up with shell-shocked expressions on their faces and scare the kid half to death.

Before Cray arrived home from work, Angela had stood at the kitchen window watching for him, trying to get her emotions in check while she had a few minutes alone.

She thought she had it under control until Cray pulled up. His lunch box was hardly on the kitchen table before her arms were around him and her face was buried in his shoulder. He smelled like pine trees and damp earth and the familiar scents comforted her. Neither had felt like saying anything in those first few moments before Paula arrived. After she felt calmer, Angela pulled away and announced, "I'll put some coffee on for us."

"Not sure that's necessary," Cray said. "This isn't a social call, Angela."

She'd ignored him as she went through the motions of measuring out the coffee grounds for the machine and filling the reservoir with filtered water. He hadn't pushed the issue. He understood that she needed to keep her hands busy in her anxiousness. When she started to arrange lemon squares she'd baked the day before on a small serving plate, Cray grabbed her by the shoulders and forced her to look at him.

"Paula just pulled up. I want you to go sit in the living room. I'll let her in." Angela looked around the kitchen for any excuse to stay with Cray. He turned her around and pointed her in the direction of the couch.

"Go."

A minute later, Angela heard muffled voices in the kitchen as Cray greeted Paula at the back door. Their muted conversation trailed off as they entered the living room to join Angela. Paula walked over to where she sat on the couch and leaned over for a quick hug. "Good to see you," she said.

"Aden will be out in a few minutes," Angela said as Paula took her seat. "He's taking a shower."

Cray joined her on the couch.

A heaviness seeped into the room that threatened to smother Angela if she didn't get relief soon. Grief permeated the walls around them and pinned everyone to their seats. The trio sat in silence, absorbed in their own thoughts as they sat and waited.

Paula didn't offer Angela and Cray any additional information, obviously waiting until Aden joined them. Angela's eyes darted around the room, taking in the neat stack of *National Geographic* magazines on the bookshelf against the far wall, Blake's baby pictures on the wall above the cold fireplace, the paisley throw rug on the floor with one corner carelessly flipped over from someone's shoe… Her eyes came back to rest on Paula, who was now writing in a small notebook that she'd retrieved from her handbag.

From the kitchen, the sound of the ice maker plunking cubes into the dispenser splintered the awkward stillness of the room. Cray used the opportunity to address Paula.

"Would it be better for you to talk to Aden alone first?" he asked.

Angela was almost hoping that she would say *yes* so that she and Cray could be excused to hide in the kitchen while Paula faced Aden. *She's much more experienced with dealing with these kinds of things,* Angela thought. *I don't know if I can hold myself together for this.* She felt Cray rub his thumb across the top of her hand as if he sensed her inner turmoil.

Paula shook her head and leaned down to tuck the small book into her bag on the floor.

"No," she said, "it's better that you're here. You've both developed a relationship with Aden the past few months—built up a level of trust. I think you would be a great support to him by being here."

No one attempted to speak after that, sinking back into brooding silence as they waited on Aden. They didn't have to wait long. A moment later, a bedroom door opened down the hall. Angela's head jerked toward the sound and she leaned forward, pushing the blanket from her lap, wondering if it was Blake venturing out of the playground she'd created for him and if she needed to intercept him before Aden came out.

"Hold on," Cray said, gripping her hand tighter. She sank back against the couch, eyes fixed with anxiousness on the hall entryway. *Blake would never come out of a room that quietly,* she calculated. Her heart thumped in her ears.

Aden appeared from around the corner dressed in fresh jeans and a red *Phillies* T-shirt, a gift Ben had sent Aden. His white socks seemed overly bright in the dim room and his wet hair was plastered against his head as if he'd hastily smoothed it down with his hands instead of bothering with a comb.

He was attempting to tuck in the last edge of his T-shirt into his jeans as he walked in, but stopped when he noticed the three of them sitting there—staring at him. Three frozen smiles greeted him at the same time. The last section of shirt was left to spill over his jeans pocket as Aden took in the scene. His expression was puzzled, like he wasn't sure if he should walk back down the hall and try re-entering the room again.

Angela felt like all the air had been sucked out of the room. She struggled to take a full breath.

Paula spoke first.

"Hello, Aden. Why don't you come on in and join us." Cray and Angela jolted into action and made room for him on the couch next to Angela. She patted the empty spot. "Right here, Aden," she said.

Aden didn't move right away. He just stood outside the hallway, looking bewildered. A clump of damp golden strands had loosened from the pasted hair and dangled over one eyebrow. After what felt like an eternity, his hands moved toward his pockets and pushed down into the openings.

"Hey, Paula," he said, shuffling toward them. His eyes danced with wariness and Angela detected both an excited anticipation and a sinking horror creep into them. The caution in each step and his shifting glance looked as if he was surrounded by wolves and was trying to gauge his escape route in case things turned bad.

"Please," Paula continued when Aden paused midstep, unsure of where to go. "Have a seat." She nodded her head in the direction of the empty place next to Angela. Angela wondered why Cray was being so quiet.

Shouldn't he be stepping up to the leader role here? She wasn't sure what she expected him to do or say, she just needed him to do *something.* Just as she felt her coffee creeping back up into her throat, Cray spoke.

"Paula has some information about your mother, Aden," he said quietly. If Cray's voice was any indication, Aden was sure to detect that Paula didn't come bearing good news. With hands still shoved deep in his pockets, Aden slid past Paula and hunkered down on the couch on the right side of Angela, tugging his hands out in order to get more comfortable. He folded them across his chest instead as he stared at Paula. Angela and Cray shifted themselves to face Aden.

Paula scooted closer to the edge of the recliner and leaned toward Aden. Her expression reflected her resolve to focus on the job she had to do. Her eyes locked on Aden's.

"We found your mother."

Angela had expected an immediate response from Aden—some sort of instant reaction of joy or shock or that he would launch right into a list of questions that had obviously been rehearsed many times in his mind over the past months.

Nothing. No response.

Paula let the words settle before continuing. She watched Aden's initial reaction so she would know how to proceed.

As Aden stared at Paula, he blinked…once…twice.

Angela saw a wall of tears mounting in Aden's eyes. *He knows.*

Her hand instinctively inched toward Aden's knee but she didn't dare touch him.

Paula went on.

"You know that we have been searching for her all these months, interviewing people on the street who knew her, asking around at businesses she visited often, checking back at her—*your*—apartment to see if she'd returned. We had very little to go on except a physical description and the police reports we have on her." Paula breathed in deeply, releasing it slowly as she chose her words. "It was as if she didn't *want* to be found."

Aden found his voice. "But you said you found her...right?" Angela watched his fingers claw into his elbows as he struggled with what he was hearing—and what he was about to hear.

Paula seemed to be at a loss for words. It felt that, at any moment, the tension could shift into a total meltdown for everyone. But, with newfound bravery and resolve, Paula shook her head and looked down briefly before lifting her eyes back to Aden. Lacing her fingers together in front of her knees, Paula scooted closer to the edge of the chair cushion. Cray was squeezing Angela's hand so hard he was cutting off her blood circulation. She pulled her hand back slightly. His grip loosened. She could smell the nervous sweat radiating from his body.

"Yes, Aden. We did," Paula answered. She paused. "About a week ago, a neighbor—you might remember an elderly lady named Marie?—saw a woman trying to enter the apartment that you previously shared with your mother and called the police. She told them that she thought it looked like a woman she called *Lauren*. Is that your mother's name, Aden? Lauren? Lauren Tennison?"

Aden nodded, his eyes wide and glassy full moons, unblinking as a single tear rolled down one cheek.

"She was there? She came back?"

His voice thin and high, like the cry of a cornered animal. He unfolded his arms and slid to the edge of the couch. An identified emotion—*Hope? Fear?*—made his voice rise while his body braced itself for whatever news he was about to receive.

"We believe so, Aden." Paula bit on a corner of her lip. She nodded in affirmation as she went on. "The police followed some leads from a few people who saw her in the neighborhood that evening and were eventually led to an abandoned house several blocks from the apartment. It's a known drug house that the police had been watching for a while. When they searched, they found drug paraphernalia but no one was in the house."

"Two days later, an anonymous call came in that someone had found two people unconscious in the basement of the house. When the police arrived, they discovered the bodies of a middle-aged man and a younger woman…" Paula broke off, searching for the right words.

"They were…deceased—dead," she clarified. "Drug overdose. There was…no reviving them." Paula reached over and rested her hand on Aden's shoulder as she delivered the final blow. "One of them was identified as Lauren Tennison…your mother."

42

The call came almost two weeks later when Ben was at Angelo's. Although he was supposed to be on light duty, Ben refused to let Mia lift the heavy canisters of flour and sugar, insisting that he could do it "just fine." Mia scolded him.

"You better not have a relapse, Ben, and fall out on me," she warned.

"The only thing that's gonna be wrong with my head, woman, is a raging migraine from all your nagging," he told her after she tried to block him from going up a ladder to get a large can of condensed cream from a high shelf. Still, he had to admit he didn't mind being fussed over too much. Mia had spoiled him over the past few weeks with meals of homemade lasagna and chicken enchiladas that he just pulled from the freezer and heated in the oven.

When she showed up to work today, Ben had presented Mia with a gift card to her favorite restaurant.

"Thanks for everything, Mia," he told her. "Tell that husband of yours that he is one lucky man."

Mia had blushed at the compliment. "Put that in writing for me

Ben, with bold letters, so I can hang it on the refrigerator and he'll be reminded every day when he sees it," she smirked.

The bakery was bustling this evening with customers getting off work and stopping in for a dessert to bring home for dinner, ordering a cake for an upcoming event, or just because they had a craving for Angelo's famous *bomboloni*, an Italian pastry filled with thick chocolate custard. It was one of Ben's favorites as well and Mia made it a point to let him know when there was a fresh batch made.

A few local deli owners also bought bread from Angelo's a few times a week. Ben noticed one of them, Carlos, who owned the deli two doors down from Angelo's, waiting by the newspaper rack inside the front door, a large canvas bag draped over one arm.

"Evenin', Carlos," Ben called out. "I'll go back and grab your order in just a sec."

Ben was covering the cash register while Mia took orders and packed up pastries for customers. He counted two fives and a handful of change out to a young woman with an adorable toddler in a stroller. The little girl waved up at him from under a lacy pink hood. Ben waved back and gave her a friendly wink.

"Mia, I'm gonna head to the back to grab that order for Carlos," he hollered, untying his apron and tossing it on the counter next to a tall stack of folded pastry boxes.

As he rounded the corner to the kitchen, the phone on the wall rang. Ben grabbed it in mid-ring.

"Angelo's. How can I help you?"

No answer.

"Hello?"

Ben started to pull the phone away when he heard a deep voice on the line.

"Uh, yes, hello. Is there a Ben Morgan who works there?" It was a man.

"Yeah, this is Ben. What can I do for you?" *Was this a bill collector or somethin'? Who would be asking for him by his full name?*

"Oh, um, this is *Ben*? Uh…this is…I'm…Jeremy."

Ben could feel the phone handset trembling against his cheek. He had to clamp both hands around the center grip to hold it steady. He anchored himself against the wall for support, his legs ready to buckle under him.

It was his turn to be at a loss for words.

"*Ben*? Hello?" the voice repeated.

For the life of him, Ben couldn't loosen his tongue. He wasn't sure why, but it felt like his entire world hinged on what he said next. This was the moment he had rehearsed in his mind a thousand times over the years and now his tongue was stuck to the roof of his mouth.

"Jeremy?" he managed to croak.

"Yeah, it's me. Um, Mom called and gave me your number. Nana…uh, my grandma, said you called looking for my mom. I… well…called your home number first and a guy answered and said I should call you at this number," he said. "Mom said she was sure it was me you were probably wanting to talk to and asked me if I wanted to call. So…here I am."

Ben struggled to connect the mature, deep voice of the man on the other end of the line with the high-pitched squeak of the eight-year-old boy who had once called him *daddy* and had looked up at him with unveiled admiration in his eyes.

He's your son…say something, Ben scolded himself.

But he honest-to-goodness didn't know what to say. When faced with the reality of Jeremy actually being on the other side of

216 | WHILE YOU WALKED BY

the phone line, trying to breach the gap between years of lost fatherhood to talking man-to-man with your son felt like crossing an ocean on an inner tube.

"I'm glad..." he said, falling over his words, "...sure glad you called, Jeremy. I hope you don't mind me callin' your grandma. I really wanted to...find you and your mom...to talk to you." The line was silent as Jeremy waited for him to go on.

What did I hope the man would do? Strike up a friendly conversation and fill me in on his life that I've missed?

"How's your momma doing? You doin' okay?" Ben scrambled for footing in the conversation. "I'm livin' out in Philadelphia now. Working at a family-owned bakery. Been livin' with an old high school buddy, Jake—you remember him—no, no..." He did a quick calculation in his head. "You wouldn't remember him. Anyhow, I, uh, I've been, well, thinkin' about you and had some things I felt needed sayin'..."

Ben stopped talking. His words were getting faster as the emotions rose in his chest. He needed to slow down—give the kid a chance to catch up.

Jeremy's voice was kind. "Yeah, uh, that's good. Sounds like you have been doing great." Ben heard an audible exhale of breath, like the ominous freight train roar that people describe hearing right before a tornado hits. "I...don't really know where to start. Obviously," he sighed, "I grew up." The pause was so long that Ben thought they might have lost connection. "Mom and I did alright."

Without you, Ben added in his mind.

"I played baseball through high school, but wasn't good enough to get an athletic scholarship for college or anything, so I decided to go into teaching. I teach math to middle school kids now."

Jeremy didn't offer anything more. Ben knew the ball was in

his court now—that it was up to him to pick the conversation up from here.

"Wow, son…Jeremy. I'm impressed. I'm, well, proud of you."

"Thanks."

"I was wonderin' if we could maybe meet and talk sometime," Ben said. "You don't have to if you don't want to. I would understand. I was just hoping to say some things, but feel like I should do it face to face. You know what I mean?"

"You don't have to say you're sorry or anything, Dad. I get that you had problems that you had to deal with. I know Mom left—not you. I also know that she did it because she knew you weren't good for us like you were. It was a bad time for all of us. I don't blame any of you really."

Ben didn't even know he was crying until he felt the wetness trickle down his chin.

I'm so sorry, Jeremy. He wanted to say the words aloud. To climb the tallest high-rise in Philadelphia and scream it for all the city to hear. But the words just slammed against the back of his throat and refused to budge.

Not here, he thought. *I want to tell him lookin' in his eyes.*

Before Ben could answer, Jeremy jumped in.

"So, I…uh, go on break from school in a few weeks. I was thinking that maybe I could drive up your way and we could…well, meet up."

The wetness covered most of his face now. "That would be perfect. I would like that, Jeremy."

Just as Ben finished making arrangements to meet with Jeremy and had hung up the phone, Mia's flustered face appeared around the corner.

Oh, no. She's been covering up front and I've been gone a long time, he thought, *not to mention that Carlos is probably wondering where his bread order is.*

There were beads of sweat on Mia's forehead and her glare bore holes into him, but when she saw his wet cheeks, she stopped short. As the anger drained from her face, it was replaced with alarm.

"What wrong, Ben?" she asked, her short legs covering the distance between them in record time. She was already reaching a hand toward him, probably imagining he had just found out that he had terminal cancer or some other horrible news.

"It's Jeremy…" He could hardly say the words.

Mia just stared. He could tell she was puzzled as she tried to place the name.

"Jeremy…my son." Recognition crept over her face and her eyes widened into saucers.

"Oh, Ben, honey, no…what happened?" Mia reached out to grab his hand.

It was Ben's turn to be puzzled. She'd misunderstood.

He squeezed her hand back. He knew his friend would share his joy.

"No, Mia. He's coming," he told her through trembling lips. "He's coming."

*a*den lay staring at the blank wall in front of him, the room engulfed in darkness except for a narrow slice of moonlight pushing its way through one edge of the window drapes. Muted shadows danced on the wall as tree branches swayed in front of the moon's glow. The elongated shadows took shape on the wall, like the limbs of skeletal bodies dancing across an invisible stage.

Aden imagined they were souls acting out a scene on his bedroom wall. Souls of the dead. *Like my mom,* he thought. For so long he'd wondered where she'd disappeared to, if she had ever gone back to look for him. Now he knew *exactly* where she was— laying in a frosty morgue thirty miles away, just an empty shell waiting to be disposed of.

NO...Mom...Please God...no!

A hot, searing geyser broke loose from the deepest part of him as sobs racked Aden's body and took possession of his fragile emotions. He tried to force it back down, but was powerless against the grief and despair that overcame him. Huddled under heavy flannel sheets, he curled his limbs into a tight ball against his chest and wept in silence.

The intensity of his grief shook the bed and he turned his head to bite down on the fabric of his pillow to keep from being heard. His clenched fists dug into his ribs and his lungs struggled to suck in air between long sobs. The pain was so penetrable; it was like a thousand shards of glass had impaled him from every angle.

Aden felt the hope he'd clung to for so long begin to drain out as his tears spilled onto his pillow, now a soggy lump against his cheek. He hadn't cried when Paula told him that they'd found his mom—he struggled to even form the word—*dead.*

How? Aden struggled to understand. *It wasn't supposed to be like this. She just needed some time to work things out so that she could bring me back home...*

A cold hardness snaked into his soul, closing tight the cavernous wound that had torn open only moments before. Aden reached up and roughly brushed the tears from his face with the edge of his blanket. Shoving the covers aside, Aden jerked up and scooted to the edge of his bed, his chest heavy with a simmering rage as he sat and stared at the shadows still tantalizing him from the wall.

It's their fault she'd dead, he thought, biting down on his bottom lip until he felt the pain. *They weren't trying hard enough to find her. If they had found her sooner, she wouldn't be...she'd still be here. I hate them. I hate them all.*

Aden stood, eyes darting around the dark room, unsure of what to do in that moment, yet positive of what he *would* do next.

I won't stay here.

Clarity settled over him as a plan formed in his mind. Flicking on the lamp on his nightstand, Aden glanced around and noticed his backpack on the floor by the dresser. It took him only moments to dump its few contents on his bed: an assortment of pens and writing paper Aden used to scribble ideas on, a blue rubber ball that Blake had insisted he hold for him, a flashlight Cray had given him. The blue notebook tumbled out last, sliding down the pile and coming to rest on the comforter, its cover bent open where it fell over on itself.

Pulling a few changes of clothes out of the dresser, Aden decided to forgo sneaking down the hall to the bathroom for his toothbrush or any other toiletries. He'd gone without them before and could do it again. Zipping the backpack closed, Aden tossed it to the floor beneath the bedroom window and walked over to turn off the light. He couldn't afford to attract any attention.

Back at the window, Aden pushed the curtain aside and looked out over the property. Paula had left hours ago, the house behind him was quiet and, from what Aden could see from his viewpoint, the world outside had slipped into a deep slumber. Fate was in his corner.

Thank God they don't have a dog, Aden thought.

Angela and Cray had talked about getting a puppy for Blake after their dog had died earlier this year. But, right now, the only warning system Aden had to worry about was that ill-tempered, cranky rooster. Aden glanced over to where the chicken coop stood —a sinister structure in the dark shadows of the tool shed. This time of the night, the flock and their ever-watchful defender were more than likely all tucked away in their nests for the night.

It took a few shoves for Aden to get the rusty metal lock at the top of the window released, but the window lifted easily when he pushed it open. Aden tugged the screen off and set it on the ground beneath the window before reaching back down for his backpack.

Glancing once more around the room for reassurance that he wasn't forgetting something, Aden lifted a leg over the window sill and slithered through the opening, careful to avoid landing on the screen below him.

He pressed against the side of the house and stared out at the dark cluster of trees that lined the back of the Pearson's property. Unlike the city, where darkness lingered in small pockets between streetlights, the black shadows of the landscape beyond the reach of the porch lights were foreboding and ominous.

He swallowed hard against the sudden dryness in his throat. Fear bubbled deep in his stomach, an unfamiliar form of unease unlike anything he'd ever felt out on his own in the city. At least in Philly he had some idea of what evil lurked behind dark corners and in empty alleys, but the sight in front of him was a completely foreign entity.

Aden thought of his mom and the anger against everyone who had wronged her—wronged *him*—rushed back at him with renewed force. He pushed himself off the wall, adjusted the bag on his shoulders, and made his way into the darkness.

———

"CRAY! WAKE UP! HE'S GONE!" Angela rushed over to the bed to shake Cray awake, but he was already throwing off the blankets and jumping to his feet. He grabbed Angela's hands to still her so he could make sense of what she was saying.

"What are you talking about, Angela? Who's gone?" Cray blinked against the sluggishness still gripping him as he waited for her to explain.

"Aden." She took several quick breaths before going on. "I went to check on him. You know...to make sure he was okay. He wasn't there, Cray! He's not in his room!" Angela pulled her hands from Cray's and started pacing the room. She thought more clearly when she could move around. "I searched the other rooms in the house and I can't find him. What do we do, Cray?" She turned back to her husband, who was already pulling on a pair of jeans. He pointed to a chair in the corner.

"Hand me my sweatshirt," he told her, reaching to pull his boots closer to the bed.

She handed Cray the sweatshirt and started toward the closet for herself. Cray stopped her with his words.

"No. You stay here with Blake. I'm going to take another look around the house and then check around outside. He might have just gone out for some fresh air."

After he was dressed, Angela followed him to Aden's bedroom. Cray flipped on the bedroom light and noticed the open window right away. Angela must have been too distracted when she didn't find Aden in his room and missed seeing it. Her hand flew to her mouth. She voiced what they both knew.

"He's run away! Oh, Cray, where would he even go way out here in the middle of *nowhere*?" Angela felt panic rush through her as she watched Cray shove the window closed.

Cray brushed past her, moving down the hall toward the kitchen at a determined pace. Reaching for his keys, he swung around to face Angela.

"Call Paula and let her know what's going on. Tell her she doesn't need to head over here just yet—give me some time to track him down. If you don't hear from me in the next half hour, call her back and tell her to decide what she wants to do next." His lips brushed her cheek before he turned and pushed out the back door.

Angela was frozen where she stood but, just before the door closed, she snatched it back open. Cray was already off the porch, headed toward his truck.

"Cray! You'll need a jacket!" she called to him from the doorway.

"Got one in the truck! Go on and make that call, Angela." Cray jumped into the truck cab, already pulling the door closed as he slid onto the seat.

Angela heard the engine start as she latched the door and turned toward the phone. She spied a dish towel on the counter next to her and reached for it. Pressing her face into the cloth, she smelled the lilac fabric softener she loved but absolutely forbade the tears to come.

Breath, Ang. You can fall apart later but, right now, Aden needs you.

Whispering a quick prayer for Aden, she lowered the towel and reached for the phone.

44

*A*den followed what looked like some kind of a rough trail through the wooded area. He wasn't sure it even led anywhere, but it was the only open space to walk that resembled a path. If it trailed off into a dead end, Aden had no clue where he would go from there. He was tempted to turn around and abandon the whole idea, but pure stubbornness kept him moving forward. He had to remind himself several times that he'd seen a lot of scarier things in his life and that he'd been just fine.

I can find my way out of here, he assured himself. *This has to lead somewhere soon.*

Aden had been walking for over an hour and was starting to lose all sense of direction. *Was he going in circles?* He could have even gotten turned around somewhere and be heading right back the way he came for all he knew.

Even though he kept up the pep talks to encourage himself, Aden was starting to feel anxious and scared. He'd felt so brave when he'd slipped out of the house earlier, heading out into the unknown—so determined to set out on his own again and leave all those meddlers who had ruined his life behind. But his resolve was weakening and being back in a warm bed kept creeping to the forefront of his mind as he trudged through the cold darkness, with only the moon's glow to guide his footsteps through the indistinct path he struggled to follow.

Finally, Aden spotted what looked like an opening up ahead. He hadn't realized he was so cold until he pushed through the last cluster of thick bushes and found himself standing on the edge of an open road, panting out breaths that left wisps of fog in the air in front of him and wrapping his arms around himself for warmth as he stood rooted on the asphalt. Swinging his head to the left to peer down the dark road, then toward the right, where the road was just as endless, he had no idea which way to start.

Standing there out in the open, he felt only slightly better than what he'd just come through—startling at every snapped twig and jumping at the sight of his own shadow on the ground. It only occurred to him just now as he stood there that he had no solid plan in mind.

Even if I run to another house nearby, it's not like I can just knock on their door and ask for help. They'd wonder where I'd come from way out here and what I was doing out alone in the middle of the night. For sure, they'd call the police.

That would never do. He needed to figure something out but there weren't many options here in the middle of acres of farmland and woods.

Aden considered crawling back into the bushes to spend the night and trying to think it through in the morning, but he was cold and shuddered to think what might be crawling around under that tunnel of overgrowth behind him.

Aden was ready to change his mind and resolved to go back, regardless of his fear, when he saw the glaring lights of a large vehicle coming toward him. He stopped to consider his options: *try his hand at hitchhiking or dive into the bushes.* Aden had a healthy enough fear of strangers—especially ones out at this time of the night—that he preferred to face the dark woods than whatever danger might be heading his way. Backing steadily into the undergrowth so that he wouldn't draw the attention of the vehicle's driver, Aden kept his eyes fixed on it to determine if the vehicle slowed or not. Pressed back into the darkness, Aden felt confident that the driver couldn't see him.

However, much to Aden's dismay, the vehicle started to slow as it came close to where he stood huddled in the shadows.

Maybe they saw me move and thought it was a deer or something and are just slowing in case it darts out in front of them.

Just as he tensed to jump into the bushes, the vehicle, which Aden now saw was a dark blue truck, pulled onto the gravel and came to a stop. He knew that truck.

Cray.

He wasn't sure if he felt relief or anger that he'd been found but, either way, Aden didn't make a move. He waited while the truck door opened and the cab light illuminated Cray's face. Aden didn't detect any sternness in Cray's expression as he hopped out of the truck and made his way toward him. Instead, Aden thought he seemed...*sad? Worried?*

How in the world did he find me out here?

They stared at each other over the glare of the truck's headlights. Cray's hands were shoved in his pockets and his stance posed no threat to Aden. It was as if he were waiting for Aden to make the next move.

Not knowing what else to say, Aden blurted out, "Hey, Cray."

Cray nodded, "Aden." He pulled a hand out of his pocket to rub the back of his neck. "You doing okay?"

Aden moved forward a few steps, more to relieve himself of the thorny branch poking him in his side than to greet Cray.

"No, not really." Even he was surprised by his honest answer.

Cray jerked his head toward the truck. "You wanna sit in the truck and talk about it?"

Aden was even more surprised to find himself moving toward the passenger side of the truck and reaching for the door handle.

Oh, well, he thought, resolve settling over him as he pulled himself up onto the seat. *I didn't have a better plan anyway.*

ADEN BRACED himself for all the questions and accusations he was sure Cray was about to lay on him, but he was wrong. *Awkwardly wrong, actually.*

Instead of launching into a tirade about how stupid Aden was to be trekking through the dark woods in the middle of the night, making Cray drive all over looking for him, and at how ungrateful Aden was for all that he and Angela had done for him, Cray just sat there staring straight ahead. He'd locked the doors and turned the truck off and was just sitting there with his hands draped across the steering wheel. Aden had been ready to bite back when Cray lashed into him, but Cray hadn't done that and Aden was unprepared for the silence.

"It's fine, Cray. You can send me back. That's where I was going anyway. Well, *trying* to go," he finished lamely.

Cray sighed deeply, and Aden got the impression he was reining in some deep, consuming response that Aden couldn't define but didn't seem to be anger.

That's it. He thinks I'm hopeless. He regrets letting me stay with them. Aden turned to look out the window. *I never asked to come here anyway. I was forced to be here.*

Aden could feel Cray shift on the seat and turned back to face him. Cray's eyes boring into him were so intense that Aden felt like a cowering dog under his stare. *Maybe this is what it feels like when you are about to get a whipping from your dad.* Aden didn't need to find out. Cray's look sobered him up fast enough.

"Send you back to *where*, Aden? To Paula? You'll just be placed in another foster home, and maybe that's what you want. The *streets*? Is *that* where you want to go back to, son? Because those are your only choices besides staying with me and my family. Tell me where you want me to send you *back* to, Aden."

Cray had one arm slung over the back of the seat while the other waved through the air as he leaned in toward Aden. Aden was faced with either jumping out of the truck or answering Cray because, with the truck parked on the side of the road in the middle of the night and them staring at each other in the dark cab, Aden was sure Cray meant to settle this right here and now.

He didn't know what to say. Cray had laid out the choices, plain and raw, before him and Aden was stunned into silence. *Where had he really expected to go from here? What choices did he have now that the only one he'd wanted all along had been stripped from him?*

As if he could sense what had driven Aden to this point, Cray leaned back against the seat, his eyes never leaving Aden, but his voice gentle as he pulled at and exposed the fine layers of Aden's heart.

"I'm sorry, Aden. You're hurting real bad right now. I understand. I lost my mom when I was a little younger than you. Sure, it was under different circumstances, but it still tore me up and changed my life suddenly in a hundred painful ways. I don't know *why* your mother made the choice to leave you—I'm sure she had good intentions—or what led her to where she ended up, but, in the end, they were *her* choices, Aden. You had no say in that."

Aden couldn't tear his eyes from Cray if he wanted to. He was locked in a trance as he absorbed Cray's words. He wasn't sure where it was leading, but he felt the sincerity in what Cray was saying. It dug into places Aden had kept buried all these months, places even Ben hadn't dared to pry into.

Aden felt his face crumbling, although he worked so hard to keep it strong and steady, like he thought a man should do. A man who could take care of himself, that didn't need anyone. All that melted sitting next to Cray while he laid the raw facts out at Aden's feet.

Before he knew it, he was leaning against Cray, crying against all the injustices life had dealt him and all the pain of loss that he'd bottled up inside. Cray patted his back and let him cry it out.

"I know life isn't what you planned it to be and you've had to face things that no young man your age should face, but there are people who care about you, who want to shoulder that load with you now. Is that okay?"

Aden sat up and looked at Cray. He felt subdued, humbled, and more weary than he'd ever felt before.

"Ben too?"

He wasn't sure why he even brought his name up. He had already forgiven Ben but hadn't really considered that it was Ben who had reached out for help when Aden wouldn't. It was because of him that Aden sat across from a stranger who had taken the time to search for him in the middle of the night instead of washing his hands of him and letting Paula and the authorities take over.

Cray was nodding, a soft smile on his lips. "Yes, Ben cares about you, Aden. And so do Angela and I. You could probably throw Blake in there too," he said with a grin. "We know you need time to heal. Take all the time you need, son."

Aden's smile was weak, but brave. "Thanks, Cray. It's going to take a while, but…I'll try."

Cray started the truck and pulled his seat belt on. "You ready to head home?"

"Yeah," Aden said. "I'm ready."

45

Thump. Thump. It was the third time Aden had heard the timid knock—and ignored it. He knew it was Blake and appreciated that he didn't just creep into the room like he normally did most mornings. Still, he wasn't up to it today.

Go away, Blake, he thought.

The knocking stopped but Aden sensed Blake's presence still at his door. He closed his eyes and drew the sheet closer to his chin. The coolness of the fabric felt comforting against his hot skin. He couldn't remember when he'd finally fallen asleep but it couldn't have been more than a few hours ago, he thought. He didn't know what was expected of him at this point. Did Angela assume he would come out and help with chores and hunker down to his school work?

What day of the week is it anyway? He couldn't remember. His brain was muddled from running through mental obstacles most of the night. As much as his body wanted to fall back asleep, his brain was already gearing itself for the day's challenges. *Tap. Tap.* Aden mumbled loud enough for the intruder to hear. "What is it, Blake?"

A slight creaking sound came from across the room as the door was inched open. Aden's back was to the door so he couldn't *see* Blake standing there as much as he *felt* him.

"Can I come in?" Blake whispered, the voice drifting from the foot of Aden's bed.

"I guess you already have," Aden said. "What do you want?" He didn't mean to be harsh. Blake was a sweet kid and fun to be around most of the time, but Aden wanted to be alone today.

The mattress shifted as Blake crawled onto the bed and sat behind Aden, his bony knees digging into Aden's spine. *Where was Angela? Doesn't she know Blake is up and bothering me?*

"I'm sorry about your mom, Aden," Blake said softly.

The adults had all said the same thing to him last night after Paula had dropped the devastating news on him, but hearing Blake, in his tiny, wispy voice say it touched Aden almost as deeply as the things Cray had said to him last night.

A fresh deluge of tears filled his eyes and he wanted to start weeping all over again. But Blake wouldn't understand. He'd probably be scared and Aden would have to end up comforting *him* instead.

Aden kept his back to Blake. Swallowing down the wad of cotton lodged in his throat, he managed to speak, "Thanks, Blake. I needed that."

A door slammed in another part of the house and Aden felt Blake shift, presumably to look and see if someone was coming to bust him for bugging Aden. He shuffled to scoot off the bed.

"I gotta go, Aden. I said a prayer for you when I went to sleep last night," he said, still whispering. The soft *tinkling* of his voice was strangely comforting. A second later, the door clicked shut and the silence closed in again around Aden.

With Blake gone, Aden felt free to give in to the eruption of grief that had been building since the first sheepish knock on his door had awakened him. As his resolve crumpled under its burden and the tears fell freely, Aden pressed back against the despair. Through the dark clouds surrounding his mind, a tiny spark of light nudged its way into Aden's heart. While grown-ups had their entire lives to practice the right words to say in grave situations, six-year-old kids don't have that level of experience. They say exactly what they feel.

Aden's tears subsided as he thought of Blake's comforting words: *I said a prayer for you...* Aden knew the boy was genuinely worried about him. In his young, innocent way, Blake was trying to help because he *cared* about Aden.

Just like Cray had told him last night.

I'm not alone, he thought, *not anymore.* Saying the words in his head made him feel better, but he knew it would take him some time before he really believed those words.

He thought about what Cray had told him about his mom and the choices that she'd made about Aden and about her own destiny.

Like a voice breaking through the walls of his mind, a revelation and understanding swept over Aden. His mother had thought she was protecting him by bringing him to the shelter where someone could help him and where he would have a shot at a better life than she could give him. She hadn't known he never went in. He wouldn't allow his mind to think that she may have gone back to look for him—that was too painful to dwell on right now.

He had to believe—somehow—that she'd done it because she *loved* him.

Ben, Paula, the Pearsons—little Blake—had all showed up in his life to help him. Fate, or maybe even God, had stepped in and given Aden hope for a better life, even if the path to get there had been the long, hard way around.

Aden dragged the sheet off his body and sat up on the edge of the bed. He stared down at his bare feet for several minutes, searching for strength to get up and face whatever lay ahead. He would do it—for her. His mom. Because it was what she really wanted for him all along. He was sure it had hurt her, but she'd tried to do what was best for him. *Like when Ben called Paula to get me off the streets. He wanted better for me.*

"I miss you, Mom. You…you did good," he said aloud, praying that, in some way, his words would travel through time and space to reach her. "I'm safe with the Pearsons. Please…don't worry about me anymore. I'm going to be okay."

Before the grief could overtake him and send him into another bout of weeping, Aden stood and walked over to the tall mirror suspended on the back of his bedroom door. He straightened the clothes that he'd slept in from the night before.

It's the best I can do right now, he thought as he opened the door.

$\mathcal{B}$en stared at the clock on the wall. The cadence of the *tick-tock, tick-tock* drilled into his head until he couldn't take it anymore. He jumped off the couch and went to get dressed.

It was already 5:30 p.m. and he'd only just now started to put presentable clothes on and that was only because he needed to run to the grocery store to stock up on food for the week before he went back to work tomorrow. Thankfully, Jake had loaned him his old jeep until he could find something to replace his totaled car.

Ben had enjoyed the long the day off. Actually, it was the last of five long, relaxing days that he'd been on vacation. He and Jake had returned last night from fishing down on the Susquehanna River, one of their favorite fishing spots located just a few hours outside of Philadelphia in Columbia County. It was one of the prime spots in Pennsylvania for pulling in smallmouth bass and catfish and he and Jake tried to make it an annual trip.

They'd had a time at it this year, bantering and acting like two teenagers. They'd opted to rent a cabin this year because they both agreed that they were too old to be sleeping in tents and—truth be told—they were both too lazy to put one up.

Jake's brother, Rick, had loaned them his fishing boat in exchange for a share of their catch. They'd had a great time gorging on fried catfish complemented with homemade coleslaw and corn bread served up by Rick's wife. When Rick pulled the lid off of the ice chest and started passing out bottles of beer, Ben caught Jake looking at him. That familiar burning in his gut and sweating palms broke over him almost immediately.

"Nah, we'll pass, Rick," Jake told him when Rick walked up with two icy bottles of beer.

Ben excused himself to go to the bathroom. Part of him was relieved Jake has stepped in and intervened, but another part of him was angry at Jake for interfering, like Ben was some pimpled-faced teenage kid that needed a chaperone.

But he'd *really* wanted that beer. It just seemed like the perfect ending to a long weekend of fishing, enjoying the fruits of their labor. *It's just what guys do,* Ben thought, sourly.

Now, standing in front of the mirror, tucking his shirt into his pants, it was hitting Ben hard again. He was facing a long night at home alone since Jake needed to stay down at the shop to catch up on paperwork.

Why were these demons all comin' back at him so hard after all these years? Deep in his heart, though, he had a strong suspicion about why.

Jeremy.

Ever since the phone call from Jeremy, Ben had wrestled the demons, his soul in torment over those past mistakes that had, once again, awaken from dormancy and perched themselves comfortably on his shoulder while they taunted his mind: *Seeing you again will only remind Jeremy of what a failure you are. He's only comin' so that you can see what you lost and how he's done just fine without you in his life.*

Ben backed away from the mirror and sat on the bed, dropping his head into his hands. He was losing his confidence, the euphoria over the upcoming reunion going up in smoke right in front of him. He didn't know how to quiet the demons...except by drowning their mocking voices under several shots of hard liquor.

Ben's heart pounded in his chest, his saliva suddenly thick and pasty. He was dressed and facing a whole night open ahead of him with nothing else to do.

He would go... No one would even know but him and he'd be back home and in bed before he would have to face Jake's disappointment and judgment.

The wheels set in motion, Ben stood and snatched his keys off the dresser. He was a man possessed and there was no turning back at this point. *I just need to get through tonight, that's all. I'll be back to work tomorrow and right as rain. Then, I'll meet with Jeremy this next week and we'll figure things out from there.*

Just as Ben reached the front door, the phone rang in the kitchen. He paused, one shaky hand resting on the doorknob. *I'll let them leave a message,* he thought, starting to turn the knob. But, his curiosity got the best of him.

Keys still in hand, Ben made his way to the kitchen and snatched the phone off the hook, "This is Ben."

"Ben, it's Paula. How are you? Sorry to be calling so late in the day but I needed to talk to you about something. Do you have a minute?" Paula's normal cheery voice had an edge to it that Ben couldn't decipher. His heart was still pounding and he was already feeling the jitters. He took a deep breath and tried to sound normal.

"Evenin', Paula. No problem at all. What's on your mind?"

"Well, it's about Aden." Ben felt the blood rush to his head. All thoughts of a drink took a back burner.

"What's happened? Everything okay?" He set his keys down on the counter.

"Yes, he's fine, well…as best as he can be. They found Lauren —his mother," she paused, "I don't know how else to say it but… she's dead, Ben. Overdosed on heroin. I drove out to the Pearson's to let Aden know. Thing is, she hadn't really been a user—not heroin anyway—when the police had run-ins with her before. They said that she was busted with marijuana possession a time or two and was brought in on prostitution charges several times, but that was it. She was also known to have an alcohol problem. But heroin use appeared to be a recent thing she'd dabbled in and it took her down fast."

"Anyhow, as you can imagine, Aden is taking it hard. That's why I'm calling. For one, I just thought you should know since you have a vested interest in Aden's life and have built a relationship with him.

The Pearsons mentioned to me that you have reconnected since your accident and, well, I was hoping you might be able to reach out to him. The Pearsons have been having some trouble with him lately. Nothing serious, except that he did attempt to run away the other night."

Ben stared across the room at the digital clock glowing blue on the coffee machine. The shock of Paula's news crashed into him like a tidal wave of icy water. *Oh, Aden…son, I'm so sorry.*

"I'm glad you called to let me know, Paula," he said, peeling his eyes away from the glow of the clock. He stared down at the floor instead. "I can imagine Aden's hurtin' real bad right now."

"Yes, he is," she continued. "I'm sure he probably would have told you eventually himself but I didn't want to wait until he did.

He may not admit it, but he needs the few people that are in his life right now more than ever. We still haven't been able to locate any other family members at this point. It's like they don't exist."

They talked for a few more minutes, Ben promising to call Aden to check on him and see about maybe going to visit, if the Pearsons—and Aden—didn't have a problem with it.

Ben gripped the phone in his fist for a moment before lifting it back onto its cradle. Dragging his weight over to a kitchen chair, he slid it from under the table and sunk down onto it. His body shook with sobs so violent that the old chair wobbled and threatened to buckle under him. Ben didn't care. Even the demons he'd fought earlier had fled and he was left to face his pain in peace.

"Oh, God…oh, God…" he said, his voice echoing off the walls of the small kitchen. "I almost…what did I almost *do?* You know where it would have led you, old man. You've been down this road before." Ben jammed his fists against his eyes in disappointment and frustration.

"Here I am, only a few days away from seeing my son after all these years and now Aden is needin' me. What if that phone call hadn't come right when you were walkin' out that door?"

But it had and here Ben was—mercifully saved from himself.

Ben sat up in the chair and lifted his eyes to the ceiling. He didn't bother to wipe away the tears running down his face.

"Thank you, Lord. I didn't think you paid this old man any attention, but all these little miracles comin' at me these past few weeks…well, I'm just gonna give you the credit."

47

*A*ngela gave her hair a final spritz of hairspray before slipping her feet into a pair of brown loafers. Cray was just walking in to check on her when she beat him to the punch. "I'm coming, I'm coming," she said, reaching for her purse on the bed. Cray was taking the family out to dinner to their favorite downtown restaurant, Fogo de Chão, to celebrate her birthday and they had reservations for 7:00 p.m.

They had fifteen minutes to get there. Cray was going to have to break a few laws to make it on time.

When Angela passed Cray leaving the bedroom, he stopped her for a brief hug. "It's going to be a great night. You'll see. Relax," he said.

Angela looked up at him and put on a brave smile. "It's been a tough few weeks. Are you sure this is the right time?" she asked, searching his eyes for assurance.

He answered with a kiss on her nose. "It's as good a time as any, Ang," he said, turning her toward the door and guiding her down the hall. Passing the boys' rooms, he called out, "Ready, boys?"

As they piled into the truck, Angela looked back at Blake and Aden through the rearview mirror and watched them buckle in, Aden leaning over to help Blake untwist his belt first. When she looked over at Cray he was already watching her with a grin on his face. "Almost like a real family," he whispered and turned to start the car.

As Angela appreciated the beautiful passing landscape from her window and listened to Cray telling Aden and Blake about a humorous story from his youth, she thought about the evening they had ahead of them.

This is either going to end awesome or be a complete disaster, she worried.

She and Cray had spent several nights lying in bed discussing the possibility of adopting Aden—if he would even want that. They had talked about it before they had even found Aden's mother and were planning to approach Paula about how to move forward with the process and about the likelihood of Aden's mother giving up her rights to Aden.

Not that she hadn't given him up already by dumping him off at a homeless shelter's doorstep, Angela thought, then scolded herself. *Aden's mother, Lauren, was an addict. A prostitute. Did she feel that she really had any choice or any other options? Would I have done better in her situation?*

But, sadly, she was gone. Angela regretted her sharp criticism and harsh judgment. Aden was hurting and broken, trying to find his place in the world. Destitute or not, Lauren was the only mother he'd ever known and he loved and missed her intensely.

She and Cray still wanted to adopt Aden—now more than ever —and it would be easier now with no family left that anyone knew of or could find, but they had decided it would be on Aden's terms. He had been denied so many choices in his life already. The poor kid had endured a great deal of unwanted baggage thrown on him that they wanted him to decide for himself if he wanted to become a part of the Pearson family.

She and Cray had agreed that, along with celebrating her birthday, tonight they would be asking Aden that very question.

ANGELA SAVORED the last bite of her prime rib, pushing it around the juices on her plate before popping it into her mouth. "I can't remember the last time I had prime rib. You grill some top-notch hamburgers, Cray, but sometimes you just have to indulge," she said, pointing her fork at her now-empty plate for emphasis.

"No argument from me, Ang," Cray told her, buttering a soft yeast roll. "I'm all for taking things up a notch from time to time."

Angela noted that Cray seemed a bit distracted and kept glancing back over his shoulder. When the waitress carried over a plate and set it down in front of her, she understood what Cray had been up to.

In the plate's center was a gigantic slice of raspberry cheesecake with fresh raspberries spilling down its sides and pooling at the edges. Bright pink syrup laced delicately across the white porcelain in a lovely script that spelled out *Happy Birthday.*

"Happy birthday!" Cray said, leaning in for a kiss. Aden and Blake wore cheesy smiles on their faces and Blake even started to sing the birthday song until Cray warned him off with a shake of his head. The diners around them probably wouldn't appreciate the interruption to their solitude. A few glanced over and smiled at their small celebration but quickly became reabsorbed into their private conversations.

Angela passed the oversized cheesecake slice around the table to share with everyone. "I want one of those for my birthday too!" Blake announced. Everyone laughed.

The table quieted as everyone shared the rich dessert. Angela could tell that Aden was especially enjoying it as he reached his fork over for several bites.

Cray cleared his throat. It was a signal to Angela, who set her fork gently down on her plate and pulled her napkin up to wipe her mouth. She looked over at Cray expectantly.

Blake was entertaining himself by constructing a tent with his napkin, pulling it up to a stiff point and forming the edges into a cone shape. Aden licked his fork as he watched.

Cray cleared his throat a little louder.

"Boys," he said, looking pointedly at Blake. Blake looked up and caught his father's expression. He squished the napkin between his hands, collapsing his creation, before pulling the napkin down onto his lap.

Cray turned his gaze to Aden.

"Angela and I wanted to talk with you about something important, Aden," he said. Looking at Blake, he continued, "We want you to listen too, Blake. No interrupting, though."

Aden nodded at Cray, lowering his fork down on the table. His face grew serious and Angela thought he looked nervous. Her maternal instinct kicking in, she reached under the table to halt Cray before he launched into his speech.

What if Aden assumes that we have more bad news? He might think we're sending him off to another foster home.

Cray must have thought Angela's hand was there to lend him support because he reached down and gave her hand a squeeze. She sunk back into her chair as she braced herself. She'd just have to ride the wave as it came.

Cray looked down at the table briefly, then back to Aden, whom Angela was sure hadn't blinked since Cray had called this meeting.

"Aden, Angela and I…" Cray rubbed his lips together, seeking the perfect words for the moment. "We love having you in our home and"—he glanced over to Blake, giving the boy a big grin —"you're just about the closest thing to a superhero in Blake's eyes. We've come to think of you as, well, a big part of our little family. We…" He looked to Angela for confirmation. She gave him a reassuring nod and her best *you got this* look.

That was all the bolster Cray needed.

"Angela and I want to ask you what you would think about making it more of a permanent thing. We were hoping you might like to join our family, well…officially."

Angela kept her eyes fixed on Cray—partly because she didn't want Aden to feel like he was in the middle of an interrogation with three sets of eyes zoned in on him, and also because she was pretty impressed with Cray's heartfelt appeal.

Cray was a man of few words and, although she knew he loved her and Blake fiercely, he didn't launch into emotional diatribes very often. He'd said more to Aden in those few sentences than she could have managed in a twenty-minute prepared speech.

She held her breath as her eyes drifted over the faces of everyone at the table. Blake looked between his father and Aden, a look of confusion etched on his young face as he tried to understand why everyone was being so serious and what his dad meant by "join our family." Angela's gaze rested on Aden.

He blinked. Once, twice…*Did she see tears? Was that a good or bad sign?*

Angela let go of Cray's hand, which was now slick with sweat, and wiped it on the edge of the tablecloth. Cray was done talking and was leaving the next move in Aden's court. Angela was sure everyone in the restaurant could hear her heart pounding in her chest.

"You want to be Aden's daddy, too?" Blake said, obviously reading the long silence as permission to join the conversation. Angela could have kissed him at that moment. Cray kept his eyes on Aden and ignored Blake.

Still, Blake had helped break the spell. Aden roused himself and chewed on his bottom lip. Angela definitely saw tears now pooled in his eyes. Blinking, he kept them in check. Angela wasn't as successful.

"Yes, honey," Angela broke in. "We want Aden to become part of our family. If that's what *he* wants." She spoke to Blake, but her message was for Aden. Aden's gaze shifted from Cray to her. Seeing Angela's tears seemed to bring on his.

"I've never had a dad," Aden said, looking down at his lap.

———

THINKING BACK over the months with the Pearsons, Aden reminisced about some of his favorite moments: fishing with Cray and Blake, playing hide-and-seek with Blake behind the house, bouncing down the bumpy road to town in Cray's truck with Blake and Cray belting out goofy country songs with the radio—he had even learned a few songs himself—rolling out dough for cinnamon rolls in the kitchen with Angela...

Then, as if someone suddenly jerked the wheel out of his hands, he felt himself being steered down a treacherous winding road of unwelcome memories: A woman passed out at the kitchen table, an empty bottle on its side next to her. He had left her there when he couldn't wake her... A young boy's face—*his* face—pressed against the glass of the apartment window as he stared down at the passersby on the street below. A chair pushed up against the kitchen counter as the boy searched for food in empty cabinets.

Then, a man. Filthy and smelling like old sweat and whiskey, leaving a bedroom. The gaunt-faced woman sitting on the bed just beyond the man, pressing fingers against a bloodied lip. The woman—his mom—bolting from the bed after the man turned on Aden, who sat on the floor outside the bedroom, lifting a heavy black boot to kick him. Aden racing to hide and cower in the hall closet while the man finished the job on his mom instead. She didn't leave the bed for two days after that.

The image of himself—older now—being kicked and beaten in a dark alley. Aden felt like he was floating on a cloud, looking down on his body, bruised and broken, sprawled across the gravel while a crowd gathered around him.

Aftershocks coursed through him as he desperately tried to thrust away the painful memories invading his mind. *No more, no more...*

He forced himself to refocus on the three people sitting at the table with him. *How long had they been waiting while his mind had wandered?* They stared back at him expectantly, but didn't push him to answer. Blake was caught up in the moment, but Angela and Cray understood how hard the decision was—what it would cost him.

But, what might he gain instead?

This family had taken him to his first fancy restaurant tonight. They shared with him his first taste of cheesecake. The Pearsons had given him a glimpse of what a real family could be like for him. A revelation washed over Aden, resurrecting a dream that had once burned and sparked within him before it fizzled and blew away in a cloud of disappointment.

They were *choosing* him, *wanted* him...

The smile was slow in coming but larger than life when it did.

"Yes," he answered. "I want to be part of your family."

48

"Can I get you a drink?" Ben looked up at the tall young woman standing over him. Her rich auburn hair was pulled up in a loose ponytail and she wore a cheerful bright pink polo shirt under a dark blue denim jumper with a matching belt. She smiled down at him and tucked a wayward strand of hair behind her ear as she waited for his reply.

Ben glanced over to the large glass window by the restaurant entrance before answering. He debated whether he should wait or not.

"I'll take a Dr. Pepper. Easy on the ice."

When the bright pink polo moved away to get his drink, Ben opened the menu and browsed the selections. He usually ordered the lamb gyro sandwich or a hoagie with double prosciutto and capicola and extra Italian dressing, but he wasn't sure he could eat with his stomach tied in knots.

Guess I could wrap somethin' up and take it home for later.

Located off Chancellor Street in Philadelphia, Giulio's Diner was an old-world style eatery with red-checkered tablecloths and a bold green with red pinstripes awning over the entrance and its menu proudly posted in a display case just outside the front door.

Ben had suggested Giulio's, not only because it was close to Jeremy's hotel and twenty minutes from Philadelphia International Airport, but also because it was a favorite of Ben's. Sometimes Eddie sent Ben out to the restaurant supply store a few blocks away and Ben would call in an order for a hoagie that he could pick up on his way back.

He set the menu down on the table and watched the door.

You can do this, Ben.

A shadow crossed the front door window just as an elderly gentleman reached to open the door for his wife. Ben heard a voice say "thank you" as a figure made its way around the gentleman.

Jeremy.

Ben couldn't have pried his eyes away from the young man even if his chair was on fire. He was tall with broad shoulders and ruddy cheeks that perfectly complemented his mop of curly brown hair. He wore black jeans and dark-chocolate loafers with a soft gray turtle-neck sweater that blended with his wide hazel eyes that Ben caught when they connected with his.

It was only when Jeremy started walking toward his table that Ben felt his heart lurch back into rhythm after he felt it had frozen in his chest.

Ben stood to greet his son. *His son...* He reached a sweaty hand out to shake hands with Jeremy. Jeremy looked at the extended hand with hesitation—as if deciding whether to treat this meeting like a job interview or a sales call—before leaning in for a quick hug instead.

"It's good to see you again," Jeremy whispered.

Ben was thrown by the intensity of the exchange. With the brief hug, Ben's senses were rocked by the earthy-scent of the cologne

Jeremy wore and the soft tickle from the fibers of his sweater. *He's really here.*

"Good to see you too, son. Real good."

They took their seats across from each other.

The waitress was just bringing Ben's drink—reminding him of how parched his throat felt—when she noticed Jeremy.

"Hi, hon. Can I get you something to drink?" Her eyes were glued on Jeremy as she placed the soda down in front of Ben. Ben pictured Jeremy through her eyes: tall, dark, and handsome—an American girl's dream. *And charming,* Ben thought as Jeremy turned a beaming smile up to the young woman. With his wayward curls twisted every which way and long dark lashes resting above those hazel eyes, Ben could understand why her undivided attention was on Jeremy.

"Just water, please."

"You got it," she said and headed off for the water and an extra menu.

Ben was first to speak. "How was your flight?" He knew it sounded generic but what else did one start off with? *Do you want to go fishing and spend Christmas together?* Ben cringed.

"I slept most of it," Jeremy said. "It's been a long week wrapping things up in my classroom before break started, so I needed to catch up on lost sleep." He looked around the restaurant, examining an old movie poster of *Goodfellas* on a far wall and a rusty newspaper vending machine in the corner as if they were relics from an ancient civilization.

"This place is cool. Kind of like one of those family-owned mobster diners in the movies," he said with a chuckle.

Ben looked around with a new appreciation for the diner.

"Yeah, this place goes way back for me. I guess I never really noticed anything special about it. Got good food, though," he said.

The waitress brought the extra menu and wiped the condensation off of Jeremy's water glass before setting it down. "I'll be back in a few minutes to take your order," she said with a wink that Ben knew wasn't for *his* benefit.

Ben searched for the words that he'd been practicing over the past few days. He couldn't think of any of them at the moment. He'd have to start from scratch.

"Jeremy," he started, "I, um...I know it's been a lot of years. You don't really know much about me except a few memories. I'm hopin' a few of those are good ones. I...I don't know what to say."

Jeremy sat looking at him. Smooth hands rested on the table, fingers laced as he took in Ben's words. Ben took it as a cue to continue.

"I wanted to look for you all these years. Let you know that I was thinkin' about you—that I was sorry. That I..." his voice softened, "that I missed you." He swallowed hard. He meant to go on but words failed him.

Jeremy was thoughtful before he spoke. "Mom never had anything bad to say about you," he said. "I was eight when we left so I was old enough to put some things together. I knew you had a drinking problem and that Mom didn't want to live that life anymore. I never thought you were a bad father, it's just...just that we lost you sometimes. I mean, when you were...sober"—he paused—"we had a lot of fun." Jeremy smiled to himself, recalling a memory.

"Do you remember how excited we were when we found that vintage Home Run Baker baseball card in Grandpa's old military chest? He had no idea that it was valuable or anything. We spent that whole week looking up his stats and how he was a three-time World Series champion." Jeremy's head nodded in wonder at the memory. "Two game-winning home runs in the 1911 World Series,

Hall of Fame in 1955... Wow, that card was quite a find." Ben and Jeremy were both grinning now.

Ben snickered. "I remember you beggin' Dan—your grandpa—to let you have it. We took it right down to a dealer in town the next day, thinkin' it was worth a fortune even though you had no intention of sellin' it."

Jeremy cut in. "Yeah, only worth three hundred bucks, but that was a million to a young kid like me." His smile faded but his expression remained kind. "Guess we have a lot to catch up on."

Ben was carried back in time to when Jeremy barely came to his shoulder. Those big hazel eyes staring up at him as he clung to Ben's every word. *Like a son should look at his father*, Ben reflected with sadness.

"I'd like that, Jeremy. I truly would."

Ben could see the waitress approaching and wished he could make her turn and go away for a few more minutes. He didn't want anything to break the magic of this moment. He hadn't even touched his Dr. Pepper and food was the farthest thing from his mind.

Jeremy nodded, a happy glow spreading across his rugged, handsome face. Ben felt a deep contentment that he hadn't felt in many, many years.

There would be more times like this. This is just the beginning, he thought. *No need to rush things.*

It was his turn to smile up at the waitress, who was now giving him her full attention.

"I'll take the Italian hoagie, double prosciutto and capicola—toasted. Extra Italian dressing on the side, please."

49

*B*en called Aden the next day after learning the news about Aden's mother being found. He had done most of the talking while Aden listened, and Ben knew he had fumbled all over himself trying to comfort the boy.

Lord knows, Ben didn't have a clue what to say to a young man whose heart had just been shattered in a million pieces—*again*. Still, he felt sure that Aden knew Ben had at least tried.

They'd talked several times on the phone since then and, each time, it got a little easier. It wasn't long before the words flowed between them and they fell back into the comfortable dialogue they'd shared back at Angelo's—before both of their paths had taken unexpected detours.

Ben was pouring his morning coffee—black as he pleased, no creamer—when the phone rang. Mug balanced in one hand, Ben reached over and snatched the phone off the hook.

"Hello, Ben speaking."

"Hey! What's up, Ben?"

He was surprised to hear Aden's voice. The boy wasn't much of a morning person. In fact, he *never* called Ben in the morning.

"Well, howdy there, Aden!" Ben peeked up at the clock above him. *7:30 a.m. What's the boy callin' me for at this time of the morning?* "I was just having my coffee and packin' my dinner for work tonight."

"Oh, that sounds like fun," Aden said.

Fun? Ben was more than a little curious now.

Setting his coffee down on the counter, Ben cradled the phone between his cheek and shoulder while he pulled open the refrigerator to retrieve the lunchmeat, cheese, and mustard for his sandwich. Talking to Aden right now kind of made Ben sad, thinking about only have to pack food for *one* these days.

"What are you soundin' all excited about? Did ya just find out that you have an extra birthday this year or somethin'?" he chuckled.

"Noooo, Ben. Don't be a goon. Everything is going good. Me and Cray finished building that garden shed for Angela that I told you about. And Blake—you remember me talking about him—kept bugging us, asking a million questions, climbing all over the piles of wood we had made. I know I never asked that many questions when I was six...sheesh." Ben could tell Aden was trying to sound like it bothered him but the lightheartedness of his tone suggested that he didn't really mind Blake hanging around.

"You don't say..." Ben pulled open a drawer to retrieve a brown lunch bag. He yanked one out and shoved the drawer closed with his hip. "Well, I'll tell you, I'm sure, Aden, that you have no idea how many questions you asked when you were at the tender age of six. Nobody remembers how annoying they were at that age."

"Whatever," Aden huffed. "Anyhow, I kind of like helping Cray work outside and around the house. I'm learning a lot of new stuff. Angela's cool too and she cooks amazing, but, well, she drives me nuts with the schoolwork. I think my mom was much better at teaching—don't tell Angela I said that," he added. "I'll probably go to public school this coming school year just to get some relief."

Ben grinned. *Good for you, Angela.*

The boy had no idea what a real school environment was like, Ben thought. He'd face some tough transitions but the friendships and memories he would make would last him a lifetime. Ben understood about tough transitions—he was working through a few himself right now.

If Aden can heal and move on, so can I. All this time, I selfishly thought it was me helpin' the boy. But, I'm guessin' that it was really the other way around.

Ben shared with Aden about his meeting with Jeremy and how they had been talking over the phone and making plans. "He wants me to meet his girlfriend," he told Aden. "I'm thinkin' that's just one step away from bouncing a grandkid on my knee." Aden's giggle was like the tinkling of chimes when a gentle wind blew through them. Ben liked the way it sounded.

"That's pushing it a bit, Ben, but I am super happy for you!" Aden told him. "I'm glad Jeremy is finally getting to know his dad again 'cause you're pretty fun to be around."

Ben felt himself grow ten feet taller.

The line grew quiet, the only sound being Aden's breathing.

Ben wondered if something had distracted Aden when he suddenly piped up. "So…guess what else."

Ben rolled the top of the lunch bag down and pushed it off to the side. Grabbing his coffee and a kitchen chair, he sat.

"Well, let's hear it, boy. You didn't just call to talk about garden sheds and pesky little boys. I can tell you're bustin' at the seams about something."

"Okaaay," Aden said. "You better sit down for this… Ready?" The excitement in his voice was so infectious that Ben was almost ready to burst himself waiting for the kid to spill it out.

"I'm already sittin', boy. Get on with it. Hang on…wait, let me guess…you got a book deal?" Ben teased. Aden had picked up his story-writing again and had even shared some of his stories with Ben over the phone.

"Nah…that'll be later," he teased back. "The Pearsons want to adopt me!"

Ben sloshed scalding hot coffee on his pant leg when he jerked up out of the chair. Coffee dribbled onto the floor too, but he ignored it.

"You don't say, Aden!" Ben felt like doing a jig right there on the kitchen linoleum, but he'd probably pop his bad knee out. "Boy, I'm smilin' big right now!"

"I know, right?!" Aden plowed on, his words tumbling out at warp speed. "Paula gave Angela and Cray the information on how to get things started and we're pretty sure they can get a court date set for next month. Angela says that it should go fast because I don't have any family or anything to protest it. Cray told me that *Aden Pearson* sounds like a lawyer or a CEO's name and that he could almost imagine it on a nameplate in an office someday." Aden sounded short of breath by the time he got everything poured out.

Ben's grin could've filled the whole kitchen.

"Well, now, I'm happy for you, son. Real happy! Sounds like that's what you are wantin' too from what I hear in your voice."

"Yeah, Ben, I think so. I…" Ben caught the catch in Aden's voice. "I miss my mom…a lot. But it's okay. I think she would be happy for me too. She would like the Pearsons, don't you think?"

Ben was deeply moved that Aden would choose to share his joy, as well as his pain, with him.

"Yes, son. I think this is a good thing and a change for the better that would bring your momma joy—maybe even peace. I don't know the Pearsons very well myself, but I can tell from what you've shared with me that they're wonderful people. I think she'd want you to have a family again, Aden."

50

*B*lake was throwing up...all over Aden's bed. The four of them had made s'mores—another first for Aden— around a bonfire in the backyard last night. Cray had to explain to Aden what a s'more was since Aden was clueless.

"All it is," Cray told him, "is a toasted marshmallow and chunk of chocolate smashed between two graham crackers. Nothin' to it."

Blake was more than thrilled to jump in and give Aden a demonstration on the proper way to toast a marshmallow over the fire and build a s'more. Problem was, Blake kept sneaking chocolate squares even after Angela had warned him not to numerous times. Hence, the barfing on Aden's bed...

"My tummy hurts, Aden," Blake managed to croak out before another heave added to the growing pool of brown slime and foam puddled in the middle of Aden's comforter. His bed would stink for weeks.

I wonder if there's a cot in the attic, Aden thought as Blake started crying when another heave washed over him.

It was Blake's bright idea to sleep in Aden's room since, as he put it, "We had a campfire and ate *s'mores*—we should have a sleepover in your room!" *If this is how sleepovers end up,* Aden thought, *I can do without them.*

Aden scooted as close to the edge of the mattress as he could without sliding to the floor and reached a hand over to rub Blake's back. He would have already gone for Angela but he didn't want to leave the poor kid in the middle of his crisis. Listening to the violent hacking coming from Blake, Aden felt bile clawing up into his own throat.

"It's gonna be okay, Blake. Just breathe and try to relax," Aden gagged. "Don't fight it."

Between hiccups and bawling, Blake managed to squeak out, "Am I done? I don't want to be sick no more." Aden continued to rub his back and reassure Blake while he waited for the calm after the storm. After a minute, Blake appeared to have emptied himself and Aden lifted him gently off the bed, propping him up against the foot of the mattress.

"I'm going to get your mom. Okay, Blake?" The room smelled putrid. Aden needed the escape.

"Noooo...don't leave. I don't wanna be by myself. Five more minutes," Blake cried, grabbing Aden's hand and turning to sit back down on the bed.

Aden fidgeted while he considered what to do. He started to pull his hand back so he could go and get Angela anyway, when Blake turned his watery eyes up to him.

"Are you really gonna stay here and live with us forever, Aden?"

Aden couldn't resist the wobbly smile and pathetic, helpless look on the little boy's face. He'd never had a brother and he guessed this was as good a time as any to start practicing. Ignoring the overwhelming sour smell drifting from Blake, Aden knelt down in front of him. *If he throws up now*, he thought, *I'll be hurling right along with him.*

"Yeah, looks like it, Blake," he told him, returning the smile. "Is that cool with you?"

Blake's eyes brightened under the dark shadows that circled them. "Yeah! I want you to stay. We could go fishing whenever we want now!"

Aden thought about how amazing it was that a kid who was throwing up and crying just minutes ago could be so chipper and pleasant all of a sudden. *Although fishing wouldn't be the first thing I'd get excited about.* But, Aden felt happy simply because Blake was happy.

"Hmmm, Blake, I have a friend who probably loves fishing as much as you do," he told him. "Maybe I'll introduce him to you sometime."

"Really?" Blake said. "What's your friend's name?"

"His name is Ben."

Blake was looking a bit green again and Aden didn't wait for him to stop him this time.

"That's it, kid," Aden said, trying not to look at the jellied mass in the center of his bed as he stood and gently shook off Blake's vise-like grip. "I better get your mom because we sure ain't sleeping here now."

Not waiting for a reply, Aden crept from the room to wake Angela and grab an extra blanket from the hall closet. He'd be sleeping on the couch for the rest of the night.

———

AFTER ADEN HANDED BLAKE—WHO had started to complain that he

thought he might throw up again—over to Angela, Aden dragged out a few throw blankets from the hall closet and settled himself on the couch. He thought back over his conversation with Blake and about how Aden should introduce Blake to Ben since they both liked to fish.

Who knows? Aden considered. *Maybe I could start to like fishing too.*

A plan formed in his mind about having Ben come over to meet Cray and Angela. And Blake, of course. Ben and Blake would get along real well, he knew. Angela had briefly met Ben at the hospital but had never really had a real conversation with him. He thought Angela would really like Ben. And he knew Ben would love Angela's cooking since he used to complain that the only home-cooked meal he ever got was when Jake tried his hand at barbequing. Ben hadn't seemed too thrilled about that either.

Yawning, Aden rolled over and tucked himself tightly against the couch cushions. He would talk to Angela and Cray about his idea and, if they agreed, he'd call Ben tomorrow and invite him to come.

51

*B*en rolled down the windows of his hunter green '95 Dodge Ram and let the cool breeze flood the cab. He'd purchased the sturdy truck from a used car lot with money he'd dipped out of his savings.

After his Thunderbird was totaled in the accident, Ben had decided to go for a larger vehicle this time around. He felt safer in a truck and, although he would never admit it, it was easier on his old knees climbing up into the truck than hunching down into a car. Plus, being at the same level as the cashier in a drive-thru was a welcome perk.

It was a beautiful day for heading out of the city on a road trip. The truck's purring rumble was music to Ben's ears as he traveled northwest on Interstate 76 out of Philadelphia, heading toward King of Prussia.

"Huh," Ben said with a grunt. "Imagine that. Kid goes from being homeless to livin' in a place called *King of Prussia*."

As he drew closer, Ben breathed in the smell of pine and wood smoke as he drove under lush tree canopies and admired spacious homes with sprawling front lawns that were larger than some of the city parks Ben passed every day back in Philly. The Pearsons lived on the outskirts of King of Prussia. Even though it was less than a forty-minute drive from where Ben lived, the view outside his window made him feel like he was on a different planet when Ben compared the uninspiring colors of concrete and brick that made up Ben's world in the inner city to the array of vibrant, bright colors of the countryside surrounding him.

Ben turned down a long gravel road that stretched on endlessly before him. He noticed fewer houses as open fields of wild brown grasses and patchy tufts of green blanketed the landscape. The clouds huddled close to the earth, casting long shadows as far as his eyes could see.

I've got a good seven years before retirement, but this place is goin' on my list of prospects, he thought, admiring a thick patch of wildflowers that jutted up against the road, their delicate faces lifted upward while they eagerly waited to greet the sun tucked behind the low-lying clouds.

It was the call he received from Aden two days ago that really made his heart sing as he drove through the magnificent countryside to the Pearson's place. For every mile away from the city that he drove, Ben felt just a little bit lighter.

If the open space had this kind of an effect on *him,* he could imagine how it made Aden feel, especially after what he'd seen and lived through. The city had its attractions—even beauty—but Aden had mostly been exposed to its ugly side.

Ben was excited about meeting the Pearson family today. He'd met Angela briefly when he was in the hospital, but he'd only heard bits and pieces about the rest of them. Aden had invited him, with their permission, to spend the afternoon and dinner with them. It had been a long time since he'd been invited to someone's house for dinner. He pranced around the house all morning trying to decide what to wear and had even slicked his wiry hair down with Vaseline to keep it in place.

Aden's last words this morning when he called to confirm Ben was still coming were, "Hey! Bring me some chocolate eclairs from Angelo's! Not the gross ones left from yesterday either." Ben thought back to the many nights he'd set aside day-old muffins and leftover pastries to share with Aden.

"Well, aren't you gettin' demanding these days?" Ben pretended to be offended. "Fine. I'll see what I can do."

"I'll pay you back!" Aden said before the line went dead.

Ben watched as the clouds drifted apart and the sun made its bold appearance, setting the somber shades of brown and mottled green fields on fire as they burst into colors of vibrant jewels, the now-golden and jade colors spreading warmth through him.

When he finally pulled into the long driveway ten minutes later, Ben admired the cozy, warm cottage-style house that stood before him. He was impressed with its rugged white stone walls and tidy rows of red and yellow flowers tucked under wood-framed windows. It looked like something out of a fairy tale.

You could walk right on by this place and never know the stories sheltered behind its walls, Ben thought.

Kind of like my own life. People see an old man who looks like he hasn't got a care in the world outside of the latest sports news and weather channel updates. If they could only see the regrets this old man carries and how long it's taken me to find the courage to make things right.

Ben shook his head to clear away his brooding mood and shifted the truck into *park.*

Looking up, Ben saw Aden standing on the back porch next to an animated sandy-haired boy who was hopping up and down at Aden's side. *I'm guessin' that's our little Blake.*

Both boys waved at him.

"Over here, Ben!" Aden called.

Ben returned the wave as he pushed open the truck door. He leaned across the seat to grab the white bakery bag stuffed with various pastries and—*bless his heart*—Aden's precious chocolate eclairs—all courtesy of Mia.

The hopping boy broke away from Aden and ran ahead, reaching the truck first and making his way around to Ben's open door.

"Hi!" A face smudged with something that looked like it could be dried toothpaste grinned up at Ben. "I'm Blake."

Ben took in his bright green eyes and the sprinkling of freckles across the bridge of his nose. He gave the boy a wink and lowered himself out of the truck.

Blake backed up a few steps so that Ben could close the door.

"Well, hello there!" Ben grinned down at Blake. "I'm Ben."

"I know. Aden told me." The boy's eyes fell to the large bag in Ben's arms. "What's that?" he pointed.

Aden had arrived and reached to take the bag from Ben. He stuck his tongue out at Blake. "Wouldn't you like to know? You gotta wait until later to find out." Blake's lips puckered into a pout.

Turning to Ben, Aden reached up to give him a high-five. "Come on, Ben. Let's go."

As the trio approached the porch, Ben saw Angela leaning against a stocky man with a short, rust-colored beard, dressed in faded jeans and an untucked blue flannel shirt. He struck Ben as being a gentle soul: unhurried, relaxed, pleasant. Ben took an instant liking to him before they had even exchanged a word. The man descended the stairs and walked up to meet them, gripping Ben's hand in a strong, friendly shake.

"Glad to finally meet you, Ben. I'm Cray. Aden's told us a lot about you," he said.

Ben heard Aden mumble next to him, "Don't worry, it was *mostly* good."

"It's a real pleasure to meet you too, Mr. Pearson. Thank you for the invite." Ben took in the property around him. "You got a nice place here."

Cray looked around with pride before patting Ben on the shoulder and turning toward the house. Blake was already fluttering around his mother on the porch, a bundle of energy.

"Thank you," Cray said, "and call me Cray." Pointing up to his wife, "And you've met Angela already." Cray turned to motion for Aden, who was standing next to him, to lead the way. "Come on into the house."

*a*den took in the scene at the dinner table.

Ben and Cray sat at the far end, engrossed in an animated conversation about the recent news of the closure of a shipyard located near the Delaware River in South Philadelphia. This led to Ben telling Cray about how he used to paint ships at a naval shipyard for a living before a leg injury forced him to change careers. Then, Cray shared that his grandfather had been a cook on a Navy ship back in World War II.

Back and forth they went. It all sounded incredibly boring to Aden. He reached over to grab a biscuit from the basket in front of him.

At his right, Angela was issuing a stern warning to Blake about not talking with food in his mouth. Blake's head bobbed obediently, while he repeated, "Yes, ma'am" several times around a mouth packed full of green beans. Aden found the exchange pretty comical and had to look away before Blake caught him trying not to laugh.

Aden didn't even mind that no one was paying attention to him right now. It was enough for him to just enjoy sitting at a table full of the people that had become an important part of his life.

Everything's changed so much over the last several months. I honestly don't know how I would have survived much longer on my own. Someone—maybe God?—was really looking out for me.

Aden could have never predicted that he'd end up living outside of Philly, waking up to a surly rooster crowing every morning, and have a little kid that had recently started calling him "brother" shadowing him everywhere he went.

And now, I'll even have a new last name—Pearson. Aden Pearson. He liked the sound of it.

His moment of reflection was interrupted by Blake, who must have overheard Cray and Ben talking about ships…which involved *water*…and, in Blake's over-active imagination… *fishing*. He shot a glance at his mother, hastily swallowing his mouthful of food before he piped, "Hey, Ben!"

Ben and Cray turned in sync toward Blake. "Aden told me that you like to go fishing." Aden saw their faces light up like two toddlers on Christmas morning. He tried hard not to roll his eyes. *Oh, brother.*

Ben gifted Blake with his full attention. Blake was all over it. He sat up three feet taller in his chair while his eyes danced with glee.

"You bet I do, son," Ben told him. He looked at Cray, then back to Blake. "You and your daddy like to go fishin'?"

Blake was now squirming up onto his knees in his chair and leaning his upper body across the table toward Ben. "Yes, sir! Daddy takes me all the time." His head swung around to Aden. "Aden went with us too. Remember, Aden?" Blake reached over and thumped Aden's arm, much to his annoyance. Turning back to Ben, he added, "I helped him catch his first fish!"

All eyes were on Aden. *Nothing like being the new kid in class.*

"Yep, Blake, you sure did," he said. Aden couldn't help but notice the obvious raised eyebrow and half-cocked grin on Ben's face as he watched Aden squirm under the attention.

"Is that right?" Ben kept his eyes on Aden though his words were for Blake. "I'm thinkin' I should plan another fishing trip up to Susquehanna now that I got me a fishing buddy to take along."

"Oh! Can I go too!?" Blake bounced in his chair until Angela stilled him with a hand on his back.

"Blake..." Cray warned. "Mind your manners."

Aden was ready to answer this one. "I think that would be a great idea, actually. What do you think about the four of us guys going on a fishing trip?"

All of a sudden, it didn't matter to Aden that he didn't care one hoot about fishing. He couldn't explain the sudden urge to go through with this. It just came out of nowhere, and Aden didn't fight it.

Everyone, even Angela—who had no desire to join them, but offered to prepare food—got excited over the idea of a fishing trip.

"Now you're talkin' boy!" Ben told him.

———

AFTER DINNER AND TRIP PLANS, Aden offered to take Ben on a tour of the property. He wanted to show him the new shed and where they would be fencing in a vegetable garden area for Angela in a few months. Cray practically had to peel Blake—who had adopted Ben as a second grandpa at this point—off of Ben, promising to play a card game of Go Fish with him to keep in the house.

Aden could tell Ben enjoyed being outdoors, surrounded by grassland and newly-blooming wildflowers that nestled up against the backdrop of woodland on the opposite side of the Pearson's homestead.

When they'd finished the tour, Ben and Aden found themselves standing at the back of Cray's old tool shed. Aden wandered over to a pile of logs and sat down. Ben joined him, nudging a log with his boot first to make sure it wouldn't roll out from under him when he sat down. Satisfied, he lowered himself onto it, stretching his legs out in front of him.

"Reminds me of my childhood," he said, lifting his face to the night sky, unencumbered by invading city lights and air traffic. "I used to love sittin' under the stars at night when I was a boy. Got me out of the house and away from my pesky sisters."

Aden stared up at the ever-shifting canvas of clouds that filled the heavens. The stars reached far beyond what he could see. It reminded Aden of just how small he was compared to the Universe. "Yeah, I kind of like it out here too."

Aden spotted a cloud that had broken free from a larger cluster off toward the west. It drifted alone, free to wander where it pleased. Dense and well-defined, Aden was intrigued by its uniqueness.

"Hey, Ben. What do you think that cloud looks like?"

Ben followed Aden's finger where it pointed. He squinted, a thoughtful expression on his face as he studied it for a moment.

"Hmmm, looks to me like an alien spaceship," he remarked.

Aden peered more closely at the cloud. It reminded him of a creamy scoop of vanilla ice cream.

"A *spaceship*? Seriously, Ben?"

Ben shrugged. "Yeah, well, that's what I see anyway, and you know what they say about aliens landing out in the middle of nowhere." His arms were stretched out wide, making a point that there wasn't anything around for miles that they could see.

Aden sighed. "You're such a weirdo."

Reaching into his jacket pocket, Aden pulled out a gallon-sized plastic baggie that held two chocolate eclairs. With Ben looking on in puzzlement, Aden carefully pulled one out and handed it to Ben.

"Sorry, I forgot napkins," he said. "I know you actually brought these but I wanted to be the one handing *you* something to eat this time. I figure I owe you." Aden felt the lump in his throat, but swallowed it down.

Ben held the éclair up in a mock toast. "I accept!" After sinking his teeth into the soft pastry, he cocked his head at Aden.

"Got a story for us, kid?" he asked.

Actually, Aden had a whole notebook full of stories in the house that he couldn't wait to share with Ben—but not right now. He had another kind of story in mind.

"Okay," he started, setting his own éclair down on the baggie at his side and pushing crumbs off of his jeans.

"There was this old crow that lived inside the hollow of a huge oak tree in the center of a busy park. He lived there alone for many years but no one really noticed because, well, he was *just* a crow and no one really notices crows like they do blue jays and robins."

"Every day, the old crow would come out of his hollow and hop to the end of his branch to watch children playing in the park and families having picnics on the grass." Aden had been watching the lone drifting cloud when he started the story, but now looked back at Ben to make sure he was paying attention.

He was.

"You probably think that the old crow was just sitting there waiting for someone to drop part of their sandwich, so he could swoop down and snatch it. But he wasn't. That old crow was admiring daddies pushing their kids on the swings and moms cuddling babies on the park bench nearby. Then, when the sun started to lower in the sky and all the children were gathered to make their way back home, the old crow would remember all the good things he'd seen that day and would hop across his branch and snuggle down deep in his hollow for the night, all the happy images melding into his dreams."

Ben's éclair was still clutched in his hand, momentarily forgotten while he listened to Aden. He looked as if he was trying to remember if he'd heard this story somewhere before. Aden could tell he was losing him. He pushed on.

"One night, the crow had an awful dream."

"Tucked away in his hollow were three small nestlings. They were curled close to their mother, who sheltered them under her broad wings. They were all alone. Her mate was nowhere to be found. He'd gone off and left them unprotected. Suddenly, there was a thunderous sound of flapping wings and the hollow opening was filled with the enormous shape of a Great Horned Owl. He stared down at the nestlings and their mother with black, predatory eyes. In one swift motion, he was on them…"

"The old crow jerked awake from the nightmare, feathers rustling against his trembling body. If birds could cry, Ben, that poor old crow would have wept right then and there."

Ben looked shell-shocked. "You and your stories about creatures getting' slaughtered, Aden. Downright depressing." But Aden could tell he wanted him to go on.

"Were those babies and that momma the old crow's family?" Ben asked. "Did that owl get them?"

Aden smiled sadly. "Good guess, Ben. Did you know that crows mate for life and raise their young together? Well, in that one fatal moment, everything that mattered to the old crow was stolen from him. Every day, he grieved for them. He didn't want to think about how he wasn't there when the enemy came and destroyed his little family. It hurt too much. To comfort himself, he sat on his oak branch and watched the families that came to the park and thought about how things might have been different."

Aden studied Ben. He didn't need to ask if Ben was getting this. He could tell by the shimmer in his eyes that the message was being received.

Ben looked down, then back up at Aden. "You callin' me an old crow, boy?" He smiled sadly.

Aden smiled back but wasn't quite finished.

"Yeah, an old crow sounds fitting, but I wanted to share this because I think that we're both part of the story, Ben. You and I have had people we loved in our lives—regardless of the good or bad that went with that love." Thoughts of his mother came unbidden. He tried to focus only on the good thoughts.

"Until an enemy swept in and stole them from us. You had a different enemy than I did, but you get what I mean."

A single tear rolled down Ben's cheek. "Yes, son, I think I know exactly what you mean."

"I don't want to be sitting on a branch all alone anymore, Ben. Sitting there looking out at everyone else's family, wishing I could have what they have. Mourning what I've lost." Aden traced a chocolate smear on his pants with his finger.

"I think that's why I'm here. The Pearsons want to adopt me and, well, you are here tonight too. I want all of you to be my family now."

Aden paused, wondering if it would be okay to say what he was going to say. He decided to anyway.

"You went all those years watching, Ben, thinking that it was too late for you too. But you found Jeremy and now he wants to get to know his dad. I think that's pretty cool."

Ben's soft gray eyes met Aden's. They stirred with deep

emotion. Aden thought back to that first night when Ben found him hiding at the back of Angelo's. He remembered that Ben's gentle eyes were the first thing that drew him in. Something about those eyes told Aden that he could trust this man. He hadn't understood back then what trust really meant. He couldn't have known how much he had needed Ben. Now, the lines between *who* needed *who* were blurred as they looked at each other.

Eyes bright as he studied Aden, Ben brought the forgotten éclair to his lips. He tore off a chunk and gave Aden a sloppy grin.

"Where'd you get to be so smart, boy?" Ben asked.

Aden gave him a smug look. "I've always been smart, Ben." He pointed to the sky.

"Smarter than you to know that cloud up there doesn't look nothin' like an alien spaceship and you know it."

Ben threw the rest of his éclair at Aden.

ACKNOWLEDGMENTS

To my husband and biggest fan, Andrew:
Thank you for keeping the dishes washed and making countless
cups of coffee for me while I worked through this debut novel.

Thank you, Felty Tribe:
For cheering me on in my writing journey.
I owe you all homemade Italian ravioli!

SPECIAL THANKS TO:
Randy Sullivan
Jean Dunstan
"Your input and encouragement have been invaluable."

ABOUT THE AUTHOR

 **Regina Felty** was born in Philadelphia, Pennsylvania, where she claims you can find the finest Italian hoagies and soft pretzels on the East Coast. Although she'd always kept a journal and wrote stories for fun, it was during her turbulent teen years in a foster home that she turned to writing as a source of therapy.

Besides dividing her time between being an author and her career as an American Sign Language Educational Interpreter, Regina also manages her personal blog, *It's a Felty Thing*, and has a special place in her heart for troubled youth.

While You Walked By is her debut novel.

To learn more about Regina, visit her website at www.rlfelty.com

facebook.com/ReginaLFelty

instagram.com/reginafelty

Made in United States
North Haven, CT
02 July 2022

20892448R00157